Praise for Reed Fa and *Walking the F*

D0546886

"Reed Farrel Coleman is a terrific writer.... a hard-boiled poet... If life were fair, Coleman would be as celebrated as [George] Pelecanos and [Michael] Connelly."
—Maureen Corrigan, NPR's *Fresh Air*

"Reed Farrel Coleman is one of the more original voices to emerge from the crime fiction field in the last ten years. For the uninitiated, *Walking the Perfect Square* is the place to start."
—George Pelecanos, best-selling author of *The Way Home*

"Among the undying conventions of detective fiction is the one that requires every retired cop to have a case that still haunts him. Reed Farrel Coleman blows the dust off that cliché in *Walking the Perfect Square* . . . with a mystery that would get under anyone's skin."
—Marilyn Stasio, *The New York Times*

"The author makes us care about his characters and what happens to them, conveying a real sense of human absurdity and tragedy . . . a first-rate mystery. Moe is a fine sleuth. Coleman is an excellent writer."
—*Publishers Weekly*

"Whenever our customers are looking for a new series to read, they often leave with a copy of *Walking the Perfect Square*. It has easily been our best-selling backlist title. Thank you, Busted Flush, for bringing this classic 'Moe' back into print!"
—Gary Shulze, Once Upon a Crime (Minneapolis, MN)

"The biggest mysteries in our genre are why Reed Coleman isn't already huge, and why Moe Prager isn't already an icon. Both are to me. Read this book and you'll find you agree."
—Lee Child, best-selling author of *Gone Tomorrow*

"Originally published in 2001 . . . *Walking the Perfect Square* has been reissued by Busted Flush Press, good news for mystery lovers, since Reed Farrel Coleman is quite a writer, and this is only the first of five books about Moe Prager. The story and the characters will hook you, and Coleman's lightly warped take on the world will make you laugh, dark as the tale is. As soon as I finished *Walking the Perfect Square*, I started the next in the series, *Redemption Street*. The only problem with the following three (*The James Deans*, *Soul Patch*, *Empty Ever After*) will be to decide whether to read them immediately or savor them over a period of time."

—Marilyn Dahl, *Shelf Awareness*

"Moe's back—if you haven't already discovered Reed Farrel Coleman's wonderful, award-winning ex-cop-turned-PI, Moe Prager, here's your chance. He's for real, and so is Coleman's handling of cases that stay with you long after the book's end. *Walking the Perfect Square*, *Redemption Street*, and *The James Deans* belong in every mystery fan's personal library, because the writing is fine, the realization is believable, and the character is true to himself. This is the man to measure the rest by, a writer with a passionate belief in giving his best, and an eye for what makes the PI novel work at a level few can match."

—Charles Todd, best-selling author of *A Duty to the Dead*

"One of crime fiction's finest voices, Edgar Award-finalist Reed Coleman combines the hard-fisted detective story with a modern novel's pounding heart and produces pure gold. Moe Prager belongs with Travis McGee and Lew Archer in the private eye pantheon. Coleman's series is a buried treasure—dig in and hit the jackpot!"

—Julia Spencer-Fleming, best-selling author of *Once Was a Soldier*

"Moe Prager is the thinking person's P.I. And what he thinks about— love, loyalty, faith, betrayal—are complex and vital issues, and beautifully handled."

—S. J. Rozan, Edgar Award-winning author of *The Shanghai Moon*

Soul Patch

Reed Farrel Coleman

TYRUS
BOOKS
F+W Media, Inc.

Published in electronic format by
TYRUS BOOKS
an imprint of F+W Media, Inc.
10151 Carver Road
Blue Ash, Ohio 45242
www.tyrusbooks.com

eISBN 10: 1-4405-4099-3
eISBN 13: 978-1-4405-4099-8

POD ISBN 10: 1-4405-6387-X
POD ISBN 13: 978-1-4405-6387-4

This is a work of fiction. Names, characters, corporations, institutions,
organizations, events, or locales in this novel are either the product of the author's
imagination or, if real, used fictitiously. The resemblance of any character to actual
persons (living or dead) is entirely coincidental.

This work has been previously published in print format by:
Busted Flush Press
Print ISBN: 978-0-935415-09-1

FOREWORD
by Craig Johnson

UNLIKE MOST WRITERS, Reed Farrel Coleman isn't looking for
compliments, and what he has in common with the really good writers
is a search for the truth. Truth means a lot to Coleman, like a
compass that points to an unerring north. Like some Brooklyn street
poet, he weaves honesty in and out of a story like a golden thread—a
tarnished golden thread that's seen better days, but is still gold.

I heard about Reed from Scott Montgomery, an individual with
impeccable taste in the genre. He said I had to read Reed Farrel
Coleman. Generally, I don't trust people with three names, but I'd
met Reed and his wife at the Edgar Awards in New York where I
complimented his wife on her dress. Coleman said he picked it out. I
complimented him on his taste. He said the dress hadn't looked as
good on him. I agreed.

When I think of Moe Prager, the protagonist of Coleman's series,
I think of Bogart's line in *Casablanca*, "He's just like any other man,
only more so." No hero here, just a guy who does a job, only more
so—a guy who knows strong D with good footwork on the b-ball
courts and who quotes Blaise Pascal in an unobtrusive way. If I'm
going to be stuck in a guy's first-person head for three hundred pages,
he'd better be interesting and he'd better be funny.

I've spent an awful lot of my life in locker rooms, squad rooms,
and hunting camps, where a certain type of humor pervades, a dark
humor that undercuts the hardness of the life. Reed's got it down
cold, and his pitch-perfect delivery is like the relish on a Coney Island
hot dog.

But I'd read him even if there wasn't a humorous word in his
books—I'd read him because there's an energy to his characters that's
contagious, a grinding hurt for the individuals that's honest to
humanity. And, like my old buddy Tony Hillerman used to say, he
tells a good story.

Any one of Reed's novels could've been pulled from the pages of
the *Daily News*. But for me, *Soul Patch* is Reed Farrel Coleman at the
top of his game: the political gambits of unbridled ambition, the
personal angst of loss for things that might have been—or worse,

never were. Moses Prager gets under your skin in *Soul Patch*, and I mean that in a good way—or maybe we are the ones who get under Moe's skin, allowing us to see the world through his eyes, and, more importantly, through the pain of his wrecked knee. Prager is a fallen knight who reached for the brass ring in the form of a gold detective's shield and came down to earth, hard. I carried a gun, lived in Harlem for a few years, and had the City of New York reconstruct my own left knee, and can vouch for the gritty realism of the world Reed Farrel Coleman shows us.

That's the thing about Reed's writing—the human element that complicates everything. He pursues and defines the universal human condition. While displaying myriad characters and their motivations, he finds a way to pull us all together and show us where we're alike, and sometimes that's a scary place to be.

He's the guy who starts getting distracted when you flatter him. You might notice his fingers paradiddling a complex pattern on the surface of the bar as he looks out the windows at the street. It's not that he's ignoring you; it's just that he's hearing the music, picking up the rhythms—looking for the truth.

Reed Farrel Coleman won't like this intro because it's too complimentary.

Tough.

Craig Allen Johnson
Ucross, Wyoming
January 2010

Craig Johnson is the best-selling author of six Walt Longmire crime novels, including *The Dark Horse* and *Junkyard Dogs*.

ACKNOWLEDGMENTS

I would like to thank Ben, Alison, and Peter Rubie for helping keep Moe alive in print. I'd also like to thank Ellen Schare, Peter Spiegelman, and Megan Abbott for being first readers, first listeners, and for their editorial advice. None of this would have been possible without Rosanne, Kaitlin, and Dylan.

This book is dedicated to the Brooklyn
that was and never was.

THOU SHALL NOT GET CAUGHT
—The 11th Commandment

[soul patch] n. 1. a small strip of facial hair, often triangular in shape, grown between a man's lower lip and the point of his chin. 2. euphemistic name given by local police (circa 1960-75) to the predominantly African-American section of Coney Island, Brooklyn.

NOTHING IS SO sad as an empty amusement park. And no amusement park is so sad as Coney Island. Once the world's playground, it is no longer the world's anything; not even important enough to be forgotten. Coney Island is the metal basket at the bottom of Brooklyn's sink. So it is that when the County of Kings is stood on end, Coney Island will trap all the detritus, human and otherwise, before it pours into the Atlantic.

Coney Island's demise would be easy to blame on the urban planners, especially Robert Moses, who thought it best to warehouse the niggers, spics, and white trash far away from the crown jewel of Manhattan in distant outposts like Rockaway and Coney Island. If they could have built their ugly shoe box housing projects on the moon, they would have. It is no accident that the subway rides from Coney Island and Rockaway to Manhattan are two of the longest in the system. But Coney Island's decay is as much a product of its birth as anything else.

Coney Island, the rusted remnants of its antiquated rides rising out of the ocean like the fossils of beached dinosaurs, clings to a comatose existence. Like the senile genius, Coney Island has lived just long enough to mock itself. And nothing epitomizes its ironic folly better than the parachute jump. A ploughman's Eiffel Tower, its skeleton soars two hundred and fifty feet straight up off the grounds of what had once been Steeplechase Park. But the parachutes are long gone and now only the looming superstructure remains, the sea air feasting on its impotent bones.

It was under the parachute jump's moon shadow that the four men ambled across the boardwalk toward the beach. No one paid them any mind. No reason to. There was a flurry of activity along the boardwalk and in the woeful vestiges of the amusement park during the window between Easter Sunday and Memorial Day. False hope bloomed like weeds as city administration after city administration promised a return to the glory days of Coney Island. But by the advent of summer, hope would be gone, another silent funeral held for a stillborn renaissance.

At the steps that led down to the beach, one of the four men decided he was having second thoughts. Maybe he didn't want to get sand in his shoes. No one likes sand in his shoes. The man standing to his immediate right waited for the rumble of the Cyclone—several girls screaming at the top of their lungs as the roller coaster cars plunged down its steep first drop—before slamming his leather covered sap just above the balking man's left knee. His scream was swallowed up by the roar of the ocean and the second plunge of the Cyclone. He crumpled, but was caught by the other men.

Once their shoes hit the sand, they receded under cover of the boardwalk itself. Above their heads bicycles clickety-clacked along the splintering wooden planks, old Jewish men played chess, teenage boys proved their worth by hurdling wire garbage baskets. Out on the beach, couples sat in vacant lifeguard chairs. Some contemplated the vastness of the ocean or calculated their insignificance in relation to the stars. Some boys kissed their first girlfriends. Some girls placed their heads into their boyfriends' laps.

It was much cooler under the boardwalk, even at night. The sea air was different here somehow, smelling of pot smoke and urine. Ambient light leaking through the spaces between the planks imposed a shadowy grid upon the sand. The sand hid broken bottles, pop tops, used condoms, and horseshoe crab shells. Something snapped, and it wasn't the sound of someone stepping on a shell.

CHAPTER ONE

RED, WHITE AND You, that's what Aaron and I called our third store. It was pretentious, but at the end of the '80s pretentious was high art, ranking right up there with big hair bands and junk bonds. *The '80s, Christ!* The decade when video killed the radio star and AIDS killed everybody else. Pretentious worked well on the North Shore of Long Island, especially in Old Brookville, where even the station cars were chauffeured.

The attendees at the grand opening party were a volatile emulsion of relatives—even my sister Miriam and her family were in from Albuquerque—broken down cops, queens, politicians, journalists, kids, clergy, and, oh yeah, the occasional customer. Throw 'em together, shake 'em up with a little alcohol, and they all seemed perfectly blended. Not so. The second the shaking stopped, the elements settled out. More like a time bomb than a party, really. Tick . . . Tick . . . Tick . . .

The devil himself, my father-in-law, Francis Maloney Sr., had deigned to grace us with his presence. Several times during the course of the day, particularly during the toasts, I'd spot him raising his glass of Irish in my direction, smiling at me with the accumulated warmth of a tombstone. My tombstone. We'd kept the self-destruct secret between us now for nearly twelve years, neither of us reaching for the red button. There were times I actually forgot about his long-missing son and how I'd come to marry his only daughter, times when I thought he'd just leave it be. Then we'd see each other at some family function and he'd smile that smile to remind me—to remind me that it was just a drawn out game of chicken we were playing, that someday one of us would flinch, that it would probably be me. I needed to breathe fresh air.

Larry McDonald, my old pal from the Six-O precinct and current NYPD chief of detectives, was already out front smoking a cigarette. *So much for that fresh air!* Something was up. Normally unflappable, Larry was sucking so hard on his cigarette I was afraid he'd inhale his index finger. He had smoked on and off for years, but it was never an addiction with him. Larry Mac's only vice was ambition and, with a little assist from me, he'd nearly satisfied his craving. He was within sniffing distance of being the next commissioner.

"Nice shindig," he said.

"Shindig! Christ, Larry, where'd you come up with that one? Did you already use hootenanny today?"

If he was laughing, it was definitely on the inside.

"Will you look at this fucking parking lot, Moe?" He flicked the filter away in disgust. "If I didn't know better, I'd swear it was the used car lot of a Porsche dealership. More Jags, Beemers, and 911s here than in all a Brooklyn. You and me, we come a long way from Coney Island, huh?"

"Not *so* long. I still live in Sheepshead Bay, remember?"

"That's not what I—" He stopped himself, lit another cigarette. Sucked on it like Superman.

"You trying to smoke that thing or swallow it, bro?"

That bounced off him too. "Yeah," he repeated, "we come a long way."

Larry was definitely off his game. He was a lot of things—preening and vain for sure, pragmatic to the point of cutthroat—but reflective and philosophical weren't generally part of his repertoire. I took a good look at him. He seemed much older somehow. I couldn't quite put my finger on it.

Wasn't in his posture. Wasn't how he fit in his clothes nor how they fit him. Tall, broad-shouldered, thin-waisted, Larry wore his clothes the way a smooth plaster wall wears wet paint. Today was no exception. His gray, light-wool pinstripe hung on him perfectly. Even when we were in uniform, his blues looked tailor made. And he was handsome as ever, maybe more so. He was the type of guy God had in mind when he created gray hair. No, the age was in his eyes, in his voice. Larry reached into his jacket pocket.

"You believe in ghosts, Moe?"

Shit! There it was, that fucking question. A sucker punch. Usually it was my father-in-law who asked it. He had asked it of me a hundred times over the last dozen years, and with each asking came a sick feeling in my belly. Most times Francis didn't even need to mouth the words. It would come in the guise of a glance or, like today, a smile. He never explained the question, never once discussed it. Didn't expect or want an answer. It was a pin pricked into the skin of a balloon, but not quite deep enough to pop it.

"Ghosts?" I repeated. "Depends. There's shit that can haunt a man worse than the walking dead. But do I believe in spirits and shit? Nah, I don't believe in things that go boo or bump in the night."

"You sound pretty confident."

"I am."

"Don't be so sure," Larry said, his eyes looking through me and into the past. He smiled. Pulled a cassette tape out of his pocket. Put it in my palm and gently folded my fingers around it. "Don't be so sure."

"What's this?"

"It goes bump in the night."

"Very funny, McDonald."

"You see me laughing?"

I didn't.

He held his right hand out to me. I put the tape in my pocket.

"Again, congratulations on the new store, Moe. Pass it on to your brother and kiss Katy for me. Listen to the tape and call me."

"Cryptic isn't usually your style."

"This isn't 'usually.' "

I thought about saying something to that. Thankfully, he'd gone before I could formulate a question. When I turned back around, Francis Maloney was smiling at me through the plate glass window of the store.

CHAPTER TWO

I COUNTED SLEEPLESS nights instead of sheep, staring up at the ceiling I knew was there but couldn't see. Katy was next to me, but a million miles away. We had hit the inevitable impasse, that stage in marriage when each day is like a long drive through Nebraska. In the absence of passion, I wondered, what distinguished love from habit? The answer escaped me there in the dark.

Once, many years back, when I was working the case that ultimately led to Larry Mac's first big promotion, I thought Katy meant to leave me. Only time in my life I felt faint. Had to prop myself up against the furniture. God, I can feel the power of that moment surging through me even now. A few months before, Katy had miscarried. The convulsion of grief and guilt that followed in its wake had overwhelmed us. After the initial tears and blame, Katy fell into a kind of stupor. I thought she was coming out of it, but she was so unpredictable in those long weeks.

The miscarriage and the months that followed caused the first subtle cracks in our marriage. They were hairline fractures, small, barely detectable. I suppose they've added up with time. But that day, the day I thought I would faint, my panic wasn't about the miscarriage. No, the panic belonged to me. I owned it. I thought Katy had stumbled upon the secret, the one her father and I kept wedged between us like a bottle of liquid nitroglycerin.

Back in December of 1977, Patrick Maloney, Katy's younger brother, had gone into Manhattan and vanished. I had just been retired from the job due to a freak knee injury. Hobbling around on a cane and looking for a way to raise some money for our first wine shop, I was hired by the Maloneys to help find their missing boy. According to the media, Patrick was never found and everyone but the Maloney family had long since moved on. The truth was both more and less than that.

I had, in fact, found Patrick, a college sophomore who had collected a trunkful of his own dark secrets. By that time I'd already begun to fall in love with Katy. But when I found her brother, he begged me for a few more days. He wanted to come back to his family on his own terms. I agreed. Biggest mistake in my life. I should have dragged him out of his hiding spot by the ears and plopped him on his parents' sofa.

Of course, Patrick was full of shit. He hit the road running and never looked back. Can't say that I blamed him. My problem was that my father-in-law knew I'd found his son. We both had our reasons for not telling Katy. Now our reasons were moot. The time for confession had come and gone. Compounded with each passing day, this was a sin Katy would never forgive.

For years I had been able to keep the panic and guilt at bay. My sleepless nights were few. Only time it used to get to me was when I'd work the odd case, or see Francis and he'd ask me that fucking question about ghosts. Then I'd relive it all over again, the past churning inside me. These days, sleeplessness was the norm and I'm not sure if guilt or panic has a thing to do with it. I suppose I still loved Katy and that she loved me, but the love just wasn't the glue it had once been. Sarah, our little girl, she was the glue now. These nights, when I stare up at a ceiling I cannot see, I wonder if I would still feel faint if Katy threatened to leave or if I would simply feel relief.

Tired of the frustration, I got up and fished Larry McDonald's cassette out of my jacket pocket. Still smelled his smoke on my suit. Went downstairs. Poured myself a few fingers of Dewar's. Sitting on the floor, hunched against the wing of the sofa closest to the stereo, I sipped scotch and rolled the cassette in my hand. It was a prayer of sorts, a prayer without words; a prayer that the cassette meant trouble, that the trouble meant Larry Mac needed my help. It was a cruel prayer. It's cruel to pray for troubles, but I was lost. Worse, I was bored.

Some cops are action junkies. They crave stimulation. If it doesn't come to them, they go looking for it. If they can't find it, they create it. That wasn't me, not who I used to be—not while I was on the job, anyway. Now I wasn't so sure. The wine business had never been my dream. That was Aaron's gig, not mine. I'd just hitched my ass to it and went along for the ride. I don't think I ever thought it through, really. But that's what happens when you're lost. You make stupid decisions. The wine business had taught me at least one important lesson, though—dust collects on many things other than just old bottles of red wine. Dust corrodes a man's soul.

I slipped my big old Koss headphones over my ears, clicked off the SPEAKER A button, and pressed PLAY on the tape deck. There were three voices, two men and a woman. All sounded far away, but I could make out what was being said clearly enough. The recording had the sound of a tape that was made surreptitiously, because no one was speaking into the mic. It became immediately apparent I was listening to an interrogation or, as cops euphemistically like to call it, an interview. The suspect's name was Melvin. Melvin didn't like being called Melvin. *Even my moms don't call me Melvin no more. It's Malik!*

A strategic mistake, telling the detectives that. The woman detective—young, with the lilt of someone raised speaking English in school and Spanish at home—jumped all over him. She started and ended each question with *Melvin*, picking fiercely at his scabs. She was the bad cop and was either a great actress or born to the part. The male detective—older, white, Bronx Irish—was the sympathetic voice. *Listen, Malik, I'm with you, man, but it's her case.*

You could tell he was the more experienced detective, not because of his age, but because he spoke less. A good interviewer knows that silence can be your best weapon. The Latina's youth was showing. She was a little too eager, too much of a shark, that one. She smelled blood in the water, Melvin's blood. She'd learn.

Funny thing is, I was a cop for ten years, but I wasn't allowed in the box except for maybe once or twice, and then only to try and intimidate the suspect. Detectives guarded their turf jealously; uniforms need not apply. For detectives, the interview room was like the ark that held the torah scrolls; only the rabbis got a free pass. The rest of us had to be invited to stand before the ark or stare from the pews in awe and wonder. It took me a minute to divine that Melvin, a.k.a. Malik, had been snagged with half a key of coke taped to the underside of the dash of his 1979 Buick Electra 225. Things quickly settled into a boring point-counterpoint:

I'm keepin' my mouf shut till y'all get me my lawyer.

You do that, Melvin. You keep quiet while I extol the virtues of the Rockefeller Drug Laws to you. Okay, Melvin?

The partner bitched about her using words like extol.

What's the problem? You afraid Melvin won't understand?

Fuck Melvin. I'm worried I won't understand!

I didn't get what this chatty interrogation about a drug bust had to do with Larry, nor why it would worry him so, but it was great for insomnia. I found myself drifting off into that netherworld between consciousness and numb sleep. I was almost fully out when the female detective began a rant about just how much of his worthless life *Melvin* would be spending in Attica thanks to the former governor of the Empire State.

Shit! Get me my moufpiece and you best bring a D.A. too.

Why's that, Melvin?

Cause I got something to deal.

Something like what, Malik?

You ever heard a D Rex Mayweather?

There was an uncomfortable silence. I could hear the hum of the ventilation system, shoes brushing along the linoleum floor of the interrogation room, bodies shifting in their chairs. I thought I might have heard whispering, but it was hard to know if I was just imagining it. The silence broke, and the older detective did the honors.

Why should we give a shit about some dead, drug-dealing nigger, Malik?

Man, y'all gimme that buddy-buddy Malik shit and then you gotta get all up in my face like that. S'not right, man. Y'all get my moufpiece and a D.A. We let them decide if they should give a shit about what this nigger got to say.

That was it. End of tape. But not, I figured, the end of the story. It was too late to call Larry. It was too late to go back to bed. Maybe it was too late for a lot of things.

Excerpted from the *Daily News*, June 5th, 1972:

BOARDWALK BODY IDENTIFIED
Terry O'Loughlin, Staff Writer

The partially decomposed body discovered last week in a shallow grave beneath the Coney Island boardwalk has been positively identified as that of reputed drug kingpin Dexter Mayweather. Mayweather, better known by his street name, D Rex, was alleged to have run the largest drug trafficking network in the five boroughs.

Mr. Mayweather had been arrested on a host of charges over the last ten years, ranging from simple possession to assault and attempted murder. Yet at the time of his death, he had never, been convicted of any crime. Detectives at the nearby 60th Precinct refused comment on either Mayweather's homicide or on his previous run-ins with the NYPD.

However, an unnamed source in the federal prosecutor's office was more forthcoming. He spoke of Mayweather with a grudging respect. "D Rex was the real goods. He was shrewd, slippery as an eel, and ruthless," the source said. "He was anything but run-of-the-mill and he had been the undisputed ruler of Coney Island. But no lion stays king forever."

Although the Medical Examiner's office has listed the death as a homicide, it has refused to release the actual cause of death. Beyond stating that Mayweather's body had been in the sandy grave for about two weeks and that it had been positively identified through the use of dental records, the ME has declined further comment.

Dexter Mayweather, the youngest of seven children, began life in a coastal South Carolina town. When his father abandoned the family shortly after his son's birth, his mother relocated to the Coney Island section of Brooklyn.

(See Body Identified on page 28)

CHAPTER THREE

I WOULD HAVE caught the winning touchdown pass or floated down some lazy country stream or tasted a woman for the first time. When I woke, the world would take me to its breast and I'd be able to hear myself think for the first time in my life. Not only would that voice inside my head know the right questions, but it would supply the answers for my way ahead. Unfortunately, it had been my experience that focusing on *ifs* and *woulds* and *should haves* was a shortcut to hell.

"Jesus Christ, Moe!"

I woke up, the touchdown pass glancing off my fingertips.

"Is this how you want Sarah to find you?"

I took inventory:

Shirtless and in my boxers.

Headphone cord twisted through my arms.

Tumbler between my legs.

Bottle of Dewar's dripping scotch onto the living room carpet.

Drool on my shoulder.

A stiff neck.

A sore back.

The stereo on.

"I guess not," I said.

"Come on, clean yourself up. Sarah's gonna be up in a little while and want her Sunday morning pancakes."

"Okay, just let me wipe this—"

"Forget that mess. I'll take care of it. What were you doing out here anyway?"

"Time traveling."

"Can't you give me a straight answer anymore?"

I let it go. Katy and me, we were a million miles apart out of bed as well. Never mind that I wasn't certain what I *had* been doing last night. Maybe Larry's tape had been a way for me to escape from the bedroom, a ready excuse to deaden my senses with a few too many fingers of scotch.

As to what was actually on the tape . . . Sure I knew who Dexter Mayweather was. Every cop who worked the Six-O in the late '60s and early '70s knew about D Rex, King of the Soul Patch. Shit, they found his body under the boardwalk where I used to walk my beat. But D Rex had been murdered in the spring of 1972, and what possible connection this could have with Larry was escaping me at the moment. Besides, I had other reasons for remembering that spring.

On Easter Sunday of 1972 a little girl went missing. Seven-year-old Marina Conseco was the youngest of five brothers and a sister. Her dad, a divorced city fireman, had left Marina in the charge of her older siblings while he went to get some hot dogs and fries at Nathan's. When he returned, he noticed Marina was missing. Three days later, she was still missing. Coney Island was never hell on earth, not even in the bad old days when I worked it, but it wasn't a good place for little girls lost.

By the fourth day, we'd made the unspoken transition from searching for her to searching for her remains. No one had to say a word. You could see it on the faces and in the slumped shoulders of the off-duty cops and firemen who had volunteered to look for her. We were running out of places to search. They'd even had the divers in to plumb the muddy waters of Coney Island Creek. They found a capsized submarine, but not Marina's body. My hand to God, there's a submarine in Coney Island Creek. You can look it up, as my sister Miriam likes to say.

Never underestimate exhaustion. As the years pass, I become more and more convinced that my exhaustion saved Marina's life. Between regular shifts, overtime, and my off-duty volunteering, I had barely slept in ninety-six hours. In spite of my lack of sleep, I was out searching with a couple of firemen. We were driving toward Sea Gate along Mermaid Avenue. I could feel myself drifting off, so I blasted the air conditioner, turned the radio up full bore, began shaking my head violently. The guys in the car with me must have been just as tired, because they didn't say a word. I began forcing my eyes open, wide open, the way you do when you sense yourself falling asleep at the wheel. I kept looking up. You know when you stare at something long enough, it either becomes invisible or you begin noticing things.

What I noticed were the old wooden water tanks on the rooftops of abandoned buildings. I slammed on the brakes and all three of us jumped out of the car. When I pointed up, they understood. We found Marina Conseco at the bottom of the fifth tank, in half a foot of filthy water, alive! She was in shock and suffering from hypothermia.

She had a fractured skull and some broken bones. She'd been molested for two days before being thrown in the tank and left to die.

That was my moment, my *one* moment on the job. It earned me a few medals, a nice letter in my file. Papers wrote about the rescue. Even rated some face time on local TV. What rescuing Marina Conseco didn't get me was a gold shield. Why not?

The city was nearly bankrupt.

Twenty-three year olds didn't get gold shields back then.

Jews, blacks and Hispanics needed to walk on water to get one.

All of the above.

Answer: (D) All of the above.

Took me a lot of years to come to terms with not getting a gold shield. Even now, I'm not quite sure I have. For some people, for the people who've hired me over the years to find their missing relatives, my not getting that shield was a godsend. It's what has driven me to prove myself for the twelve years since the NYPD put me out to pasture. And proving myself has helped me keep my sanity while I sold wealthy schmucks bottles of wine that cost more than my first two cars combined. Funny thing is, I've twice come closer to getting that gold shield since my retirement than I ever did for saving a little girl's life. Life's fucked up that way, I guess.

After breakfast, I listened to the tape once again to make sure I hadn't missed anything obvious. The replay was no more enlightening than the first go-round. I called Larry McDonald at home. He picked up in the middle of the first ring, as if he'd been sitting at the edge of his bed by the nightstand, arm coiled. Alternately impatient and distant, he had the sound of a man who hadn't slept much lately. I was well familiar with the symptoms.

"You told me to listen and call. I listened, now I'm calling."

"You heard?" he asked.

"I listened. I'm not sure what I heard, but I listened."

"What . . . What'd you say? You listened to the whole thing, right?"

"Twice."

"And . . ."

"Some desperate skell is trying to play let's make a deal with a weak hand. Wouldn't be the first time. D Rex is old news. It's like trying to cut yourself a deal by saying you know who killed King Tut. Who gives a shit?"

"Murder's never old news, Moe."

"It is when the victim's a fucking drug dealer."

"Not always. This is one of those 'not always' kind of situations. People can get hurt by this."

We were close, Larry Mac and me—as close as you can get to an ambitious bastard like Larry. It's sort of like being friends with a mercenary; you're only as good a friend as your market value can sustain. So when Larry said something about people getting hurt, I knew it was code for himself.

"People, Larry, or you?"

"People."

"You gonna explain this shit to me or what? This cryptic nonsense is pissing me off."

"Not on the phone."

"How then, by fax, or the Pony fucking Express?"

"Can you meet me in an hour?"

"Where?"

"The boardwalk, by the parachute jump."

"See you in an hour."

It took him a lot longer to ring off than it had to answer.

CHAPTER FOUR

MY DAD USED to take Aaron and me to Coney Island on spring Sundays. I don't remember him taking Miriam. My dad was a good man in an old-school sort of way. He loved Miriam, maybe more than he loved his sons, but I'm not certain he knew how to handle a girl. He suffered from China Doll syndrome. Dad was always frightened that Miriam was somehow more breakable than his boys, that she needed to stay home and have tea parties with her stuffed animals. Sports, roller coasters and the like weren't for delicate little girls. Miriam, a mother lion in a previous life, needed very little protecting.

Dad loved the parachute jump.

"*La Tour Eiffel du Brooklyn*," he'd say, in an accent less French than Flatbush.

"What's that mean, Dad?"

"The Eiffel Tower of Brooklyn, you idiot!" Aaron would snap. "You ask that every time."

"Aaron!" my father would bark.

"Sorry, Dad."

"Don't apologize to me. Apologize to your little brother."

"That's okay."

We did a variation of this exchange each time we came. Steeplechase Park was still open back then. They had this really cool ride with wooden horses on tracks, and you could fly around the park as if you were in a real steeplechase race like the kind they had in England. But by the time I took the oath and was assigned to the 60th Precinct, Steeplechase Park had been razed and the wooden horses sent to the scrap heap. They don't make glue out of wooden horses, just splinters.

In 1968, as today, the only thing that remained of Steeplechase Park was the rusting hulk of the parachute jump. I wasn't like my dad. I hated the damned thing. It was an unfortunate vestige like the human appendix, its decay calling attention to a purpose no longer served. Sometimes I think they should have just taken a bulldozer to the whole amusement park area and put up a fucking plaque like they did at Ebbets Field. In this way, the romantic vision of the place would be all that remained. There are reasons beyond stench why we don't let the dead rot above the ground.

I watched Larry McDonald's approach. He came up the Stillwell Avenue stairs onto the boardwalk. Where Surf and Stillwell Avenues collided was where Nathan's Famous had stood for about seventy-five years, but the wind was strong out of the west and blew the fragrant steam of Nathan's griddles and fryers away from me, towards Brighton Beach and Manhattan Beach beyond. The sudden aging I'd noticed in Larry's eyes and voice the previous day had begun to affect his gait. He took the measured steps of an old man who had always been sure on his feet, but had suddenly lost confidence not only in his stride but in the solidity of the ground beneath his shoes.

As usual, he was sharp dressed. Larry was the only person I'd ever met who could overdress for any occasion. He wore a finely tailored camel hair blazer over an ivory silk shirt and beige slacks with a crease so sharp it could cut diamonds. His brown alligator loafers probably cost more than my entire wardrobe.

"Italian?" I wondered, pointing down.

"What? Huh?"

"The shoes, shithead."

"Oh yeah, they're Italian. What else would they be? And that's Chief of Detectives Shithead to you."

"Sorry." I made the sign of the cross and said, "Forgive me father for I have sinned."

"You heathen fucking Jew. You're gonna rot in hell for that."

"Jews don't believe in hell."

"Believing's got nothing to do with it. It exists." He lit up and smoked away.

"So . . ."

"You know they found him over there."

"Who?"

"Mayweather." Larry walked to the rail along the beach side of the boardwalk, and I followed. "He was half buried in the sand right under where we're standing. Some *alter kocker*'s dog dug his hand up like a hidden bone. Did you know he was tortured before he was killed? They broke every single finger on both hands, snapped 'em one by one. And his knees! They were smashed to bits."

"That must've been unpleasant. Trust me, I know from knee pain, but what the fuck, Larry? This is all very fascinating, but I don't really give a shit," I said, putting my foot up on the bottom rung of the

16

rail, resting my arms across the top, my chin on my arms. I watched the little waves roll ashore, stared at the container ships slowly moving toward the mouth of New York Harbor. "You gonna tell me what's going on?"

"There were rumors . . ."

"What kind of rumors?"

"Just rumors. Rumor rumors."

"Hey, that clears it all up, I guess."

"Ugly rumors."

"Yeah, well, the world is full of whispers and innuendo," I said. "I don't usually concern myself with that stuff and you never struck me as the kind of guy who paid them much mind."

"There's a chance some of our old friends maybe can get hurt by this shit getting dredged up again."

"Then maybe you wanna tell me about those rumors, Larry."

"The word on the wind back then was that some of our guys were on D Rex's pad. You remember what the Soul Patch was like. No one could touch Mayweather in the day. He was like Robin Hood in Sherwood Forest. And we were clowns in blue, the Sheriff of Nottingham and his deputies, with our thumbs stuck up our asses. You understand what I'm saying?"

"I can do the math. Maybe some of *our* guys are at or near twenty years on. Maybe some of them would do a little gun eating if they lost their reputations and pensions now."

"It's one of the things I always respected you for, Moe. You were quick on the uptake. Shit never had to be explained to you."

"Did anybody ever look into these rumors?" I wondered.

"Of course. Those were the Buddy Boy days, the time of the Knapp Commission. They looked into every fucking thing. If some dick complained that a cop farted in his direction, they looked into it. But I.A. was bullshit back then. They assigned every eager schmo to the bureau, even the ones who couldn't make a case with a road map."

"I was around, Larry, remember? I was the one who knew Serpico a little."

"Yeah, that's right. Frank fucking Serpico, the only honest cop in all New York City. Fuck him! I think the guy was half a fag myself."

"Pity I don't have his number anymore. We could call and ask."

"Doesn't matter. Serpico really is a harmless piece of shit. He hurt whoever he was gonna hurt a long time ago. Only time people even remember him is when that bullshit movie is on cable. D Rex is something else. I don't want him reaching out of the grave to hurt anyone."

"You really are worried, aren't you?"

"What makes you say that, Moe?"

"You're talking too much. You're making speeches." I stood straight up, took my foot off the railing, grabbed Larry by the sleeve, and made him face me. "So, how much were you cut in for?"

"Huh?"

"Don't play dumb with me, McDonald. You forget, I know you. I know who you are and I know what you are. I think sometimes maybe that's why you trust me, because I know. So please don't insult me."

"I'm not gonna make excuses to you, Moe. A lot of us earned a little on the side from D Rex. You worked the street. You know we weren't gonna make a fucking dent. It was big business even back then."

"I thought you weren't gonna make excuses."

"You're right, but I think you might be surprised to find out just whose pockets D Rex's money found its way into."

"Right now we're talking about your pockets, Larry, and being on a drug dealer's pad wouldn't look good on your résumé for beatification."

"I'm no saint!" He jerked his sleeve out of my grasp.

"Doesn't mean you don't aspire to the job."

A broad, sad smile briefly forced its way onto Larry's face. "You *do* know me, you prick."

"Yeah, maybe, but what I don't know is what I'm doing here."

"I wanna hire you."

"To do what?"

"To save my career and the reps of the guys we served with."

"No."

"You haven't even—"

"No. The answer's no, Larry. This is a dirty business."

"What, you're quoting *The Godfather* to me now? Talk about being a martyr . . ."

"The answer's still no."

Killed me to say it. I think if he had asked me to do almost any other job, I would have jumped at it. I was desperate to escape the boredom of the stores and to occupy my mind with something other than the growing distance between Katy and me.

He turned to the beach again, reached into his pocket much as he had the day before, and slapped something down atop the rail ledge. Although his hand obscured my view, I felt confident it wasn't a cassette tape. Pretty sure it was metallic, as it had made a pinging sound when he hit it against the rail. And I was also pretty sure I knew what it was. He lifted his hand and proved me right. A gold and blue enamel detective's shield glistened in the afternoon sun.

"Do this for me and it's yours. Detective first; no physical, no range qualifying, no questions asked."

Larry McDonald and I had done this dance once before. Six years earlier, in 1983, with Larry's help, I'd discovered what had happened to Moira Heaton. Moira, an intern for an up and coming politician, had been missing since Thanksgiving Eve 1981. Though there was no physical or circumstantial evidence linking the politician to her disappearance, he had been tried and convicted in the press, his once promising career placed in limbo. After we found out the truth about Moira Heaton and the politician was cleared of any wrongdoing, Larry got his big bump to deputy chief. A few years ago, he got chief of detectives.

All of us involved with that case made out. Politicians and their wealthy backers can be a generous bunch. But a few weeks later, when I began feeling uneasy about the facts of the Heaton case and started nosing around, Larry Mac called out of the blue to offer me the one thing I yearned for: a gold shield. I took it. It was both the perfect distraction and the ultimate bribe. And if it hadn't been for a stupid fender bender with an out of state car, I'd still have that gold shield in my pocket.

Later, when the original facts unraveled and Larry stood to lose his shiny new promotion, I questioned him about his motives in offering me the shield. He claimed it wasn't his idea, that he had no idea I'd reopened the investigation. I chose to believe him, because with Larry, faith was always a choice. I knew he trusted me. I'd earned it, but like I said before, trusting Larry was transitory and involved the equation of sell-interest.

"You can get me a shield?" I asked. "Even now, even at my age? You can get all that shit waved?"

"You'd be amazed."

"Sorry, Larry, no. I guess I don't want the shield that bad anymore."

He didn't argue. Instead, he scooped the shield up and placed it back in his pocket.

"That's a pity, Moe."

"Why's that?"

"Dirt's a funny thing, pal. It rubs off all over the place, on lots of people too."

"You're getting cryptic again."

"Maybe so. Let me tell you a story about my late Uncle Finn. Uncle Finn lived with the guineas near Arthur Avenue up in the Bronx, and he loved to sit out on his stoop at night, having a beer or three, watching the world pass by. One night there was a helluva car crash in the gutter out in front of Finn's house. A bumper flew off one of the cars right up onto Uncle Finn's stoop. Nearly decapitated him."

"Is there a moral to this story?"

"I'm getting to it."

My sense of humor was at low ebb. "Get to it!"

"In this world, the greatest injustices are done to the innocent. No?"

"You're threatening me now, Larry? That's what we've come to?"

"It's not what we've come to. It's where we've always been."

"I guess I didn't know you as well as I thought."

"Yes, you did. Don't act so surprised. We've both used each other over the years," he said, lighting up another cigarette.

"I never threatened you."

"That's because you never had to. People who eat three squares a day don't pick through the garbage, but take those three meals away for a week or two and . . ."

I shook my head at him. "Jesus, and I thought boredom was rotting *my* soul. Is this what ambition did to yours?"

"This isn't about ambition anymore. It's about survival. Yours and mine."

"You'd hurt me, Katy and Sarah just to save your own ass?"

"It's a start."

"You know what, Larry, go fuck yourself! You think you can hurt me, go ahead. There's some stuff related to the Moira Heaton business you don't know about that will make you look pretty fucking bad. I can spin it so that it looks like you got your bump on the strength of covering up a murder. So be my guest, start spreading the dirt. We'll see who comes out looking cleaner."

"See how easy it is to make threats, old buddy. You're a natural."

"Fuck you!"

"Yeah, Moe, you said that already."

I took the cassette tape of the interrogation out of my pocket, thought about tossing it onto the sand below. "I don't know how you got this tape and I don't care. What'd you expect me to do, anyway, wave a magic wand and wash away your old sins? If I had that kinda power, I'd wash away my own." I slid the tape back into my pocket.

I turned to go.

"Moe!"

"What?"

"You know I couldn't hurt you or your family. I just didn't know who else I could go to with this. For some reason, you're the only person I've ever really trusted. And when you said no, I . . . I guess I panicked. I'm sorry, Moe. But please, can't you do this thing for me, for old time's sake?"

"Our old time's sake ran out about two minutes ago, right around the time you threatened my family."

I started walking along the boardwalk into the heart of Coney Island. I'm not sure whether I was more upset at him or at myself. He was right, after all. We had used each other over the years. Maybe I was just jealous that he had used me to better effect than I had him. And I had always known what Larry was at his core. But his threat— there was no getting over that for me. No amount of backpedalling, rationalizing, or apologizing was going to make that right. There are things said and done in this world from which there can be no retreat.

When my legs stopped moving, I turned back to look. Either Larry had gone or I was just too far away to make him out. On the other hand, the parachute jump seemed just as big as if I were still standing directly beneath it. Fucking thing seemed to follow you like the full moon on a clear night—or your own guilt. I think maybe that's why I hated it so.

CHAPTER FIVE

A RUINED MARRIAGE is a peculiar thing. After the dust settles, I think you can look back and see that both parties had a fair amount to do with the collapse. At first blush, it's easy to point the finger at one party or the other, especially when there's cheating involved. And even though that wasn't the case with Katy and me, I'd have to confess to having known a few people who would have cheated regardless of what their spouses did or did not do. But a lot of the time, cheating is as much a reaction as an action. I guess it's not only cheating that works that way.

I'd been thinking about this shit a lot lately. Maybe a few of our troubles can be traced back to the miscarriage, maybe most of them. Sometimes, though, I think the fatigue was structural, a flaw in the design. It's like when there's an undetected crack in the airframe of a jet as it first rolls out of the factory, but it takes thousands of flight hours before the aluminum fails and the plane disintegrates. Were we like that, I wondered, Katy and me? Were the cracks there even before we took our vows?

I mean, it's not like Katy and me got together under the best of circumstances. Her big brother had been killed in Nam. She'd been recently divorced and Patrick was missing. Me, I was lost without my job and so drugged up from the pain medication for my knee that I could barely see straight. Jesus Christ, the first time I met Katy we were standing over a body—the cops thought it might've been Patrick—that had washed up in the Gowanus Canal. Now how many people have a Guess *How I Met My Wife* story like that one? Pretty fucking romantic, huh?

Then Katy went and converted to Judaism. Don't look at me! Wasn't my idea. Worst of all were the secrets. Yeah, *secrets*, plural. There was the big one between her dad and me, but there were others—things I'd uncovered about Francis Sr., and Patrick, about myself even, that I kept locked away where no one else but me could see them. All the ingredients except the miscarriage were there from the very beginning. What more proof do you need for the blinding power of love?

But for the two days since I'd told Larry McDonald to go fuck off, the shaky legs of my marriage were all I could think about.

Paradoxically, his threats had made me ponder what I'd be losing if Katy and I stopped pushing the boulder up the hill and let gravity have its way with us. In one sense or another, people had been threatening me my whole life and I hadn't gotten any more comfortable with the process. Nothing like being pushed to make a man push back.

Red, White and You was my baby for the time being, so on Monday and Tuesday I'd schlepped out to the new store and settled into the same boring routine that had, for the preceding dozen years, passed for my life's work. "Same shit, different venue," that's what Ferguson May, the late philosopher of the 60th Precinct, used to say. He would have laughed his big black ass off at the thought of me explaining the differences between Australian and South African Chardonnays. Too bad he got a shiv shoved through his eye and into his brain while trying to break up a domestic dispute. There were days I wondered if he wasn't the lucky one.

As it was, I was fiercely regretting Larry having threatened me. If he had only had a little patience and given me a few days back in the stupefying world of wine sales to come around. Don't think I hadn't been tempted to call him and tell him as much. I'd played the scenario out in my head during the few moments break between the boredom and my contemplations on marriage. I never got the chance.

"Moe, line one." A voice woke me from my torpor.

"This is Moe, how can I help you?"

"Moe, how are you?"

It was a woman's voice, a vaguely familiar one, and the words it spoke belied its tone. This voice was worried, and not about how *I* was doing.

"Margaret! Margaret McDonald, is that you?"

"It's Margaret Spinelli now."

The woman on the phone was Larry Mac's ex-wife. They'd split up about four years back and we'd lost touch.

"I guess congratulations are in order then."

"Thanks, Moe."

"But this isn't a wedding announcement, is it?"

"It's about Larry. I'm worried about him."

"Why?"

23

"I hadn't heard from him for a few years. Then about two weeks ago he started calling out of the clear blue. He just kept apologizing for the way things had turned out between us and how if he could only take it back . . . Things like that. And last week, there was this one call when he just broke down. He asked me to come out to dinner with him, just so we could talk. He said he needed to tell me some stuff in person."

"What happened?"

"At first I told him to stick it up his ass. He really hurt me, Moe. The man turned his back on twenty years of marriage. One day, what, he decides he's had enough? Do you know what that felt like? After I got done throwing up, I thought they'd have to sweep me off the floor in pieces."

"I'm sorry. Did you tell him this?"

"Every word and more."

"And . . ."

"He took it. Then he did something I never thought I would ever hear Lawrence McDonald do."

"What was that?"

"He begged me."

"He *begged* you?"

"See, you can't quite believe it either, can you?" She sounded relieved, like someone being told they weren't crazy after all. "I was stunned, because as ambitious as my ex-husband is, regardless of the things he's done to get ahead, the one thing I was always sure he would never stoop to do was beg."

"Did you agree to see him?"

"Yeah. Frank, he's my husband, he's down visiting his mom in Florida. So I agreed to meet Larry this once, at the Blind Steer in the city."

"I know it. He took me and Katy there once."

"How are you guys?"

Don't ask! "We're great. Sarah's getting big. But what about last night?"

"He didn't show. I checked with the maître d' and Larry had made reservations, but he just never came. I waited at the bar drinking red wine for hours. I used their phone to call every number I knew, but . . ."

"Did you—"

"I tried every number, Moe, even the police special contact numbers. Nothing. No one's seen him. They tell me he's taken some vacation time and he won't be back for a week."

"Maybe he just forgot about dinner, or thought better of it and flew down to the islands," I said, not quite believing it. "You know how he loves the islands."

"You trying to convince me or you? He would never do that, not after begging to see me."

"I guess you're right, Marge, but I'm not sure what I—"

"Moe, check around for me, please. He really sounded awful. Something's wrong, very wrong. I can feel it."

"Maybe something is wrong, but why should you care?" I asked, the vapor from the chill in my voice almost visible.

"He left *me*, Moe, not the other way around. He stopped loving me, but I never stopped loving him. That's why it hurts so much." Her use of the present tense wasn't lost on me.

"Okay, I'll ask around and see what's what."

She gave me her numbers and address, then hung up. Her worry hung in the air around the phone like ground fog. Margaret was right about there being something wrong, only I don't think she had a clue that her chief-of-detectives ex-husband had started his storied police career in someone's pocket. There's a lot of shit a cop's wife doesn't know, and even more she doesn't want to know.

No one had any idea of Larry Mac's whereabouts. Margaret was right about that. I called everyone I knew who knew him. Well, almost. Told them I was hunting him down because I was thinking of having a Six-O reunion party and wanted his input. Cops are wary of anything but a party especially when the guy throwing it owns liquor stores. They're always up for that. Even put in a call to a black chick I knew he used to visit down in Atlantic City. She hadn't heard from him in a year or so, and she seemed far more interested in Larry fucking himself than her.

Then there was that last call, the one I'd avoided making. I picked up the phone, dialed, put the phone down. There are just some things a man has to do in person. This was one of those.

"Jeff," I called to my assistant, "I'll be gone for the rest of the day."

Rico Tripoli had once been closer to me than my own brother. We had been through the war years in Coney Island. We'd patrolled the boardwalk, done drug raids in the Soul Patch. And as my dad had once schooled, nothing bonds men together like combat. Along with Larry McDonald we were known as the Three Stooges: Moe, Larry, and Curly. Rico's hair had actually been thick, black, and wavy, but wavy was close enough for our precinct brethren. Cops are like newspaper reporters in that way. They shape the facts until they fit.

Rico Tripoli had shaped the facts of his life into a chronic disaster. He'd gotten his gold shield on the pretense of a huge case. The truth, as always, was far more complicated. The Grinding Machine Mob were a bunch of wiseguys who had become the modern equivalent of Murder, Incorporated. They not only killed their own targets, but became the sub-contractors for most of the five New York families. After luring their victims to a convenient spot and executing them, they'd destroy the bodies by running them through industrial meat grinding machines. But as was always an occupational hazard, they began enjoying their work a little too much. They started murdering for the sake of murder and dispensed with bullets. Word on the street was they'd developed a taste for throwing their victims into the grinders while they were still alive. Rico played a major role on the task force that finally brought these sick fucks to justice.

Unfortunately for Rico, he often chose his friends and lovers unwisely. When he got me involved with the search for Katy's brother, Rico already had one divorce under his belt and was well on his way to another. He'd also gotten mixed up with a crooked politician who had plotted to ruin Francis Maloney's political career and who used me to do it. He tried buying me off with a gold shield and a pat on the back. Apparently this pol figured all cops were like Rico and would sell their souls at discount prices. I told him and Rico to drop dead. The pol obliged, dying in a plane crash upstate. I'd barely uttered a word to Rico in the last decade.

Some of that was my doing, but Rico was mostly responsible. For the past five years, he'd been at the state correctional facility in Batavia. In the early '80s he'd been assigned to Midtown South Narcotics. He'd started drinking heavily and once again sold himself cheaply, this time to the Colombians. Rico alerted them to drug raids on their big stashes and shipments. In return, they threw him some midlevel busts, spare change, and all the hookers he could handle. When one of the Colombians got collared, it took him about fifteen seconds to give Rico up in exchange for a reduced sentence. Prison is hell for a cop. And for his own protection, Rico did his stretch in isolation.

I'd heard through sources, mainly Larry Mac, that the time in stir had really taken a toll on Rico. It was the isolation mostly. Rico was a social animal. I think sometimes that's why he sold himself so cheaply. His payoff wasn't the power or the pussy, but the hypnotic blend of danger and newfound alliances. He got off on meeting new people, making new buddies. I know it sounds crazy, but there it is. I mean, I knew the guy better than anyone; at least I used to.

In N.Y.C., S.R.O. has two meanings. On Broadway or at Shea, it means standing room only. On the street it means single room occupancy. If you're more familiar with the latter, it also means you're fucked, big time. New York City may not be a factory town, but we are a city of warehouses. And the commodity we warehouse least effectively are the homeless and poor. S.R.O. hotels are a landlord's ultimate wet dream. Dilapidated, shitbag buildings on the verge of collapse are miraculously transformed into money machines. Between city, state, and federal agencies, landlords are paid thousands of dollars per month per room for filthy, crime ridden, cesspits that couldn't be given away for free. See, in New York, it's the buildings, not the streets, that are paved with gold.

Rico Tripoli lived, if you were generous enough to call it living, in the Mistral Arms. You gotta love that name, a holdover from a time when romance and whimsy had a place in American life. I tried picturing it as it might have looked new, with Gatsby and Nick driving quickly past in a flashy yellow Rolls Royce on the way to lunch with Meyer Wolfsheim. See what a few years of knocking around the city university system will do for a broken down cop? It gives him pretentions. Shit, maybe I *was* cut out for the wine business, after all.

All pretense had been beaten out of the Mistral Arms long ago. You needed a sharp eye to see that its plywood and graffiti entrance had once been a grand work of wrought iron and thick, green glass. Inside, an ill wind was indeed blowing as whiffs of crack smoke that had leaked out the sides of careless mouths rode into oblivion. In the lobby, the white marble floor and decorative pilasters were chipped and broken and defeated. A chubby Hispanic girl sat in a chair, ignoring me and rubbing the belly of a one-eyed cat. The chair wobbled on legs as sturdy as a junkie's veins.

"Whaddya want?" A man's voice bounced around the marble and landed on my ear.

I didn't look at the front desk, just held up my old badge. "Tripoli!" I barked.

"Three F." I took a step. "Elevator don't work," he said.

What a fucking surprise! "Thanks."

Cops may look back on their careers with a rose filter, but no cop misses places like the Mistral Arms. It's hard to muster up fond memories of stepping in shit. I knocked on Rico's door.

"Yeah, what the fuck?"

I saw an eye in the peephole, listened to locks clicking, a chain unlatch. The door pulled back. Framed by the empty jamb, a virtual stranger stood before me in a haze of blue smoke. If I had passed him on the street or stood next to him on a subway platform, I wouldn't have recognized him as the man I had once loved above all others. Back when we first started on the job, Rico was sort of a better looking, more solidly built version of Tony Bennett. Rico could sing, too, but his heart hadn't gotten as far as San Francisco. He had ridden the first wave of "white flight" upstate to Duchess County. He'd lost that house to his second wife.

This man, the man in the blue smoke with a wasted skeletal physique and loose, yellowy skin, his hair thin and gray and lifeless, looked nothing like Tony Bennett. He barely looked human, more a twisted root grown vaguely into human form. He tried not to smile. I didn't have to try.

"Moe! Jesus, come in." He offered me his hand. I took it, if not out of friendship, then out of pity. He scrambled about, tossing dirty laundry onto his cot and chucking empty beer bottles into a D'Agastino's bag. "Can I get you a beer or something?"

"No thanks."

He lit another cigarette, but didn't smoke it with quite the same gusto as Larry. I surveyed the room. Old cop habits die hard. It was what you'd expect, only more so: peeling paint, splintered floorboards, junkyard furniture, a coffin-sized bathroom. Above his cot was his only memento, a picture of The Three Stooges in our dress blues.

Choked me up, that. In the next room, a headboard was being pounded against the wall.

"*Ay, conjo!*" a woman screamed.

The pounding stopped.

"Twenty bucks or four vials of crack and she'll do just about anything you want," Rico said, tilting his head at the now silent wall. "Marisa's still pretty new at the game. She tries to enjoy it. I let her suck my cock once in awhile. You see the little fat girl downstairs? That's her kid."

I needed a shower.

"So to what do I owe the pleasure of this visit?" he asked, the inevitable bitterness leaking into his voice. "Wanna talk old times, buddy?"

"In a way, I guess, maybe I do."

He wasn't ready for that, seemed to stumble reaching for an empty bottle to use as an ashtray.

"Don't fuck with me, Moe. You don't have that much credit with me to fuck with my head."

"So I've got *some?* That's good to know."

"Was you who gave up on me, brother. Not the other way around. You were a big part of my life and the next day . . . *pfffft!* I was cut out like a tumor."

"Your metaphor, Rico, not mine. And it's not like you had no part in that. You tried playing me. You—"

"Yeah, I used you. Blah, blah, blah. You're like a broken fucking record, man. What's it been, like ten years since you seen me? In the hospital, right, when your father-in-law had that stroke?"

"Eight year. 1981, I think."

"Eight fucking years and you still can't let it go. Well, you can stop playing that tune. I'm bored with it. I played it over and over again in my head when I was inside. We're not friends anymore. Okay, I get that. So what is it you're doing here?"

"Larry Mac."

"What about him?"

"No one can find him."

He burst out laughing. It was wild, manic laughter. His sluggish brown eyes came to life, darting madly. His lips curled back exposing his stained teeth and thick, grayish tongue. The laughter took its toll and he launched into a coughing fit that seemed to last for hours. These were coughs from down deep, coughs so raw and raspy they hurt my throat. When the coughing finally died down, Rico made smooching sounds.

"*Mmmhhhh! Mmmhhhh!* Larry, where are you?" he looked under the dirty laundry on his bed. "Come out, come out wherever you are."

"Very funny."

"He ain't here."

"I didn't think he was."

"So what do you want from me?"

"I gave up wanting that in 1978."

He winced. I knew the tough guy shit was an act. He missed me as much as I missed him. Only difference was I'd had a life to fall back on. He'd pissed his away.

"I thought you might know where he is," I said, not interested in inflicting any more pain. "I know you two are still close and that you keep in touch."

He was thinking that one over. It was an opening he chose not to take. I guess he'd had enough hard feelings, too.

"Haven't heard from him since last week. He did tell me you and that asshole brother of yours opened another store."

I let it go. He never liked Aaron much, especially because my big brother refused to let Rico invest in the business when we were first starting out. Aaron was smart that way.

"Yeah," I said, "out in Brookville."

"Congratulations."

"Thanks. So did Larry sound okay? Did he seem like the ambitious prick we both know him to be?"

Rico thought about that, dragging his fingers and palm across a week's worth of beard. I could read the answer in his expression, but I let him say it anyway.

"Nah, something was up with him. He was quiet-like, you know, sorta thoughtful and philosophical almost. That ain't Larry. Ferguson May, maybe, but not Larry Mac."

"Anything else? Did he actually say anything out of the ordinary? Do anything out of the ordinary?"

Rico hesitated, a veil of genuine concern on his face. "Yeah, well . . . He . . . He threw me an extra hundred bucks. But he did that sometimes."

"This time was different, right? I can see it in your face."

"Different, yeah, but I can't say how. An extra c-note is an extra c-note is an extra c-note. I can't afford to be, too. . . . You know how it is."

I didn't, but I could guess. He noticed the pity on my face as I stared at the appalling condition of his room.

"Better to live in a shitbag room like this than in a fucking cell, Moe. A cell's no place for a man. Once you go in, you never really get out."

The conversation was going in a direction I wasn't willing to follow.

"Can I use the head?"

"Sure," he said.

I closed the door behind me. After I pissed, I ran the water a little and took five twenties out of my wallet. I slipped them under Rico's disposable razor and closed the medicine cabinet. When I came out, I handed him a business card and asked if he needed a few bucks to hold him over.

"No thanks, Moe."

"Okay. You hear anything from Larry, you call me."

"I'll call."

This time I put my hand out to him. He took it, but not too eagerly. Ten years of hard feelings and hurt weren't going to disappear in ten minutes.

"I didn't ask about Katy and Sarah because Larry tells me about them," he said, embarrassed.

"That's okay, Rico. Let's just worry about Larry for now."

As I walked down the hall I heard the locks clicking shut. When I reached the stairs I nearly ran into the chubby girl who had since shed the one-eyed cat. Her impassive expression had been replaced by one of loathing and disgust. Her near-black eyes cut deep. I thought she might spit at me, but she moved on. I understood. She had mistaken me for one of her mother's johns. I wondered if that little girl would ever see men as anything more than twenty dollar bills or four vials of crack. In the lobby, the one-eyed cat brushed against my pant leg.

CHAPTER SIX

IT WAS NOTHING, a small piece in the *Daily News* that only a few days before would have meant less to me than the death of a moth. At first, the words didn't quite register. I read past the article and accompanying photo, and went back to it. Two hikers in the wildlife preserve area of Gateway National Park had stumbled over a body. The unidentified man had some holes in his head besides the ones God included in the original design. It's not like dead bodies never turned up in the preserve.

Once, decades ago, before the coastal area that stretched from Flatbush Avenue in Brooklyn to the Rockaways to the approaches around Kennedy Airport had been turned into a national park, the reeds, marshes, and murky inlets along Jamaica Bay had been a favorite dumping ground for the prematurely dead. But since the area was now federally protected and the nearby Fountain Avenue landfill closed, murderers had had to find alternative, less conspicuous places in which to discard their trash. I didn't give the subject much thought.

I was too busy staring at the black and white photo of what was described as a gold and diamond encrusted ID bracelet. The bold block letters spelled out the name MALIK. Malik was described as a light-skinned black male, five-foot-seven inches tall, weighing one hundred and fifty-five pounds, approximately thirty years of age. He had light brown eyes, no facial hair, and a close-cropped haircut. Although these days Malik wasn't exactly an uncommon name, I suddenly felt very uneasy. I sensed the fan blades spinning faster and that the shit was moving in their general direction.

Another round of calls to all the people Larry and I had in common netted me nothing. I had avoided getting back to Margaret until now, but no news plus time equals panic. She took my lack of results well enough, though she couldn't quite stop the fear and worry from leaking into her voice. I promised to keep looking, and got off the phone before she had time to think out loud. Once she gave full voice to the worst of her fears, they would be hard to shove back down.

Those calls, the ones to Margaret and my old acquaintances, were easy compared to the one I was about to make. The single condition of my partnership with my brother was that I be allowed to work cases whenever I wished. The reality of it was that I averaged about one case every two years, and even then I used vacation days to account for my time away from the business. In my heart I knew that Aaron had agreed because he believed my passion for the job would fade like the taste of a first kiss. He was a smart man, my brother Aaron. Money in a man's pocket, a nice house, a new car, and a comfortable life can kill passion as effectively as a thousand different poisons. But what Aaron forgot is that the taste of some first kisses never fade.

Originally, I'd gotten my P.I. license as a way to salve my wounds, a way to lie to myself that I wouldn't let myself be swallowed up by the wine business. It was a conceit, a hedge against the "ifs" in life. Now, as I dug my license out of my sock drawer and stared at it, it felt like a lifesaver. I blew the light covering of dust off its black vinyl case and slipped it into my back pocket.

"City on the Vine," Aaron answered on the second ring.

"Hey, big brother."

"What is it? Is something wrong? Something's wrong! I can hear it in your voice."

"The Amazing Aaron, four syllables and he predicts all."

"What's wrong?"

"You always think something's wrong."

"So," he said, "am I usually right?"

"Yes, you're usually right about something being wrong. In this world, that's an easy guess. But, this time, you're wrong about something being wrong. I'm taking a few days to work on a—"

"What? Are you completely *meshugge*? We opened a new store less than a—"

"It's a case. It's our deal. No going back on the deal."

"For chrissakes, Moe, grow up already! You're off the cops twelve years and your chances have come and gone. This is your business now. *This* is your life."

Ouch! That landed solid as a chopping right hook over a pawing jab.

"The deal's the deal, Aaron. Kosta's in town and he'll cover for me."

"But we—"

"I'll be in the store for my shift later today and I'll arrange everything with Kosta," I promised. "Don't worry about it."

"Don't worry, he tells me. Am I allowed to ask what this is all about?"

"I'm not sure what it's all about. Maybe nothing."

"Why *do* I ask?"

"Good question. Why do you ask?"

The truth was, I didn't know whether there really was something here or whether I just wanted there to be. I think maybe it was a little bit of both. If Larry Mac turned up tomorrow morning sporting a new tan and this stiff in the paper with the gaudy jewelry was a different Malik than the one I heard being interrogated by the cops, it was back to the sock drawer for my P.I. license and back to my exile in the French Reds aisle. Katy, a graphic designer, was down working in her basement studio. It was my turn to drop Sarah off at school. As I sipped my coffee, waiting for her to come down the stairs, something else occurred to me, something ugly that refused to be ignored. If those two hikers had in fact stumbled over *the* Malik, a.k.a. Melvin, then his death stood to do a lot more for Larry Mac's constitution than a week in the Caribbean. Dead men don't hold up well under cross-examination.

ROBERT HIRAM FISHBEIN bore an unfortunate resemblance to the late Groucho Marx, but in spite of his looks, he'd once been a political high-flyer. The District Attorney of Queens County was an even more ambitious man than Larry McDonald. And that is really saying something. Fishbein, perhaps beyond any of us connected with the Moira Heaton investigation, had benefitted from its conclusion. Of course, if the real facts were ever made public, it would have done very few of us proud.

That said, D.A. Fishbein had parlayed the good press that followed in the wake of the Heaton case into a lot of goodwill, political capital, and, most importantly, into a nice fat campaign chest. Unfortunately, he'd ignored his handlers' sage advice to run for state attorney general and overplayed his hand. Instead, he mounted a feeble campaign for the Democratic gubernatorial nomination, and got squashed like a bug. His message played about as well upstate as a minstrel show in Brownsville. That was the difference between him and Larry Mac. Fishbein had let his ambition control him. Larry had the knack for modulating his ambition so that he could keep his eye on the individual steps on the way to the penthouse.

Fishbein, having squandered his big chance, had settled into a kind of comfortable purgatory. He could be Queens D.A. forever, and never anything more. But I understood ambitious men and knew he would not, *could* not accept his fate. For years, no doubt, he had tormented himself with false hope that there must be some way for him to crawl out of his dungeon and regain the spotlight. That's why I knew he would take my call. I was a good luck charm. I'd gotten him to the main stage once before. Why not again?

The Queens D.A.'s office might seem like an odd place for me to start, but frankly, Fishbein was about my best option. A cop may be a cop for life in his own head. The rest of the world, however, stops seeing him that way the second he takes off his uniform. As time passes, his old buddies barter their badges for golf bags and he's left with no connections on the force. Of course I knew lots of cops, but unlike guys who moved around a lot, I had spent my entire abbreviated career in one precinct. The only guys I'd ever been really tight with had served with me in the Six-O. With Larry missing, Rico disgraced, Ferguson May dead, and the rest of my ex-precinct-mates possibly under suspicion for taking bribe money from a murdered drug lord, I didn't have a lot of places to go.

"Prager, how the hell are you?" Fishbein, normally cool and shrewd, couldn't contain his enthusiasm. "What can I do for you?"

"Maybe I can do something for you, Mr. D.A."

There was a profound silence on the other end of the phone. His prayers had been answered. *Praise the lord!*

"Like what?" he wondered, more composed.

"I can't really say now, but it could be big. I'll need your help."

"You've gotta give me more than that, Prager." He was anxious, not a fool.

"Drugs and cops," I said.

More silence. Then, "What do you need?"

"For now, I need to know everything about the body that was found in Gateway National Park last night. I mean everything."

"That's federal."

"C'mon, Mr. D.A., let's not dance that dance, okay?"

36

"Do you have a fax machine?"

I gave him the number.

"You'll have it within the hour," he promised. "Anything else?"

"Just one thing."

"And that is?"

"If this amounts to anything, you might have some jurisdictional issues. In the end, you might be stepping on some very sensitive toes."

"You let me worry about that," he said. "I can step very softly when I have to, or step down really hard when it suits the purpose. If you catch my meaning."

I caught it all right. The flip side of his desperation was fury. I was being warned about playing with fire—hellfire. If I was involving him now in something that resulted in a second public embarrassment, he wasn't going to suffer it alone. I was going down with him and I was going down hard.

"I was a good gloveman in baseball," I said. "Caught almost everything hit my way."

"I'm glad that we understand one another, Mr. Prager. Because, to extend your baseball analogy I'm the manager of a team on the wrong side of a one-run game in the bottom of the ninth, and we're down to the last strike. We lose the game and—"

"—you're looking for a new managerial position," I said, regretting I had started us along this metaphorical road.

"Yes, we'll both be out of the game for good."

Time to put an end to this. "I'll be waiting for your fax."

I rang off before he could give me the bunt sign.

I SAT AT my desk in the office of Red, White and You, watching the fax machine. As a way to pass time, it ranked right up there with reading James Joyce. At least I didn't have to pretend to enjoy it. Fishbein was prompt. The machine began chittering away less than twenty minutes after we'd gotten off the phone. I resisted the urge to read the fax sheet by sheet. I had already gotten too far ahead of myself and didn't see the point of drawing and redrawing conclusions with each page received.

The unease I felt at the breakfast table proved well-founded. The body discovered in the reeds between Rockaway Boulevard in Brooklyn and Crossbay Boulevard in Queens had been positively identified as Melvin Broadbent, a.k.a. Malik Jabbar, born May 26th, 1959, in the maternity ward of Coney Island Hospital. By the look of his rap sheet, Malik's favorite pastime seemed to be getting arrested. Most of his arrests were for petty crap and he'd done the bulk of his penal tour at local venues: first Spofford as a kid, then the Brooklyn Tombs, then Rikers. Many of his arrests were for minor drug offenses, but he walked on almost all of those. He had done a short bid in Sing Sing or, as it was referred to these days, Ossining. Funny thing was, there seemed to be no record of his recent arrest for that coke taped to his dashboard.

I moved on to a less amusing section of the fax; his autopsy photos and report. No wallet or other ID had been found on the body, but the bracelet was discovered in the wet sand beneath him when the cops rolled him over. Good thing the fax had included a photo of Malik from one of his myriad arrests, because homicide had taken a toll on his boyish good looks. The two hollow-point loads put into the back of his head had removed large swaths of his face on the way out. And what the bullets had started, sand crabs and insects had finished. The autopsy photos were hard to look at, even for me. I decided to have a seat and to keep my lunch where it belonged. I'd gotten the gist of the report. I took down Malik's address, phone numbers, etc., and placed the fax in a folder.

"You all right?" a customer asked me as I stepped out of the office. "You're pale as can be."

Nauseous. "Fine," I answered.

"Good, then can you please explain to me exactly why you charge a full three dollars more for Moët White Star than Crates and Carafes in Roslyn?"

"I would be happy to."

And for the first time in years, I was.

CHAPTER SEVEN

2951 WEST EIGHTH Street, that's the address of the 60th Precinct. It's one of those hideous prefab buildings that lacks looks, character, and just about every other aesthetic quality you might think of. Its only saving grace is that it is located directly across West Eighth Street from Luna Park, one of the ugliest housing projects known to humankind. The precinct house is also right next door to a firehouse. Now there's some sharp thinking, huh? It's like putting the hyenas and the lions next door to each other at the fucking Bronx Zoo. There were times during my service I thought lions and hyenas were more congenial.

There was a civilian employee—a heavyset black woman with lacquered hair—who greeted me as I entered. She was so impressed by having an ex-member of the Six-O show up at her desk that she nearly fell asleep mid-sentence. Not that I blamed her, mind you.

"Can I help you?"

"This used to be my precinct?" I said, feeling immediately like an idiot.

"Y'all want it back?"

Then I compounded my stupidity by showing her my badge. Oh man, that really impressed her.

"You wanna see mine?" she said, showing me the laminated credentials she had clipped to the overburdened waistband of her slacks. "Not as pretty, I know, but it don't set off metal detectors or nothing. Now is there something I can help you with?"

I thought about it. My showing up here wasn't exactly part of some master plan. It's not the way I worked. Like I had any idea about that. Unconventional was a polite term for how I went about my business. Fact is, I'm a stumbler; a lucky stumbler at that. Everyone who ever hired me mentioned that I'd been lucky and that they turned to me only after they had tried competent detectives. As Thomas Geary, the rich man who had hired me to look into Moira Heaton's disappearances had said, "We've had two years of good with no success. Now it's time to try lucky." At least, that's what I remember him saying.

Didn't matter. Whenever they came to me, it was always with the *Gotham Magazine* article in hand or in mind. After my future brother-in-law went missing in 1977, some hotshot investigative reporter did a cover piece on the mystery surrounding Patrick's disappearance. It was a natural. Francis Maloney Sr., was a big *macha*, a mover and shaker in the state Democratic party and one of its biggest fundraisers. His eldest son had been shot down over Hanoi and his youngest son had vanished off the face of the earth. But what it always came down to was Marina Conseco. Within the body of the article about Patrick's mysterious disappearance was an inset with my picture, Marina Conseco's, and a brief description of how I'd saved her life back in '72.

"Hey, mister!" She snapped her fingers. "Y'all want me to call the control tower for landing instructions or what?"

"Sorry."

"No offense, but I am kinda busy here," she explained.

Well, that was bullshit, but I couldn't blame her for wanting to get rid of me. I had come here only because I knew I would eventually have to.

"So is there somebody you wanna see?"

"Yeah, is Rodriguez around?" I asked.

"Retired last year," she said. I knew that.

"Lieutenant Crane?"

"Captain Crane now. He at One Police Plaza."

"Stroby?"

"Never heard a him. Listen, Dancer and Blitzen, Doc and Dopey, they ain't here neither. So—"

Just when she was getting going, the door opened at my back and the room filled with noise. I turned to look over my left shoulder. There, cursing up a storm in both English and Spanish, was a stunning woman in her midtwenties with coffee-and-cream skin. She had thick, pouty lips, straight, jet black hair, and brown eyes that were at once both fiery and cold. She was busy waving a rolled up *New York Post* at an older, pencil-thin man in his forties. He dressed old-school Sears. She was Macy's, but One Day Sales only. Her voice was familiar. I'd heard it before. Once. On tape.

"Jesus, enough already," he said out of desperation. "Whaddya want from me, I didn't kill the schmuck."

Another familiar voice, definitely Bronx Irish.

"Fucking Melvin! My big case down the crapper and this is how I find out, through the fucking *Post*!"

Fishbein's help hadn't gotten me much of a head start. Though I had more details than the papers about the life and demise of the late Mr. Jabbar, a.k.a. Broadbent, the daily rags had the essentials. I knew because I read about it myself this morning over coffee. The news of his identification and the scant details of his very small life weren't exactly the stuff of banner headlines. The networks weren't going to preempt their afternoon soaps and the world would continue turning on its axis. But some people would notice. Some already had. His was the kind of death that would cause a ripple on the surface of a silent sea. The ripple might quickly weaken and fade, forgotten like a fallen leaf. Or the ripple might plow the water into a wave, a wave to crash onto our heads, to sweep its victims into the sea without regard to their relative guilt or innocence.

"Yo! You got a problem?"

It took me a few seconds to get that the Latina detective was talking to me. I also realized I had been staring at her. Well, I'm not sure staring is the right word, precisely. I was more than staring. It was like the rest of my visual field went blurry at the edges while her image was hyper-sharp, almost painfully so. And my hearing took on that muted, head-under-water quality. Yes, she was very pretty but something else about her commanded my attention. Even after she barked at me, I could not turn away.

"Do I know you?" she asked impatiently.

"I'm sorry, no, I don't think so," I heard myself say, and finally looked away.

She and her partner walked by, the partner shaking his head but relieved for a few seconds of distraction. Then, before they got all the way down the hall, she started up again.

"I got enough shit on my plate without some middle-aged shithead stalking my ass."

That hurt. No one enjoys being called middle-aged. It's like when you turn forty you begin the long process of being dismissed. You're no longer your own person, but just another ant in the colony. Fergie May used to say that a man knew he was middle-aged when he became invisible to hippie chicks. Well, hippie chicks might have gone the way of the Edsel and moon landings, but there was no arguing the essential truth of his philosophy. I was invisible, and if I hadn't exactly been dismissed, I was being handed my coat and gloves.

"Who was that?" I asked the woman at the desk.

"Her? That's Detective Melendez. Bitch!" she whispered, loud enough for me to hear.

We both smiled at that.

I DROVE TO Bordeaux in Brooklyn, our store in Brooklyn Heights. Situated on the lower floors of a lovely old brownstone on Montague Street, it was my favorite of our three locations. With its gilt lettered signs on green pane glass, globe fixtures, and intricate woodwork, the place had a distinct nostalgic feel reminiscent of the Jahn's Ice Cream Parlors that used to dot the borough. There were many reasons to love that store: the weird customers it seemed to attract, its proximity to the Brooklyn Bridge, the breathtaking views of lower Manhattan from the Promenade. I can remember a hundred spring days when I felt as if I could simply reach across the East River and rake my fingers along the ridges of the Twin Towers, or take a running jump and land on the South Street Seaport.

In my heart of hearts, I know I loved that store best because of Klaus. Klaus, the store manager, had been with us for years. He knew more about music and fashion and popular culture than anyone I had ever met. Born out west somewhere, Wyoming or Utah, I think, Klaus came to New York to escape his family, or maybe it was to let them escape him. The two thousand or so miles between son and family served both parties well. The distance made it easier for his folks to deny his gayness, and he could love his folks back without constantly chaffing against their beliefs.

When he started with us he was a total punk. He was all ripped clothes, piercings, weird haircuts, and attitude, but he made it work. Klaus spent more time at Dirt Lounge, CBGBs, and Mudd Club than at work. Yet he was never late, never called in sick, and learned how to peddle wine a lot quicker than at least one of his employers. I hired him as a sort of petulant "fuck you!" to my brother. I'd show him for getting me involved in a business I always knew I'd come to hate. In the end, Klaus was the best hire either of us had ever made. Not even Aaron could deny that. Klaus had long since forsaken his Dead Kennedys t-shirts for silk shirts with French cuffs, and power ties.

"Excuse me, mister, you got any Ripple?"

"Hey, boss!"

Klaus came around the counter and hugged me.

"Please, I'm a married man."

"Oh yes, and how's that working out for you?"

He knew what he was asking; Klaus had become one of my closest friends. He was familiar with the rough spots in my life. It's odd, but it seemed that I had spent the last dozen years shedding most every old friend I'd ever had. That's what aging is, I think, shedding your old lives like snake skins. And what represents a man's life better than the friends he's made and lost along the way? Along with Klaus, there was Kosta, Pete Parson, Yancy Whittle Fenn, and Israel Roth; a gay, a Greek, an old cop, a drunk journalist, and a concentration camp survivor. Not exactly the A-Team, I know, but men who I could trust more than Larry McDonald.

"How's it working out?" I repeated. "We're still married. That's how."

"That bad."

"Worse."

"If you want my opinion, it's not Katy."

"No?"

"No, it's you."

"Can we go back to that part about wanting your opinion?"

"You're bored," he said.

"Thank you, Dr. Freud, but that's not exactly breaking news."

"Alan, he's my lover, he—"

"I know who Alan is, for chrissakes! You don't need to tell me that every time you mention his name."

"Okay, boss, put your claws back in. He's a psychologist and he's about five years your senior."

"Yes, I know. We've met. Is there like a point to this or are you gonna make me wish I had gone to the Manhattan store and let Aaron aggravate me instead?"

Klaus ignored that. "Well, before me, Alan had been in a ten-year relationship, and he said when he hit forty and he'd been with his partner for a long time . . . He just lost it. He felt bored and lost and wanted to jump out of his own skin."

"Did he buy a red 911 and start sleeping with cheerleaders?"

"In a manner of speaking, yes. Why, don't you think a gay man can have a midlife crisis?"

"I wouldn't know. I figured you'd tell me when the time came. So, that's what you think this is, a midlife crisis?"

"Why, did you think you were immune? Being aware of the phenomenon is no protection against it."

"I suppose."

"Okay," he said, "I can see it's time for a change of subject."

"Nice segue."

"If you prefer, we can go back to—"

"No, that's fine."

"So what are you doing here? There's a rumor that we have a new store and that you're supposed to be there now."

"Christ, you're starting to sound like my brother."

"Bite your tongue!"

Aaron thought the world of Klaus in a business sense, but they weren't the same kind of people. It wasn't Klaus' being gay that bothered Aaron so much, though I don't think he was completely comfortable with it either. It was that Klaus was obsessively plugged in, so much an animal of fashion and music, of what was coming next. Without really trying, he tended to make you feel out of it, passé. And Aaron was very much his father's son, a traditionalist. My big brother was old when he was young. He felt way more comfortable with Elvis Presley than Elvis Costello and couldn't have imagined any set of circumstances that would have allowed for the words sex and pistols to be in close proximity in the same phrase. As Klaus had once said of Aaron, he was more fugue than a frug kind of guy.

"Sorry," I said. "But I took a few days off."

His face lit up. "You're working a case! But what are you doing *here*?"

"Kenny Burton."

"Sorry, you've lost me."

"We used to work together when I started out as a cop. Now he works for a private security firm that has a contract with the Marshal Service over at the Federal Courthouse on Centre Street. I'm going over there to talk to him in a little while."

"So, you're killing time."

"Couldn't think of anyone I'd rather kill it with."

"Yet another sad commentary on your life."

"Fuck you, Klaus!"

"Ah," he said. "There's the Moe I know and love."

TEN YEARS MY elder, Kenny Burton had the old-cop look, somehow grizzled and clean-shaven all at once. Except for my recent phone call, we hadn't spoken or seen each other in many years, but I was unlikely to miss him. Everything about him, from his get-the-fuck-outta-my-way strut to the you-don't-want-a-piece-of-me manner with which he blew cigarette smoke into the faces of oncoming pedestrians, screamed asshole. Or maybe I saw that in him because I knew him a little bit from when I had started on the job in the late '60s.

Priding himself on things most other cops would hide like a crazy aunt, Kenny Burton was a brutal, thick-skulled prick who was trained in the ways of pre-Knapp Commission, pre-Miranda Rights policing. He never paid for a meal, a cup of coffee, or a blow job until word came down from on high. He never arrested anyone who wasn't guilty or didn't deserve to have the crap beat out of them. His motto might well have been: Why use your head when you can use your fists instead?

"Caveman Kenny Burton, is that you?" I said, walking up to him outside the courthouse. He flicked a still-burning cigarette at the open window of a waiting cab. The cigarette barely missed, bouncing harmlessly off the cab's door.

"Who wants to know?"

"Moe Prager wants to know."

Burton grunted, one corner of his mouth turning up. From him this was a hug and a kiss on the lips. "What you doing around here?"

"Waiting for you. Can I buy you a drink?"

"Sure. There's O'Hearn's on Church."

O'Hearn's was your basic New York version of an Irish pub. What did that mean? It meant it was just like any other shithole bar in the city, only with cardboard shamrocks on the walls in mid-March and the occasional barman who understood that hurling had meaning beyond vomit.

Burton's malicious blue eyes pinned me to my chair as we sipped at our drinks. We were boxers staring across the ring before the bell for round one. He was doing the silent calculations. I could hear the gears churning nonetheless. The mistake people make about judging brutes is to assume they're fools. Kenny Burton was no fool. We had never been close, even during the few years we served together. Larry Mac, on the other hand, always considered Kenny a pal. Only after I'd come to know Larry well did I figure out that odd coupling. Kenny Burton appealed to Larry's ambition, not his heart. Ambitious men are like baseball scouts, they can spot everyone's special talent and how that talent can serve them. Frankly, I didn't want to know how Caveman had served Larry's ambition.

"This about that party thing we spoke about on the phone?" Kenny asked, knowing it wasn't.

"Nope." I waved to the waitress for a second round. "That was bullshit."

"I figured. We ain't exactly blood brothers, you and me. What it's about then?"

"Larry's missing."

He didn't react, but I didn't read much into his deadpan. The gears continued churning. Then, "Missing? Missing how?"

I ignored the question. The waitress came, plopped our drinks down. When she tried clearing Kenny's first glass, he stared at her so coldly I thought she might freeze in place. "Leave it!" She did.

"He was acting weird the last time I saw him," I said.

"Weird?"

"Nervous. Jumpy. Not like Larry at all. Then . . ."

"Then what?"

"I don't know. We got together back in Coney on the boardwalk and he started talking crazy about the good old days."

"Good old days, my ass. Fucking job!"

"I know what you mean," I said, just trying to see if he'd say something on his own. He didn't disappoint.

"You do, huh? I remember you being a cunt, Prager."

"Nice."

"Ah, you was like all them new cops, more worried about the skells and scumbags than the victims."

"For every corner guys like you cut, you create two more. I was worried about following the law."

"Fuck the law! The only law is the law of the jungle. You pussies never understood that."

"Was Larry Mac a cunt?"

Kenny actually laughed, an icy breeze blowing through O'Hearn's. "Larry was a lot of things."

"Was?"

"Don't be such a fucking asshole, Prager. You know what I mean."

"I do?"

"What, you want me to throw you a beating? With that bum leg a yours, it'd take me like ten seconds to kick your ass twice around the block."

"Now there's something to be proud of."

"Get to the point, asshole."

"Larry missing is the point."

"That's what you say, but even if he is, I don't know shit about it. I owe Larry Mac," he said, taking his eyes off me for the second time since we sat down. "He kept me on the job till I made my twenty. It was a fucking miracle that he pulled it off. I was like a poster boy for I.A.B. for the last half of my career. Then after a few years, he got me this gig with the Marshal Service. Job's a fucking tit."

I had made the acquaintance of two retired U.S. marshals during the Moira Heaton investigation. One killed himself. The other tried to kill me. Only time in my life I exchanged gunfire with anyone. I think I hit him, but I didn't stick around to check. Got the hell out of there and didn't bother looking back.

"Okay. You hear anything, let me know." I threw my card and a twenty on the table. I made to go.

He grabbed my forearm. "You really think something's wrong?"

"I don't know."

He let go of my arm and studied my card in earnest. "I hear anything, I'll call." He slipped the card into his wallet.

I took a few steps and turned back around.

"What?" he growled. "You gonna annoy me some more?"

"You remember D Rex Mayweather?"

If I thought I was going to catch him off guard with that, I was wrong.

"That dead nigger? Yeah, what about him?"

"Nothing."

I became acutely aware of the few black faces seated around O'Hearn's. Burton had been purposely loud. It served the dual purpose of embarrassing me and of challenging anyone in hearing distance. Kenny Burton hadn't changed. He was the same asshole I had known twenty years before. You could set your watch by him.

That night as I stared up at the ceiling, it wasn't Kenny Burton's face I was seeing in the dark. It wasn't Larry's. Not Katy's. Not what was left of Malik's either. What I saw was a pair of almond-shaped brown eyes burning with a cold fire set against dark, creamy skin. I saw an angular jaw, a perfect, straight nose with slightly flaring nostrils above plush, angry lips. All of it framed in hair blacker than the darkness itself.

CHAPTER EIGHT

COPS IN CARS can't follow suspects worth a shit. Even if they were to possess the requisite skills, the damned unmarked cars would give them away. Unmarked cars are about as inconspicuous as the Goodyear blimp. So it didn't take more than a glance in my review mirror to spot the unadorned blue Chevy as it pulled away from the curb. The whole way to Sarah's school, the car trailed half a block behind, the driver trying to keep other traffic between us.

I kissed Sarah, watched her walk into the schoolyard and up the front steps. When she had disappeared behind the heavy metal doors, I rolled slowly into traffic, making certain to get caught at the first red light. My tail was four cars back in the right hand lane, the same lane as me. I scanned the cross street for oncoming cars and, seeing it was clear, put my foot to the floor. With tires smoking, I swerved across the left lane, through the red light, and onto the cross street.

With my foot still hard on the pedal, I drove a further three blocks before making a sharp left down a dead end street that ran perpendicular to the Belt Parkway. About a hundred feet from the dead end, I backed up an empty driveway until the houses on either side obscured my car from view. I waited. Either they would give up before cruising this street or, as I hoped, they would roll down the street, distracted, annoyed, simply going through the motions rather than searching for me under every stone.

Neither hearing it nor seeing it, I sort of sensed their car coming. Then I caught a glimpse of its nose as it rolled down the block. Went right past me. As it passed, I pulled out of the driveway, slammed on the brakes and put it in park. In a moot display, the cop at the wheel of the Chevy threw it in reverse. Too little too late. My car was width-wise across the street, making it impossible for the cops to turn around or back up past me. I hopped out and strolled up to the driver's side window of the unmarked car, rapping my knuckles against the glass. The sun was strong and the refraction off the glass made it difficult for me to make out the face of the person at the wheel.

When the window disappeared halfway into the door, I recognized the driver. I had seen her face on the backs of my eyelids and suspended in the dark air above my bed only a few hours ago. But before I could react, Detective Melendez threw her door open, smacking it hard into my bad knee. Reflexively, I backed up and bent down to rub it. Big mistake. Melendez and her partner were out of the car and on me like wolves on a crippled lamb.

"All right, dickweed, you know the drill," said Bronx Irish as he threw me into the side of their car.

Still favoring my bad leg, I hit the car awkwardly, the right side of my rib cage taking the full force of impact. Hurt like a son of a bitch and it didn't do much for my respiration.

"Assume the position," she barked.

Still trying to catch my breath, I was slow to follow her instructions. Big mistake number two. My arms were being yanked up and thrust forward, palms slapped down on the hood of the Chevy. Bronx Irish kicked my legs apart and back. He frisked me, removing my wallet and .38.

"So, Mr. Prager," Detective Melendez said, "you always speed like that in a school zone?" It was a question for which she wanted no answer. "That was quite a display of stupidity you put on back there."

"I noticed I was being followed. How was I supposed to know you were cops?"

"Don't be such an asshole, Prager," said Bronx Irish. "What should I do with him, Carmella?"

"Cuff him and throw him in the back."

"Hey, I—"

"Shut the fuck up!" she cut me off. "Keys in the car?"

"What?"

"Are your fucking keys in the car, Prager?"

"Yes, Detective."

"John, you take care of him. I'll park his car right."

Bronx Irish cuffed me and slid me into the rear of the unmarked Chevy. He got into the passenger seat. As we waited for Melendez to reposition my car, I tried striking up a conversation.

"What part of the Bronx you from, Detective?"

"Pelham."

"Am I allowed to ask your last name?"

"Murphy."

"John Murphy, now there's a rare name on the NYPD."

I could see him smile.

"What were you guys tailing me for?" I wondered.

"You'll see," he said. "We didn't wanna discuss it in front a your little girl. We were waiting for you to come out, and then you come out with your kid. So we figured—"

Just then, Detective Melendez opened the driver's side door. She put the Chevy in reverse and tore down the street, tossing my car keys out the window as she went. I hoped I got back to my car before dark. Finding those keys wasn't going to be easy. She hit the siren, pulled into traffic, and up onto the Belt Parkway heading east. When she shut the siren off, I tried to get back to my chat with her partner.

"So, Murphy, when you saw me come out of my house with Sarah, you—"

"Didn't I tell you to shut up?" Melendez stared at me in the rearview. "We ask the questions."

I ignored that. "You're a real hot head, huh?"

"Shut up and enjoy the drive."

"You're kinda young to be a detective, aren't you?" I pressed on. "Christ, when I was on the job—"

"Don't gimme any of that old timers' bullshit. It's all you old guys do, talk about how it was back in the day. What you got to worry about is that I *am* a detective, not how I got to be one."

Murphy's head was turned sideways, away from her. I could see he was rolling his eyes. Wanted to ask him how he'd ended up with the young hotshot, but I didn't figure she'd much enjoy that line of questioning.

"Back in the day or today, people don't usually make detective at your age."

She bit the bait hard. "If I was a man, you wouldn't even be asking me this shit about my age. It's not about my age! I got to put up with this crap all the time 'cause dinosaurs like you think it's about whether you stand or squat to pee. I'll tell you what it's about, it's about if you're a good cop."

Murphy, making sure his head blocked her view, pointed his right hand at me and motioned like a quacking duck. He'd heard this speech before. I egged her on.

"So it's not about your being Hispanic either, then? Not even a little bit?"

Taking her eyes off the road, she turned to give me the cold stare. Murphy crossed himself. I'd done it now.

"Listen, *viejo*, I was waiting for that. See, you assholes are all the same. In your eyes, my gold shield is about my pussy or Puerto Rico, not about if I'm a good cop."

"Did I say that?"

"You didn't have to. I was always a big reader, but I read best between the lines, grandpa. Besides, you ever make detective?"

"Nope."

"So, you're just a resentful old fuck, huh?"

"I had my shot," I said.

"What happened?"

"In '72, I rescued this missing little girl from the roof of an old factory building. Everyone had given her up for dead. It was a big story. These days, they'd throw me a ticker tape parade. Back then—"

"This is it!" Murphy barked.

Melendez hit the siren and lights and yanked the wheel hard right, cutting the Chevy across two lanes of traffic. Several cars smoked their tires as they broke and swerved trying to avoid smacking into the flank of the unmarked cruiser. We pulled up around the Pennsylvania Avenue exit of the Belt Parkway.

The Fountain Avenue Dump had been a working landfill for about the first twenty years of my life. I don't know how long before that. When we were kids, Aaron and I used to call it Stinky Mountain. You didn't have to see it to know it was coming up. Depending on wind direction, you could tell you were in the vicinity from several miles away. And even when the wind blew the stench of rotting garbage and methane in the other direction, you could always spot the swirling clouds of thousands of gulls and other birds that feasted at the banquet of our moldering debris. Freaked me out more than a little, those swooping, spinning, wheeling clouds of feather and flesh, of bills and bony feet. Used to like to watch the tractors and bulldozers, though, perched atop Stinky Mountain, blending the newly dumped piles of garbage into the compost.

Then, a decade or so back, the city just shut it down. I think someone got the brilliant idea that maybe it wasn't such a good thing to have a huge dump in the wetlands around Jamaica Bay. Across the way from the dump, some developers had built a maze of apartment buildings, called Starrett City. Like everything else in Brooklyn and the city itself, Starrett City blended in with the surrounding landscape like a pile of puss in a vanilla milk shake. Even I had to remind myself that in New York, it's always about the money and never the beauty. Beauty was a commodity affordable only to people who foisted eyesores like Starrett City upon the rest of us.

But just because the dump had been closed, its mounds of fetid garbage tarped over, its methane vented and burned, its clouds of birds relocated to Staten Island, it didn't mean people had forgotten what it once had been. As Rico's task force had proved many years ago, there were plenty of bodies beneath the tarpolines. Now, apparently, there was one outside its gates. As soon as I saw the other "official" vehicles lining the road, I knew this wasn't going to be pretty. This wasn't a drug bust or a speeding ticket or a Patrolmen's Benevolent Association barbeque. There were no flames or aircraft debris strewn about. No plane had gone down on its approach to Kennedy. This scene had homicide written all over it. Disquiet wrapped me in its arms and squeezed tight.

As we rolled along, Melendez navigating us through the throng of uniforms and suits, I got that sick feeling in my belly I know that's something people just say, but I meant it. This wasn't any old crime scene either. There was a lot of brass in attendance, a lot of suits, a lot of worried white faces. We veered off the road and into a patch of tall, blond reeds and cattails. A blue and white NYPD chopper flew tight circles overhead, the downwash from its rotors toying with the reeds like a fickle plain's wind blowing Kansas wheat to and fro. We came to a full stop. Detective Melendez threw the Chevy in park.

"Okay, get him out," she groused at her partner. Murphy's clenched jaw indicated just how much he loved being ordered around.

I slid over to the rear passenger door and Murphy helped me out, making sure I didn't crack my head on the car frame. He looped his left hand around my right bicep and marched me through the tangle of tall weeds and cops. Melendez walked ahead of us, never looking back. The ground was muddy, black, and slick. Murphy and I fought not to slip down. About fifty feet ahead of us, over Melendez's right shoulder, I saw a line of yellow tape strung across a clearing in the cattails. The chopper wash blew the stink of the dump into our faces as we approached. A row of men in dark suits stood just inside the tape. Closer now, I recognized the profiles of several of the suits:

Police Commissioner Cleary, Deputy Mayor Brown, Brooklyn D.A. Starr, and—shit!—Queens D.A. Fishbein. He'd already dealt himself in.

Almost to the yellow perimeter, Melendez ducking under the tape in front of us, I turned away from the line of princes and to my left. There, in the midst of the reeds, hundreds of feet away from the closest paved road, was an incongruous blue Chevy, not dissimilar to the one I'd just gotten out of. A swarm of men and women moved around it like worker bees attending to the queen. When one of the worker bees moved away from the driver's side window, I noticed a figure slumped against the wheel. I couldn't make out his face, but I knew in my heart it was Larry McDonald.

They say energy can neither be created nor destroyed, and I guess I'll have to take their word for it. But when a man with that much ambition dies, there has to be fallout somewhere—an earthquake, a tsunami, an erupting volcano, something. Or did Larry have ambition in place of a soul? Did it pass into the body of the first cop on the scene or the person who found him? Did it inhabit the first ant that crawled by or the first gull to swoop over? If so, the other gulls had better watch out.

"What are you smiling at?" Murphy wanted to know.

"Seagulls."

"Whatever."

He guided me under the tape. It took a few seconds for the assembled minions to notice me, my police escort, and my NYPD issue jewelry. When they did, Fishbein scowled.

"Detective, what is Mr. Prager doing in cuffs?" he asked Murphy in a less than cordial tone. "You were ordered to bring him to the scene, not arrest him."

Melendez started to answer. "I told him to cuff—"

"Get them off. Now!" Fishbein ordered.

"Hey, Hy," D.A. Starr said, "this is my borough. Don't be ordering my cops around."

"They're *my* cops!" corrected Police Commissioner Cleary. Ah, the world of New York politics and fiefdoms. "Well, Melendez, why the cuffs?"

"I—he—When we went to get him, he, uh—he," she stuttered, flushing slightly.

"Spit it out, Detective. Sometime this week."

"He ran a red light."

Fishbein, Starr, Cleary, and Brown sneered disapprovingly, shaking their noggins like four bobble-head dolls on the back deck of the same car.

"If you're so desperate for traffic enforcement, Melendez, we can put you on Highway Patrol," Cleary said. "You'd cut a fine figure in those tall black boots and riding pants."

By the look on the men's faces, the image of Melendez so dressed had universal appeal. Christ, it appealed to me. But I saw that some of what Melendez had said to me on the ride over was true. She might carry the shield, but she was always one misstep away from being dismissed as portable pussy and nothing more.

"I did worse than blow through a red, Commissioner Cleary. I cut across a crosswalk and sped in a school zone. I saw I was being followed and overdid it, I guess."

But instead of being pleased or impressed by my jumping to her defense, Detective Melendez shot me a look that would scare the numbers off a clock. *I don't need rescuing.* She was tough to figure, and now wasn't the time to try.

"Cut him loose," said Cleary.

Murphy let me go. I wanted so hard not to rub my wrists, to show everybody, especially Melendez, how tough and cool I was. I immediately rubbed my wrists.

"You know who that is in that car over there?" Fishbein asked, ignoring the icy stare of his Brooklyn counterpart.

"I can guess."

"Guess."

"Larry McDonald."

"Give Mr. Prager a cigar!" Fishbein joked. "Commissioner, you smoke cigars, don't you?"

"How'd you know?" D.A. Starr got a question in before Fishbein could breathe.

"I didn't know. It was a guess."

"Why guess Chief of Detectives McDonald?"

"If it was a 1930 DeSoto or something instead of an '89 Chevy, I would have guessed Judge Crater."

"That's not an answer," Starr growled. Fishbein didn't do a good job of hiding his delight at the displeasure of his Brooklyn counterpart.

"Because I knew Larry was missing."

"You did, huh?" said Cleary.

Decision time. I had to choose my words very carefully. There's lying, and then there's the truth. Lies are lies, but you can filet the truth all sorts of ways depending on the dish you're cooking. For much of my life, I'd been a bad liar and an unskilled butcher of the truth. Patrick Michael Maloney's disappearance had changed all that. I'd since learned s-e-c-r-e-t-s was just an alternative spelling of l-i-e-s. And, God help me, I could parse the truth like a Catholic school nun with a run-on sentence.

"I did. I knew he was missing."

"How'd you know?" Cleary kept on. "The chief was taking vacation time, so there'd be no reason to believe he was missing."

Time to start parsing. "His ex-wife called me up."

"And . . ." Starr said.

"And she told me she was worried about Larry. That he had called her recently to apologize about their divorce. They had made a date to talk it over, but Larry never showed up."

"It's a big leap from standing up your ex to going missing, Prager," Fishbein piled on.

"I guess," I agreed. "But he never got back in touch with her. That wasn't Larry's style. He could be a selfish, ambitious prick, but never an impolite one. Not to Margaret, not after what he'd done to her."

They nodded again in unison.

"Is that all, Mr. Prager?"

"Is that all what?" I turned the question back on Fishbein.

"Let's not be coy. Was there anything besides his ex-wife's call that might have led you to believe something was up with Chief of Detectives McDonald? It's no secret that you and Larry were close friends."

"Close?" I asked. "Was anybody really close to Larry Mac?"

For the first time, I saw something in Detective Melendez's eyes that looked like admiration. She enjoyed how I kept deflecting their questions with questions of my own.

"Well then, closer than most," Fishbein said.

"Okay, yeah, Larry and me, we were closer than Larry and most other people, but he had a lot more layers than an old onion, so I'm not really sure there's much I can tell you."

Fishbein screwed up his face as if he were working hard to think of a follow up, but it was all an act. He was questioning me for appearance sake. I guess he was also trying to give me cover. Because, whether I liked it or not, whether I had intended to or not, I was now Fishbein's boy. By going to him the way I had, he had the inside track. I'd got almost nothing out of the relationship so far except an autopsy report and yellow sheet on Malik, but with me he might knock one out of the park.

"You know, Mr. Prager," D.A. Starr picked up, "you don't seem awfully broken up about your friend's suicide."

"The ground ain't wet from your tears either, Mr. D.A.," I said, trying to hide the shock. *Suicide! Larry McDonald?* "If it's all the same to you, I'll grieve on my own terms."

"Of course," said Cleary.

"You sure there's nothing else?" Starr said.

"Nothing else like what? Sometimes Larry played his cards so close to the vest, they were inside his shirt. Maybe there's something you guys know that you're not telling me. Is that it?"

Silence. Kind of enjoyed watching four grown men paw at the wet earth with their expensive shoes.

Now there was no mistaking it. There was full blown admiration in Carmella Melendez's eyes and fuck me if my heart didn't race at the sight of it. I had done magic before her. But like all magic, it was an illusion. I had heard the tape. I had spoken to Larry. I knew probably more than any one of them about Larry's past sins.

"Do you mind if I go over and pay my respects?" I asked.

"It ain't pretty, son," Deputy Mayor Brown spoke up.

"Nothing ever is, beneath the surface," I said.

"Just stay out of the way. It's still considered a crime scene, remember that," Cleary warned.

"How about if Detective Melendez comes with me to make sure I keep my nose clean?"

Cleary nodded. Melendez wasn't stupid. She didn't jump at the chance. She sneered as if Cleary had told her to carry me over to Larry's Chevy on her back.

"You were good back there," she said.

"Thanks. And you were right about what you said in the car on the way over. Maybe we could sort of start over."

She hesitated. "Where should we start over from, Mr. Prager? From your stunt driving this morning or your unexplained presence at the precinct yesterday? I'm thinking it's kinda odd that you turned up over there outta the blue and then the Chief kills himself, no? The suits and the brass back there might buy your line a shit, but I'm not a big believer in coincidences."

"That makes two of us."

"So where does that leave us? You gonna tell me why you were at the Six-O?"

We had reached the car. The driver's side door was open. Larry's head rested on the steering wheel, his lifeless eyes looked past me into an unfathomable distance. Even in death, he didn't look quite peaceful. His ambition had left a residue on his corpse as real as gun powder. As the chopper moved further away, I caught the stink of his death. In spite of being surrounded by several million tons of decay, the ripeness of it was unmistakable. It was like hearing one particularly sour note from a tone deaf orchestra.

"How'd he do it?" I asked.

"Look at the tailpipe," one of the busy bees said. Sure enough, a flexible black hose ran from the mouth of the tailpipe, beneath the car, around the passenger side, up into a slit in the rear window. Neat strips of duct tape covered the opening in the window left to accommodate the exhaust tube. "My guess is he swallowed some sleeping pills, washed 'em down with some bourbon, and went to sleep. There's a half-empty bottle of Jack Daniels on the floor."

"Any note?"

"We haven't found one yet."

"Thanks," I said.

I felt Melendez's eyes on me, studying me.

"You don't like it," she said, "do you?"

"He was my friend. Nobody likes it when a friend kills himself."

"Don't be that way. You know what I mean. You have doubts."

"There's shit you never want to accept at first. I was never at a shooting scene where the dead guy's mom thought he was a bad kid. No one wants to believe bad stuff about the people they lo—about

58

their friends. I think they think it reflects badly on them somehow, like it's their fault when bad things happen, like *they* failed. You know what I mean?"

I turned to look at her. Her expression went blank, her eyes nearly as distant as Larry's. "I don't think anyone knows better than me."

"What's that supposed to mean?"

Melendez ignored the question. "Come on, we'll take you back to your car."

"Gimme a minute."

"I'll wait over there."

I kept staring at Larry. It wasn't denial, but I was having trouble with his being dead. When a parent dies, you pretty much know how you're supposed to feel. Even if the feelings are mixed and confused, you've decided; or, at least, your heart has. With Larry, it was different. I realized that for the twenty plus years I'd known him, I had never quite decided how to feel about him. I'd always waited for some sign, some gesture on his part that would let me know it was really okay to love him, to hold him close. I took a long last look into his vacant, unfocused eyes, hoping that in death he could give me the thing he seemed incapable of giving in life. Of course, like most wishes, it went unfulfilled. As far as my heart was concerned, I thought, the jury would always be out. The verdict never in.

D.A. Fishbein was the only one of the princes still standing inside the yellow tape when I was done with Larry. Melendez stood a few feet to his left, paying very little attention to either one of us. Fishbein shooed her away.

"Can you excuse us for a second, Detective?"

"I'll be by the car," she said.

The Groucho Marx smile vanished from the D.A.'s face when Melendez had strolled far enough away. "Did it end here?"

"What?"

"Don't play stupid with me, Mr. Prager. You came to me, remember?"

"I remember."

"Then answer the question. Is the chief's suicide the end or the beginning?"

"Don't look now, Mr. D.A., but your hard-on is showing."

Fishbein actually looked down. "Asshole!"

"The truth is, I don't know whether this is the end or the beginning. I'm not thinking too clearly right now. That's my friend lying dead in that car over there, not the ass end of a cow."

"You can sit *shiva* later, *totaleh*. I've got no time for your tears right now. I need to know if this case has some legs. Besides, I don't for a second believe a man like Larry McDonald would have killed himself. You knew him better than anyone."

"That's not saying much."

"Stop fencing with me, Prager. Your Puerto Rican girlfriend's not around to be impressed."

Because of his clownish looks and buffoonish overstepping, Robert Hiram Fishbein was an easy man to underestimate. But what he had just said reminded me that he was neither a clown nor a buffoon. He was sharp and cunning and hungry. Very little escaped his notice, not even the subtleties of early attraction.

"No, Larry never struck me as the kinda man to kill himself."

"That's better. Then let's see if we can't find out what really happened here and if this case's got any legs."

"What case is that? I don't know that there is a case. And," I felt compelled to remind him, "if there is one, it takes place deep in the heart of Brooklyn."

"You let me worry about that. In the meantime, you're working for me."

"Officially?"

"Unofficially officially."

"Yeah, what's that pay?"

"What it's worth."

"Now who's fencing, Mr. D.A.?"

"*En garde!*"

"Sorry, my only interest in this was Larry. Whether he committed suicide or not, he's dead. My interest ends there."

"How about if I could give you some incentive to come work for me?"

"Incentive. Incentive like what, a gold shield? Money? The shield doesn't interest me anymore. That ship sailed years ago. Money? Between my pension, my wife's income and my business, I already make more money than I need."

"Money, yes, Mr. Prager, but maybe something else, something you might not have more of than you need."

"That would be?"

"Information."

"Information. What kind of information?"

"The kind you want, but don't have."

"You're fencing with me again, Mr. D.A."

He whispered, making me draw near. "How about your brother-in-law?"

"Patrick!"

"What if I could tell you what's become of him? Would that be worth—"

"You know where he is?"

"Did I say that, Mr. Prager? I asked would your involvement be worth it *if* I could tell you what's become of him. Well, would it?"

Fishbein had pushed the right button. I was dizzy. The thought of Patrick reappearing out of the blue was one of the things that kept me up nights. Yeah, sure, he had been gone for a dozen years now. Did I think he'd ever come back? Probably not, but there was always a chance. And if he did return and he told Katy about what had really gone on, about how I had found him and let him go, about the things I knew about Francis . . . That would be it, the end of our marriage, and the end for Katy and her dad. With our marriage at low ebb, maybe it wouldn't have been such a bad thing. But what about Sarah? She was eleven years old. She would never understand. Christ, I still didn't understand why I hadn't just brought Patrick in when I found him.

"Okay, Fishbein, you've got my attention."

"Good." He patted my shoulder like we were old buddies. "Go home. Get some rest. Go to the wake. We'll talk."

The ride back to my car was decidedly more quiet than the ride to the dump and, given that my wrists were uncuffed, decidedly more comfortable. Murphy was less than his chatty self. Detective Melendez seemed completely distracted, lost in a world of her own thoughts, a world with no visas, visitors, or border crossings. I was pretty lost myself. For so long, Patrick Michael Maloney's disappearance had been the persistent buzzing in the background of my life. Now I didn't know how to feel about what Fishbein had said.

Was it cause for utter joy or utter panic? That old question rang in my head, this time spoken by the late Larry McDonald.

"Do you believe in ghosts?"

CHAPTER NINE

FOR SOME INEXPLICABLE reason, I'd slept well. Neither Larry's question nor his ghost kept me from sleep. I was vaguely aware of Katy tossing and turning. Her relationship with Larry Mac was less complicated than mine. Because my wife offered Larry no usable career commodity, they were free to enjoy each other's company without holding bits of themselves back for purposes of negotiation. And for this reason, Katy felt Larry's loss in a way I was incapable of. I envied her that.

The morning was not quite so peaceful for me. Larry McDonald's name and face were splashed all over the TV, news radio, and papers like green on St. Patrick's Day. A regular cop's suicide is big news, never mind a chief's. When a chief does himself in, it's a cross between the first day of hunting season and a shark feeding frenzy. Every aspect of his life becomes fodder for speculation. And the fact that the police had yet to turn up a suicide note only added to the smell of raw meat in the air.

I had called Margaret as soon as I got into the house yesterday afternoon to tell her the bad news, to warn her before the pit bulls could latch on and pull. I was too late. Police Commissioner Cleary had laid the word upon her. Between her tears, all Margaret could do was ask me the same simple question over and over again. *Why?* Questions are often simple, I thought. Answers seldom are. It was just so weird, but a line from a Beatles' tune rang in my head: *And though I thought I knew the answer, I knew what I could not say.* Funny, in that same song they sing about leaving the police department to find a steady job. Moe Prager, my life in imitation of song.

Then there was the earlier exchange between Melendez and me as we both searched along the curb for the car keys she had earlier tossed out her window.

"You still haven't told me why you were at the Six-O yesterday."

"I didn't, did I?"

"Don't be smug, Mr. Prager."

"This isn't smug, it's silence."

"Yeah, well, before this thing is through, we're gonna need each other."

Detective Melendez didn't seem interested in explaining herself any further. I found my keys. We left it at that.

I DID WHAT any self-respecting detective would have done when investigating the suicide of his friend—I ignored it. With the press so busy crawling over Larry's corpse, I figured there was little to gain and a lot to lose by my nosing around. The press tended to use cleavers when scalpels were called for, but they could be pretty effective. The problem was that they, too, often left huge scars on the lives of people they mowed down as they struck out blindly in pursuit of the story. Time was a luxury not afforded the press, so they sacrificed innocence for expediency. Other people's innocence, their expediency.

I was also worried about being noticed. It was one thing for me to show up at Larry Mac's wake, at the cemetery at the memorial, if there was to be one. But if some stringer or crime beat reporter caught wind of me nosing around in Larry McDonald's past, the red flags would fly and it would only serve to confirm any suspicions about dirty dealings in my dead friend's closet. Instead, I called in a favor.

There was noise on the other end of the phone, but not human speech.

"Wit? Wit, for chrissakes, is that you?"

"God's day may launch come dawn, but mine does not get into swing till well after morn." You had to admire an angry man who woke with poetry on his lips. "This had better be of consequence."

Yancy Whittle Fenn, Wit to his friends, was like Truman Capote pulled back from the abyss. Well, that's an inexact description if you knew the man, but it served those unacquainted with him. When I met Y.W. Fenn in 1983, he was just as famous for his brand of celebrity pseudo-journalism as his taste for Wild Turkey. That's the kind you had shots of, not shot at. A Yale-educated society-brat, Wit had once been a topnotch journalist, but addiction and tragedy had nearly pushed him over the edge.

Never quite as beautiful or wealthy as the company he kept, Wit had invested unwisely, married badly, and began drinking. He became a hanger-on instead of one of the crowd, but as I was once told by a crony of his, "He used to be fun back in the day, a life of the party sort—funny, biting, and bitchy." Then his grandson had been kidnapped and brutally murdered. Wit had always done crime reportage, but dealt with his grief by becoming vindictive and focusing on the rich and infamous. He'd write exposés for the big magazines whenever crime—murder in particular—money, and celebrity aligned.

He had been assigned to the Moira Heaton investigation. By *Esquire*, as I recall. Of course, neither Wit nor his editor gave a flying fuck about Moira. It was the wealthy and handsome State Senator Steven Brightman who had their eye. Until Moira Heaton went missing, Brightman had been the up-and-comer, the next Jack Kennedy. Talk about a curse. Somehow they all begin as the next Jack and end up as the next Teddy. But during the investigation, Wit found something to grab onto, something to stop his slide into an early grave and snickering obits. I think maybe he remembered his grief and forgot about his rage.

"Not only is it of consequence," I said, "there might even be a book in it for you."

"Enlightened self-interest is what makes the world go 'round, my friend. Maybe you should begin speaking now."

"Anyone ever tell you you were more fun when you drank?" I teased.

"I tell it to myself every day when I gaze into the mirror. Then I'm reminded that I would not be here at all had I continued my lifelong quest for the perfect gallon of bourbon. Or maybe, sir, you are looking for me to thank you once again for saving my life."

"You know better than that, Wit."

"Yes, I do. How are the lovely Sarah and Katy? Well, I hope."

I didn't answer. "Go get your morning paper. I'll wait."

He put the phone down. I listened to the retreating slaps of Wit's slippers against his hardwood floor. A minute later, the sound of his slippers returned.

"Oh, I am so sorry, Moe. I rather liked Larry, though I wouldn't have trusted him as far as I could drop-kick a polo pony."

"I know a lot of people who might say the same thing about you."

"And they'd be right. But you and I needn't worry about that. I owe you more than I can say."

"Save it for my eulogy."

"Let us not discuss such things," he chided. "Is this call about the late Chief McDonald?"

"Yes and no. Yes, in that he's part of it. No, in that he's not nearly all of it."

"We're being rather cryptic, are we not?"

I could only laugh.

"Do I have a career in stand up, do you think?" he asked.

"Maybe, but it's just that I said the same thing about being cryptic to Larry the last two times I saw him."

There was an uncomfortable silence on the line. Then, "You know, Moe, I don't think I can recall the last thing I said to my grandson."

"Probably, I love you."

"Yes, probably."

"I think I told Larry to go fuck himself."

"Well, I don't mean to be insensitive, but he seems to have taken your advice quite literally."

I hadn't really thought of it that way, but I wasn't exactly consumed with guilt.

"I think that's what I'm getting at, Wit. I'm not sure he did the fucking himself, if you get my point. And there's too many of your *mishpocha* around for me to—"

"Say no more. I'll handle it. Give me a day or two."

"Thanks."

"None required, my friend. I'll get back to you."

He was off the line.

As soon as I placed the phone down, it rang. It rang until I left the house. First, it was Aaron calling, then Klaus, then Robert Gloria, the detective who originally caught the Moira Heaton case, then Pete Parson, then . . . They were all calling to say they were sorry and all wanted to know what had happened. Popular question, that. I took the phone off the hook and went about finding the answer, ass backwards of course.

NO ONE ON Surf Avenue had hung black bunting out their windows or off the railings of their terraces for the late chief of detectives. I made sure not to crane my neck as I passed West Eighth Street to see if the old precinct had so honored him. My soul, at least, was at half staff. Grief is a harder hurdle when it's for someone you're unsure of. *How much of it was I supposed to feel? How much would he have felt*

66

for me? For how long? Why? There were those easy questions again, the ones with the complex answers.

The block was once right in the heart of what we used to call the Soul Patch, but the drugs of choice back then—pot, ludes, black beauties, acid, mesc, a little heroin and even less coke—seem almost innocent by today's standard. Crack—coke's ugly little brother—and junkies sharing needles in the time of AIDS had ravaged much of the area. The row houses all looked on the verge of collapse. But all was not lost. On some of the surrounding streets, signs of rebirth were taking root and, if the sea breeze blew just right, you could detect the chemical scents of vinyl siding and construction adhesive.

I pressed the three bells at the row house that Malik Jabbar had listed as his last worldly address. None of them worked.

Such was the nature of poor neighborhoods—lots of bells, none of 'em work. So I pounded the door. Black faces stared suspiciously out dirty windows and through frayed curtains. I could feel their eyes branding the word COP on the back of my neck. Hell, I was white and pounding on a door like I owned the place. Old habits die hard. So much of what you do as a cop is a matter of training and practice. I stopped pounding.

I heard light footsteps coming down the hallway toward the door.

"Who is it?" a muffled and unexpectedly polite woman's voice wanted to know.

"I came to talk about Malik."

A lock clicked open, but the door didn't immediately pull back. I heard the telltale scraping of a wedge pole being removed from its place. To most folks outside big cities or high crime areas, the thought of gating your own windows in steel and keeping a metal rod wedged between your hallway floor and the back of your front door must seem barbaric. Those folks don't have a crack den two doors down.

Finally, the door opened. A slender black woman of sixty dressed in a tidy flowered house frock and incongruous white socks stood before me. She was all of five feet tall and wore half-rim spectacles tied earpiece to earpiece around her neck with a cheap silver chain.

"My name is Moe Prager."

"Are you from the police?" she asked, her eyes wary.

"No ma'am. I retired years ago."

"Then I don't understand."

"I'm not sure I do either, Mrs. . . ."

"Mable Louise Broadbent. I am—I was Melvin's mother." That shook her some. "I don't know how to say that yet. How is a mother supposed to talk about her own dead child? He is alive to me. I have gotten used to a lot of hateful things in my lifetime, but this . . ."

"May I come in, Mable? I only want to talk."

She didn't answer. She stood aside and made a weak gesture pointing down her hallway to the parlor. The apartment was a reflection of the woman who lived within its walls: tidy, small, incongruous. The furniture had survived more presidents than I had, but it was clean, the upholstery worn shiny in spots, the wood polished, and the air ripe with the tang of artificial lemon. The wall art was of sail boats and Caribbean fishermen. The rug, however, was a day-glo orange shag that matched very little I'd seen in my lifetime, other than a hunter's vest. Mable noticed me taking stock.

"This is my apartment. We let the basement apartment sometimes. Melvin lived upstairs with that whor—with his girl." She soured with that last word. "Can I offer you something to drink, Mr. Prager?"

"No, thanks. You call him Melvin, but he changed his name to Malik Jabbar."

"I'll never get used to—" She caught herself. "For his sake, I called him Malik, but now . . . He's my Melvin. Melvin got involved with some ungodly people who put bad ideas into my child's head. He was weak that way."

"He was easily swayed?"

"Like a blade of grass."

"But you continued living with him."

"Where was I supposed to go? This is my home. I own it. I let Melvin stay, even with that sassy whore he calls—called a girlfriend. When I'm done mourning, she'll be on the street where she belongs. Girl's got no more morals than an alley cat."

I pointed up. "What's her name?"

"Kalisha."

"Is she home?"

"No, thank the lord. She's out doing who knows what with God knows who. Good riddance!"

"Melvin had trouble with the law."

"Son, every young black man on these streets has trouble with the law. Some of it deserving. Some not."

"Okay, Mable, you got a point. But Melvin had a lot of drug arrests and petty thievery and all."

"Like I say, Mr. Prager, he was easily swayed. He hungered to be accepted, so he did stupid things."

"Did you know he was arrested a few weeks back for half a kilo of cocaine?"

"When was this?" She screwed up her face and twisted her head to one side as if trying to avoid a punch and failing.

"I'm not sure exactly. Two, three weeks ago, maybe."

"He never said word one about it, but it does explain some things."

"Like what, if you don't mind me asking?"

"That other police."

"No offense, Mable, but when a family member is murdered, the cops have to come ask about—"

"Not those police!" she cut me off. "I know they had to come. I'm talking about that pretty chiquita."

"Detective Melendez?"

Mable twisted her head to one side again. This time to stare at me, cold and hard, to see if she had been right to trust me.

"I thought you said you weren't from the police."

"I'm not. I swear."

"Then how would you know about this woman, this Detective Melendez?"

"We've met. Was she with a skinny, older, white guy?"

"She came alone. Why? Who is she?" Mable's voice trembled slightly.

"She was the detective who arrested Mal—Melvin for the cocaine."

"I keep telling you, he didn't say anything about such an arrest to me. And besides, where would Melvin get the kind of money it would take to buy a half kilogram of cocaine? I may be just an frumpy old church lady, but I am not a naïve nor ignorant soul, Mr. Prager. I know that drugs cost lots of money and I know money was something that my son never had much of."

She had a point. "Did Melvin know a man named Dexter Mayweather? He used to be called D Rex around this area."

"There's not a person over the age of twenty-one who lived on these streets who didn't know of Dexter Mayweather. To hear the fools talk about him, you'd think he was Robin Hood."

"Yes, but did Melvin know him, not just *of* him?"

"I doubt it."

"Why's that? I know there would have been a big age difference, but your son would have been thirteen or fourteen years old when D Rex was killed in the spring of '72."

"Because after he got into his first serious trouble as a boy of eleven, when he got out of Spofford, we sent him down to Georgia to live with his aunt, my sister, Fiona. He didn't come back home till the fall of 1972 to go back to school."

"You're sure?"

"A mother remembers when her child comes back to her."

"I suppose it's still possible they knew each other, but I guess you're right."

"Of course, I'm right."

"Do you have any idea who would have wanted to kill Melvin?"

"I'm no policeman, Mr. Prager, sir, but I would think maybe I would start with the people who had the money for half a kilo of cocaine."

"Could be."

"And like I say, Melvin knew some ungodly people."

"As you say."

She stood to signal her time and patience had run out. "Now, if you don't mind, I have to get back to my house chores."

"Not at all, Mable. Thank you for your time. I'm sorry for your loss."

"Do you have children, Mr. Prager?"

"A little girl. She's eleven."

"Same age as Melvin when . . . You hold on tight to that little girl."

"I promise."

"No parent should outlive her child."

I agreed. "Just one last thing before I go. Do you have a ballpark figure of when Kalisha will get back home?"

"When the alley cats are finished screeching in heat is usually when she crawls back in."

"Thanks again."

There was a grieving woman, but a woman with dignity. You needed a lot of that in order to survive in such a hard place, with a son in trouble with the law. In a way, she reminded me of my old friend Israel Roth. Mr. Roth was a camp survivor who had made a meaningful life for himself, a man who had literally breathed in the ashes of his dead family and come out the other side mostly intact. I'd met him in the Catskills in 1981 when I was working an old arson case. He had pretty much adopted my family as his own and had tried, with some success, to have me meet God halfway. I'd have to call him. I pulled away from the house and decided that I'd come back and talk to Malik's girl, Kalisha. Maybe not tonight, maybe not tomorrow, but sooner rather than later. In the meanwhile, I decided to kill some time at the local park. I knew there'd be some games to watch and information to be had. There's always information floating around the park, you just have to know how to listen.

THE COURTS IN the shadows of the big housing project built at the west end of Coney Island were the best kept outdoor courts I'd ever seen anywhere. We're talking glass backboards, padded support poles, unblemished court lines, and not a piece of litter on the playing surface and surrounding area that wasn't windblown. There were two full-court runs in progress, but it was a little quieter than I expected. Only a few guys waiting "winners," spying their likely competition and contemplating who they could pick up from the losers to give them the best shot at staying on. Some of the guys on the sidelines were no older than Sarah, some were older than me. Mine was the only white face inside the cyclone fencing that lined the perimeter of the park.

My appearance caused about as much commotion as a passing cloud. Mostly, the players just shook their heads. My guess was their assessment of me fell into one of three categories:

I was a cop come to bust their balls.

I was an old, washed-up white guy come to tell war stories about how I had played against Lew Alcindor, Connie "The Hawk" Hawkins, and Preacher "The Creature" Simmons when I was younger.

I was some recruiter or street agent come to spot and exploit young talent.

I just sat down on one of the benches and watched. If there was information to be had, my announcing my interest in it was not the way to go. Curiosity would eventually take hold, and then I might have a shot at learning something.

The games were typical Brooklyn street fair—a lot of tough, one-on-one defense and hardass rebounding. Shit, even the guys I grew up playing with believed in the *No Autopsy, No Foul* rules of the street. But there was a whole lot of trash talk, too. Way too much dribbling, very few picks, not enough distribution or movement without the ball. Almost every trip down court featured a hesitation move, a crossover dribble, a drive to the rack, and a dish. Now and then there'd be a steal in the backcourt and someone would fly down the other end for a showy jam.

There was a big range in talent level and size, but the best player on either court was a fifteen-year-old kid with a close-cropped do on a too-big head atop a stumpy body. Everyone called him Nugget—for the size of his head, I guess. Nugget didn't have the body, but he had game. He saw the whole court, could handle the ball, had range on his shot, fast hands, and was deceptively quick to the hole. His defensive footwork left a lot to be desired, but a good coach and an ounce of desire could fix that. Nugget had the gift. What Nugget didn't have was the best squad. He sat down next to me after his team got their asses handed to them.

"Whatchu want, grandpa?" Nugget asked, slapping the bench in frustration. *Good, he was curious.* "You ain't no coach. I seen every white high school, AAU, and church coach in the five boroughs."

"Maybe I'm not from the five boroughs."

"Nah, man, you all Brooklyn. I seen how you carry yourself, how you come in here. You police?"

"A long time ago."

"So, whatchu think a my game?"

I told him. He was less than thrilled with my assessment of his defensive liabilities.

"Man, you seen how many balls I steal? Shit! You ain't no coach is right."

"Keep playing defense with your hands and not your feet, you'll never get a full scholarship at a big time school. You'll score a million points at some NAIA school and never get drafted. You'll wind up like the rest of these guys, playing ball when you should be out earning some money. You want that for yourself?"

"Das bullshit, old man. You don't know the game."

"Nugget," I said, looking at him fiercely so that it made him uncomfortable, "I know a whole shitload about this game that you may never know. On the other hand, I never had one quarter your skills. You have what can't be taught, but you don't have what can be."

He waved at me dismissively, "Later for dis!" And walked away.

I'd blown it. Whoever said the truth shall set you free didn't gather information for a living. If I had kissed up to Nugget a bit, stroked his ego just a little, I might have gotten somewhere. But once I alienated him, I'd alienated the park. I was dead in the water. No one was going to talk to me now, but I had a way to remedy that. Maybe I'd be seeing Nugget sometime soon.

When I got back to my car, Carmella Melendez was sitting on the hood. She was in her off-duty duds: tight jeans and a silky black halter covered by a loose denim jacket with exaggerated shoulders and silver studs. Her hair was pulled back tightly and corralled into a pony tail with a red band. Expensive sunglasses with opaque lenses covered her eyes. She wore running shoes, but it didn't kill the effect. Even if she were wearing my dad's brown vinyl slippers, it wouldn't have detracted from her raw beauty.

"Detective Melendez." I nodded. "You working undercover?"

"I'm not working."

"Maybe not officially, but you're working."

"So you gonna tell me what you were doing at the precinct the other day, or what?"

"Or what. Maybe it's like you said, I was stalking you."

"You didn't even know I existed."

"You're wrong about that. I knew. I just didn't know what you looked like."

"You know, Mr. Prager, you talk in riddles a lot," she said, sliding down off the hood. "That's not polite."

"I thought you were good at reading between the lines, Detective."

"I said I was good at it. I didn't say I enjoyed it."

"If you're really not working, then let's call each other by our first names, okay? Mine's Moe."

"Carmella," she said, offering me her hand.

It was all I could do not to bow and kiss it. My heart was actually racing as I grasped her hand, but I managed to shake it, not too firmly, and give it back.

"Come on, Carmella, you like walking on the boardwalk?"

"Sounds good."

We walked east along the boardwalk toward Nathan's. Maybe she was finally learning her lesson about the effectiveness of silence. I'd learned it a long time ago, but I spoke first.

"Where you from?"

"I grew up in Flatbush on Lennox Avenue till I was about eight. Then my mother took me back to Puerto Rico to live with my grandmother. When I turned eighteen, I came back with my *abuela* and we lived with my pops. You?"

"From right around here. Ocean Parkway."

We stopped and stared out at the Atlantic, much like I had with Larry the last time we were together.

"So why become a cop?" I asked.

"Always wanted to be a cop and do good."

"Is that what you're doing, good? I thought you were just following me around because you were bored."

"Look, Moe," she said, taking off her sunglasses and catching my eyes, "I had a case, a big fat, juicy fucking case and then it disappeared. Everyone, I think, is too happy about that."

"Everyone except you."

"Except me, that's right."

"Is that why you went and talked to Melvin's mom on your own?"

If I thought I was going to get her off balance with that, I was wrong. "You blame me?"

"Not really, but I don't know what detectives should or shouldn't do. I don't even play one on TV."

"That's almost funny. You mentioned something about making detective in the car. What really happened?"

"It's not worth talking about anymore. That's all in my past."

"Suit yourself," she said. "So how's it you even know about Melvin?"

"The same way I knew about you."

"Riddles again. Come on, Moe. We're gonna need each other before this is done."

"That's the second time you've said that, but I don't see why."

"All right, be like that." Her sunglasses went back on and she turned to go.

"First Melvin gets wacked. Then Chief McDonald does himself in and everyone seems more relieved than sad. Makes you wonder," I said. That stopped her in her tracks. "And you don't like it, do you?"

"Hell no, I don't."

"Come on, walk me back to my car."

As I started back across the street to where my car was parked, Melendez lagged behind to retie her sneaker. Suddenly, I was conscious of screeching tires, but I was distracted, turning back to see after Carmella. Instinct and engine noise made me stop and look to my right. A blur was coming at me and I froze. A split second is enough time to think of a thousand things. All I could picture were my knees being crushed beneath the weight of the car. All the long forgotten pain came rushing back in like an insistent sea.

Bang! My head snapped back and my body tumbled forward, arms flailing. I tucked them in time and hit the pavement with a shoulder roll. Something fell on top of me. *Melendez!* I came up with my wits and reached around my back for my .38. Detective Melendez had already assumed firing position and had her off-duty piece aimed at the rear end of the fishtailing Camaro. I slapped her arms down as the car sped away.

"*Conjo!* What was that for?" she growled.

"Ricochet. It's not worth the risk. Did you get the plate number?"

"No rear plate."

"Fuck!" I slipped my .38 into its holster. "You saved my life, Carmella."

"I couldn't afford to let you get killed. Not yet."

"That's a real comfort."

"You seem to be the only fucking person who gives a shit about what's going on, but maybe now you'll share with me a little."

"If I was a cynical bastard, I'd say you staged this. I mean that untied lace was pretty convenient."

"Fuck you, Moe! Just go fuck yourself!"

"Did I say I was a cynical bastard?"

"Are you?"

"Yeah, but I don't believe for a second you had anything to do with that."

"Then why say it?" she asked, dabbing blood off her scraped knees with the sleeve of her jacket.

"Because you make me a little nervous."

"I make you nervous. Why?"

"I may be invisible to you, Carmella, but you're not to me."

"Am I supposed to understand that?"

"Yeah, you are."

She just shook her head. "So we're just gonna forget about this little incident, right?"

"Why bring any more attention to what we seem to be doing than we have to?" I said.

"Okay, I'll be in touch."

"You okay?"

"It's a scraped knee," she said. "I'll live. Watch your back."

By the time I was fully across the street and to my car, she had moved to the boardwalk side of the street. When I looked again, she was gone. I was none the worse for wear, not even a ripped jacket or pant leg. Maybe a little dusty, but basically intact.

Why then, I wondered, did my hands shake so when I clamped them around the steering wheel? This time the answer was as easy as the question. Someone had just tried to kill me. That's why.

Only once before had anyone tried to kill me, and that was six years ago in Miami Beach. After the night of the shooting I'd barely given it a second thought. And now it seemed so unreal to me that I found myself questioning whether it had actually happened. It had, of course. Those bullets slamming into the body of the dead man I'd taken cover behind were meant for me. The shooter told me so. But this was different. It had happened on my home turf. It was more personal somehow.

CHAPTER TEN

THE FUNERAL WAS a muted affair, a coward's burial. No one said it or even implied it, but to claim otherwise was to lie. Lawrence McDonald was afforded all the honors, pomp, and circumstance—the flag-draped coffin, the Emerald Society pipes and drums, the white-gloved pallbearers, the dignitaries, the strained faces and tears—that came with the death of a man in his position. All, that is, but respect and a church burial.

Without a suicide note to explain his actions, the church had no way to make the case for special dispensation. And it's not like Larry was a beloved figure within the department. No one at City Hall or One Police Plaza was putting in the call to Cardinal O'Connor. Oddly, when a regular cop does himself in because his wife's divorced his cheating ass and moved the family to Ohio or because he mistakenly shot an innocent bystander, the department will do what it can to intercede on his behalf. But when a man like Larry, a man with looks and style and power—things all men want—kills himself, he earns only disrespect.

An Army vet, Larry Mac was buried in the military graveyard out on Long Island along cemetery row in Pine Lawn. Strangely, most of the dignitaries, it seemed, had lost their way on the trip out to exit 49 for this part of the day's proceedings. Funny how that happened. If he had died a hero, the brass and every politician from the Tri-State area would have made sure to show up and shove their way into any photo opportunity. No one elbows the crowd to be associated with a coward.

It wasn't a lonely burial. The bugler's "Taps" fell on many ears, most of them civilian. Margaret was there, of course. She received the flag from his coffin, stained it with her tears. Wit had come. Detective Gloria too. Pete Parson had flown up and sat with his son. John Heaton, Moira's father, was there. Drunk so that he was barely able to stand. His face a garden of gin blossoms. The only two guys from the old Six-O in attendance were Caveman Kenny Burton and Rico—the storm trooper and the felon. Nice tribute, that. I was happy to see them nonetheless. Melendez was there, flitting around the fringes of the ceremonies, hanging back. It was bizarre, but I felt vaguely ill at ease with her presence. I didn't like the idea of her watching me hold Katy.

When things broke up, Katy went over to be with Margaret. Wit nodded to me and pointed to a row of low stone crosses about fifty feet east of Larry's gravesite. I made my way over, shaking a hand here and there as I went.

"Hey, Wit."

"Moses."

We hugged, not something he was usually comfortable with. Stepping back, he held onto my arms. I was being inspected.

"What's wrong, Moe?"

"What's wrong? That's Larry McDonald back there in that box. He allegedly killed himself, remember?"

"That's not what I mean and you know it. You seemed awfully distracted during the burial."

"There's a detective here that is a little too interested in my business."

"The dark-haired beauty?" he asked.

"How'd you—"

"Moe, please, give me my due. I have been reporting on crime for longer than you wore a badge. I can smell a cop from the adjoining county."

"Yeah, her. Name's Melendez."

"I can see why she would be a distraction to any man. Do you think she would appreciate the charms of a former society hack?"

"And Pulitzer Prize winner."

"Yes, there is that."

"I wouldn't know, why don't you ask her yourself, Wit?"

"Perhaps I shall. But there's something else, something you are keeping from me."

"Someone tried to kill me. I was in Coney Island and a car came straight for me. And no, Wit, it wasn't an accident."

"Would you like to inform me or shall I be forced to play twenty questions?"

Thought about playing coy. For as much as I had grown to love and respect Yancy Whittle Fenn, it was not lost on me that he had press credentials in his chest cavity where most people have beating hearts. I didn't think he'd screw me, but the pull of a good story was as strong as the pull of bourbon. It would only take one slip.

"First tell me what's the buzz and then we'll discuss it," I said.

"That's just it. There isn't any buzz."

"Get the fuck outta here! The chief of detectives gasses himself, leaves no note, and everyone is happy with that?"

"The silence is quite astounding, Moe. I have good sources, the best sources, and none of them has anything to say."

"Okay, let's forget the cops for now. You can't tell me that the media isn't all over this thing. I mean, it's got 'big story' with a neon sign and fireworks on it."

He removed his tortoiseshell glasses and rubbed his twinkling blue eyes. "That's just it. The press is all over it, but no matter how they shake it, squeeze it, kick or bribe it, nothing is coming out. Usually, there is someone in the department, some disaffected fool who has been passed over for a promotion or assigned to the rubber gun squad, who is simply clamoring to gripe and talk off the record."

"Not this time?"

"It would seem not. Not a soul is talking and that is most peculiar. Cops love to gab. It is how I used to gather half my stories. A seat at the bar and bottle of Jameson can go a long way with a pub full of cops."

"Cops and booze! Who'd'a thunk it? So, you think it's a dead issue?" I said, knowing he'd take it as a challenge.

"No need to insult me. Just because no one is talking today, doesn't mean the same will be true tomorrow or the next day. Someone always talks."

"So you're intrigued?"

"For the moment, yes," he said. "Now, would you like to tell me the entire story that I might do my part in this more effectively?"

I told Wit about the tape Larry had given me at the opening of Red, White and You. I described the interrogation, the meeting with Larry on the boardwalk, his threats. I detailed Malik Jabbar's assassination, my meeting with his mother, my dealings with Carmella Melendez.

"Well, Moe, this does get curiouser and curiouser, but it does explain the tight lips, does it not?"

"Yeah, well, no one likes a cop scandal except the press. This isn't just some old cop who took a few free cups of coffee and spare change."

"Drugs and murder, nice tandem. Juicy headlines."

I agreed, sort of. "Maybe, but it's not that simple."

"Never is. I am certain that if the department felt they could simply sacrifice Chief McDonald's memory and limit the damage to his reputation—"

"—lips would be flapping all over town. After all, the best kind of scapegoat is a dead one."

"Indeed. Moe, have you any idea who this Malik character gave up to the D.A.?"

"Not a clue. All I know is that it shook Larry to his core. But I don't even think there's a record of Malik's arrest. That's why I need to figure out a way to deal with Melendez about what I know without giving too much away."

"An interesting challenge."

"Thanks."

"You go do whatever it is you have to on your end, and I will do my share," he said. "Not to worry."

"I never do, not about you," I lied.

I shook Wit's hand and had walked a few paces when he called after me.

"Moe, watch out for the black-haired beauty. Don't repeat a mistake so many men, including yours truly, have made."

"What mistake is that?"

"Looking somewhere else for what you already possess."

I thought to question him, but reconsidered. Wit was possibly the most intelligent man I'd ever met. Sage advice or not, I'd always been better at learning from my own mistakes.

When I rejoined the crowd, I noticed Kenny Burton and Rico Tripoli milling about. I asked them to wait for me while I arranged for Pete Parson and his son to drive Katy home. Pete, Katy, Sarah, and I had plans for dinner in a few hours, but what I had to discuss with my former precinct mates needed to be said out of earshot of any of the other funeral attendees.

When everyone was gone, the three of us stood around watching the backhoe driver unceremoniously dumping bucketfuls of dirt on

Larry's coffin. Got me thinking about how disconnected we were from death. It was easy to blame drugs, movies, TV, and video games for violence and the devaluation of human life. Bullshit! The real culprit was our lack of intimacy with death. When you're unfamiliar with death, you're disrespectful of life. No one dies in his or her bed anymore. People die in hospitals now, or in hospices or nursing homes or alone in cars along the side of the Belt Parkway. Kids don't go to funerals. Strangers clean our bodies, dress and groom us. Machines dig our graves. Why should any of us respect death when we make it as remote as the mountains of the moon?

I have often wondered if it would be a little harder for a killer to pull the trigger or shove the blade in a second time if he had washed his dead brother's body or dug his mother's grave. What if he had watched his dad die an inch at a time from cancer and sat by the deathbed day after day after day? What if there was no church, no funeral home, no hospital, no way to pass the responsibilities of death off to strangers. How much harder would murder be?

"Fucking machine!" Burton growled. "I thought cemeteries was supposed to be quiet."

"Larry don't hear a thing," said Rico.

"Yeah," I said, "he's too busy angling for a bump to archangel."

We all laughed at that. The backhoe went silent and suddenly our laughter was the loudest thing in the universe.

"So, you guys think he killed himself?"

Rico frowned. Burton grunted.

"Yeah, well I don't like it either," I continued, "but there's no evidence to say different. What they say is he drove over to Fountain Avenue, swallowed some pills, drank some Jack, and gassed himself."

"The only part I buy is the Jack Daniels," Rico said. "Why would Larry kill himself anyways?"

"That's what I was hoping you or Kenny here could tell me."

"What's that s'posed to mean?" Burton wondered.

"What do you think it means?"

"Just like I said at O'Hearn's, you're a cunt, Prager. You know something, say it. Don't dance around like a fag in a forest fire."

Rico was confused. "A fag in a forest fire? What the fuck is that supposed to mean?"

"Okay, Kenny. Here's what I know. Larry came to me and told me that when Rico and me started out, some of the guys in the Six-O were on Dexter Mayweather's pad. He was worried that this was all gonna get dragged up again."

"Shit, the day D Rex bought it was a sad fucking day for me," the Caveman said. "Did you think I got that house in Breezy Point on my cop salary? You kiddin' me? We made . . . What's that Jew word, Prager?"

"*Bubkis?*"

"That's the one. We made *bubkis* back then. Maybe I shoulda sent flowers to the funeral home or something, you think?"

Rico's eyes got big, but he said nothing. A guy who took money, drugs, and hookers from the Colombians in exchange for protection was in no position to throw grains of sand, let alone stones. But Burton noticed Rico's expression.

"Don't even say nothin'!"

"What the fuck did I say? Moe, did I say anything?"

"No, but you wanted to, you lowlife skell motherfucker. Me, I took a little 'scarole on the side to look the other way so a few niggers could deal some weed and ludes to their own. You gave fucking cover to the goddamned Colombians! Asshole spics near ruined the city. Hey Moe, good thing the Nazis weren't dealing coke or your best bud here woulda sold you and—"

Smack!

Rico, as shabby and gray as he looked, still had quick hands. His right was already down at his side by the time Caveman reacted to the backhanded slap. At first, Kenny just rubbed his face, licked the blood off his bottom lip, and smiled. It was the kind of smile that wilted flowers.

"I hope you hit harder than that when it was shower time in Batavia."

"Fuck you, Burton!"

Rico's right shot out again, but I caught it.

"Cut this shit out. Larry's fucking dead and I need to know if either of you believe he killed himself."

"He's dead either way," Burton said. "Leave it be."

"You would say that," offered Rico.

Caveman positioned himself so that he held both Rico and me in his stare.

"Some cops the pair of you made—the bar mitzvah boy and the skell. Think, the both of ya! How could any of us get hurt by Mayweather's murder getting dragged up now? Where's the paper trail? You think old D Rex kept neat little ledgers, for fuck's sake? If Larry McDonald suicided, it wasn't over a few thousand bucks that a drug dealing nigger threw his way or my way twenty years ago."

He was right, of course. I hadn't really thought it through before and I decided I wasn't going to hash it out. Not here, not now, not with these two. I kept playing the suicide card.

"What do you think, Rico?"

"I don't know. Maybe Burton's right. Maybe Larry had other shit on his mind. I don't know. I can't think right now."

Rico couldn't think because he was in full thirst and needed a drink, bad. He had that whole body hunger thing going on that you see in drunks and junkies. He was swaying, twisting, bouncing slightly on his knees, caressing himself.

"Okay, I gotta get home. I'll give Rico a lift," I said.

"Well you didn't think I was gonna drive the cunt, did you?"

No one shook hands. Caveman lit a cigarette and blew some smoke in our faces. He flicked his unfinished cigarette onto Larry Mac's grave as he passed. A fitting farewell from a man like Burton.

I didn't talk to Rico in the car. That seemed to suit him just fine, consumed as he was by his aching thirst. I found a bar on Route 110, pulled over, and handed him all the cash I had in my wallet. He didn't hesitate, not for a second. Neither did I, pulling away from the curb without glancing into my rearview mirror.

When I did finally look back, I noticed Melendez's blue Impala on my bumper, waving for me to pull over. Like Rico, I didn't hesitate. We both got out of our cars.

"Thanks for not making trouble today," I said. "Larry was a good guy in his way and his ex didn't need any extra aggravation."

"Hey, the chief helped make my career. You think he didn't take shit for putting that shield in my hand? I wasn't going to show him any disrespect, not today."

"So what were you doing there? Don't you have any real cases to make?"

"Murphy's out today," she said, as if that explained it.

"And . . ."

"And I need you to talk to me or no justice is gonna get done here."

Man, she *was* young. Justice is a word that gets beaten out of most cops before they make detective. I searched my memory trying to recall when I'd lost my "justice cherry." The moment was lost with a million other forgotten milestones.

"Justice! Christ, Carmella. It takes more faith to believe in justice than in God."

"I believe."

"Why?"

"I have my reasons."

"Wanna tell me why this case, if there even is a case, means so much to you?"

She showed me her shield. "This is why."

Argue that. I couldn't.

"Okay," I said. "This is important to me too. What are you doing tonight?"

She blushed slightly, looking suddenly like a shy little girl.

"Nothing."

"Eleven o'clock. You tell me where."

"Drinks?"

"Drinks would be good."

"Crispo's, do you know it?"

"You mean Rip's in Red Hook?"

Her smile was my answer. I turned to go.

"Moe!"

"Yeah."

"You're not invisible to me either."

CHAPTER ELEVEN

THE RED NEON sign— *RIP 'S*—was like a bright smile with missing teeth. Crispo's or Rip's, on Visitation Place, was a dive. *Name me fifteen bars in Brooklyn that weren't.* But there's a kind of comfort in a dive, comfort like in a pair of ugly old shoes or a messy room. Rip's was all of that. Inside was perpetual sepia. Neither the bar nor the plank floor had been refinished since the '40s. The wobbly barstools were held together with white adhesive tape and glue, which, since the floor pitched and fell from foot to foot, was probably a good thing. Only place in Brooklyn you could get seasick sitting at a bar. Rip's was the kind of place where old lipstick on your bar glass passed as garnish.

Red Hook, once the toughest neighborhood in the city—and that's really saying something when you're talking about New York— was a place in transition. Isolated from the rest of Brooklyn by the Brooklyn-Queens Expressway, its lack of a subway line, and spotty bus service, Red Hook had once been the thriving center of the borough's waterfront. These days, the docks were inert and the memories of the tough guys that had once unloaded ships with hooks and ropes had receded into the cracks between the cobblestones that still lined its dead end streets. As its fortunes fell, low-income housing projects rose up. For the majority of the '60s, '70s, and '80s, Red Hook, with its Civil War Era infrastructure and faceless factory buildings, was left to rot. It was as if the city hoped it would simply detach itself from the western tip of Long Island and sink into the East River.

Just lately, the yuppies—with their nose for cheap real estate, rustic charm, and loft space—had taken notice. It would probably be another ten or fifteen years before the last black, Puerto Rican, and artist was driven out by gentrification, but as sure as the sun would rise tomorrow, it was coming. Inevitability comes in all manner of forms. One was waiting for me at the bar. Inevitability had an intoxicating smile.

"Over here!" she called above the din of the crowd and Johnny Maestro's sour ruminations on the prospects of marriage.

That was the thing about the jukebox at Rip's. With the solitary exception of Sinatra, every selection on the box was written or performed by a Brooklynite. Either that or the song title or the band name featured the word Brooklyn.

"Dewar's rocks," I shouted at the barman after working my way through the tangle of bodies.

Melendez held up her bottle of Heineken to show me she was fine. We clinked bottle to rocks glass.

"This is weird," she said.

"What's weird?"

"Us."

"Us?" I repeated. "What about—"

Everything! "Nothing," she lied. "Forget it."

I would have lied, too, had she pursued it. All through dinner with Pete Parson and Katy, this moment was all I could think about. Now that it had come, I felt about fifteen years old. There was no denying she made my heart beat faster, that since she had shoved me out of the path of that car my appreciation for her had taken a decidedly more personal bent than simple recognition of her charms.

"Look at this place," I said, just to say something. "If the city mixed like the crowd in here, we'd have a lot less trouble."

"Yeah, I guess," she agreed, looking out at the jumble of black, brown, and white faces. "Not many places in the city like this."

"Not many places like Red Hook."

"None."

I guzzled my scotch. "C'mon, let's get outta here for a little while so we can talk."

"Okay."

We walked to the corner, turned left on Van Brunt, and strolled toward Conover. In stark contrast to Rip's, the streets were eerily silent and a thick veil of fog obscured the normally brilliant lights of lower Manhattan. We, too, were silent. Now we stood at the end of Conover Street, where moot trolley tracks curved directly into oblivion. On most nights you could look right out into the harbor from here and behold the Statue of Liberty standing up before you. Not tonight. Tonight, nature had conspired to soften the usual distractions.

"My brother Aaron and me, we own wine shops," I said, smooth talker that I was. "And we just opened up a new place on Long Island. Larry—Chief McDonald—was there for the grand opening party. We were outside talking and he handed me a cassette tape. He told me to take it home and listen." I pulled that same cassette out of my jacket.

"What is it, a mix tape of ELP, Jethro Tull, and Pink Floyd?"

"A sense of humor, huh? You forgot Yes and the Moody Blues. How do you know from those bands?"

"You think I dance around my house with fruit on my head to Tito Puente and Menudo records? Some kids like dinosaurs. I liked dinosaur rock."

"No, Carmella, it isn't a mix tape." I handed it to her. "It's a recording of two detectives interviewing a drug suspect."

"Detectives?"

"You and Murphy, specifically. The suspect was Malik Jabbar or Melvin, as you seemed to like to call him."

Her face went blank, any hint of playfulness vanished.

"I don't know how he got it, but there's definitely a hidden mic somewhere in that interview room. You'll hear for yourself."

"Fuck!"

I might just as well have smacked her with a two-by-four. She stared at the cassette like it was radioactive.

"I know, Carmella. It raises a lot of questions."

"We need to talk and I need a drink."

"Come on, let's get back to Crispo's."

"No!"

"Where then?"

"Walk me back to my car."

I LOVED FOG. I always found a drowsy calm in it, a comforting embrace. Tonight the calm was lost on me. Following Melendez's car through the twisty womb of silent streets, I could not quiet my thoughts or the heart thumping in my chest. I turned the radio up to where it might have drowned out a subway collision on the el above my head, but it could not drown out my guilt. I couldn't think of anybody, not even Rico Tripoli, who would have approved of where I was going or the road I was about to travel. Well, that's not exactly true. Of all the people I knew, there was one; only Francis Maloney, my father-in-law, would have understood. How exquisitely perverse, I thought. It was to laugh, no? I felt the devil throw his cold arm around my shoulder and whisper, "Go for it, lad."

Melendez lived on Ashford Street just off Atlantic Avenue; still in Brooklyn, but barely. With the wind at your back, you could smack a golf ball and hit the horses turning for the finish line at Aqueduct Raceway, just across the nearby Queens border. Here the fog smelled of the sea tinged with the scent of spent kerosene as jets followed the shoreline of Jamaica Bay, swooping low toward Kennedy.

Carmella turned back to me, placing a finger across her lips.

"My grandmother lives downstairs." I preferred her whisper to the devil's.

We climbed a steep flight of unlit stairs. Cranky with age, the steps complained at each footfall. Carmella seemed not to notice. I think maybe my guilt had given me rabbit ears, that what I heard in the creaks and moans in the old wood were admonitions. I heard, but did not listen.

With laundry strewn on the living room floor, open Chinese food containers on the coffee table, Melendez's apartment was sloppy and disorganized and not so very different from any other single, lonely cop's. Though I had difficulty imagining Carmella Melendez ever being lonely.

Then again, I was probably confusing loneliness and solitude. She would have had all the company she ever wanted; but I understood better than most about loneliness in the heart of the crowd. It's what's inside that keeps us apart. Over the years, the secrets I kept had isolated me. And it dawned on me that the secrets I kept had pushed Katy away. Build a fortress well enough and it even keeps love out.

Sometimes, like at the grand opening party, the only other person I could see in the crowd was my father-in-law. We were alone together. I wondered if Carmella Melendez had secrets, too. For her sake, I hoped not.

"Drink?" she asked.

"Scotch."

"I'd try the beer."

"Yeah, why's that?"

"It's all I've got," she said. "Come on in the kitchen. It's neater in there."

She was right. The kitchen was immaculate. More likely from lack of use than anything else. She noticed me notice.

"I can cook, but . . ."

"No one to cook for. I know."

"My grandmother brings stuff up for me sometimes and we eat together a few times a week. She's getting old and is beginning to forget things sometimes. This way I can keep an eye on her."

I sat down at the little round-top table as she fished two Coronas out of the fridge.

She handed me a bottle. "No limes, sorry."

"I'm not a lime sort of guy." I took a pull on my beer and waited. I'm not sure why or what for, but I hadn't felt this awkward in a very long time. Melendez stood her ground, leaning against the refrigerator. Things were rapidly progressing from awkward to downright uncomfortable, when Carmella threw me the sharpest breaking curveball I'd ever seen.

"I want you to like me." There was that whisper again.

"What do you think I'm doing here?"

"No. I want you to *like* me, Moe, not just want me. I know how to make men want me. That's something I could do even before I knew how."

"What's that supposed to mean?"

"Nothing. Forget it. Just that I know I'm pretty."

I got up and stood close to her, softly brushing her cheek with the back of my hand, tucking a wayward strand of silk black hair behind her ear. "You're more than pretty, Carmella."

Leaning forward, I rested my lips gently on hers. It was more a caress than a kiss, really, neither of us willing to take it further. Still, it was electric. Carmella slid her lips along mine and nestled her head in the crook of my arm and against my chest. She threaded herself through and around me, holding me desperately tight. I can't explain it, but there was an old yearning in her touch, something way beyond simple attraction. When she finally relaxed her hold and looked back into my eyes, it was one of the most disquieting moments in my life. *Guilt?* No, not this time. I don't think so. I recognized something almost frightening in the depths of her stare.

"What's wrong?"

"I'm going to ruin it," she said.

"Ruin what?"

"This . . . *Us*, if I tell you . . ."

"If you tell me what?"

Now she completely freed herself, ducking under of my arms, and walked away. Gazing out into the darkness through the little window above the kitchen sink, her back still to me, she said, "Remember the other day in the car on the way to Fountain Avenue when I was saying that getting my shield had nothing to do with my being Puerto Rican or my—"

"I remember. You were giving me a song and dance about being a good cop."

"I *am* a good cop."

"I believe you, but what's this got to do with—"

"I am a good cop," she repeated, trying to convince the both of us. "But maybe I did make a compromise I shouldn't have. I just wanted that shield so bad."

Yeah, tell me about it. "What kinda compromise? Who'd ya —"

"—fuck?" She turned toward me. "That's what you were gonna ask, right? It always comes down to that—who I fucked to get ahead. I didn't fuck anybody! This ain't about pussy or passports."

"Okay, I'm sorry. You're right. So if that wasn't it, what was it?"

"I knew about the wire in the interview room," she said, looking anywhere but at me.

"How?"

"I put it there."

"You *what?*"

"I put it there," she repeated, head hanging low.

Now I understood her reaction when I told her about what was on the tape. She was worried about being found out.

"Whose idea was it?"

"Not mine."

"That's not what I asked."

"Chief McDonald. He put me up to it."

"You're shitting me, right?" I seethed. "The chief of detectives has a bug planted in his old precinct house and he winds up an apparent suicide, and you don't think to say anything!"

"I knew this would ruin it."

I was at her in a flash, my hands grabbing her shoulders and spinning her around.

"You've got a lot more to worry about than us, Carmella."

"Don't you think I know that?" she growled, pulling out of my grasp. "I just wanted my shield. You can't understand."

I ignored that last part. "Okay, okay, let's start from the beginning. When did Larry first come to you?"

"Technically, I went to him." She took a long sip of her beer. "About eighteen months ago I got called into my C.O.'s office at the Seven-Seven and he told me to report to One Police Plaza."

"And Larry Mac was waiting."

"He said he'd been keeping his eye on me since I got outta the academy. Had my personnel jacket right in front of him. I thought he was going to put the moves on me, you know? I mean, it's not like every dick with stripes or brass buttons hadn't used a variation of that 'keeping my eye on you' line since the day I got on the job. What's that look for?" she asked, noticing the smile spreading across my face.

"Believe me, Larry loved women, but you had to understand him. He was an ambitious bastard. If he saw a way you'd be of use to him, your looks would have become beside the point. That was just who he was. And if he saw you were hungry . . . watch out! That was his talent, spotting peoples' hungers. So what happened?"

"So he asked me if I thought I'd make a good detective."

"What'd you say?"

"I said no, that I'd make a great detective."

"Let me guess. He put a small box in front of you on the table and told you to go ahead and open it up. Inside, you found the thing you were desperate for, a shield, and Larry said something like, 'Congratulations, Detective Melendez.'" I could see by her expression I'd gotten it about right.

"He said he might have special assignments for me from time to time."

"But not right away. No, he would want to see if you could handle the job and the abuse you were bound to take for getting the bump so early in your career."

"That's some spooky shit, Moe, the way you knew him. You even say the words he said."

"It was hard-learned, what I know about Larry. We came up together. So when did he come back to you with the special assignment?"

"About six months later, when I was in the One-Eleven, he asked me to do some minor crap. He had me check up on someone, another detective. I wasn't supposed to say anything to anybody, no matter what. Then like a week later, two guys from—"

"—I.A. showed up and wanted to speak to you about this other detective. You didn't say a word, did you?"

"No."

"Larry was—"

"—testing me. Yeah, I knew that. It was bullshit. After that, he didn't call for a long time."

"How long?"

"I got transferred to the Six-O almost eight months ago. I guess it was four or five months after that."

"And . . ."

"And he met me at some Cuban-Chinese dive in Hell's Kitchen. Gave me some equipment, told me how to install it."

"Did he say why he wanted a wire in—"

"I didn't ask. I didn't wanna know. I'm not sure I woulda believed him anyway, no matter what he told me."

"Clever. Believing Larry was about percentages. But what happened next?"

"Nothing. Chief McDonald and I never spoke again. Most of the time, I even forgot that the wire was there. I never even saw the chief again until . . . You know."

"Fountain Avenue."

"Yeah."

"Okay, is that all of it?"

"That's it! Tomorrow, I'll pull the wire."

"No you won't. Leave it there," I barked. "Right now it's all we got. Maybe we can use it. Does anybody else know?"

"Not from me, but I can't say if Chief McDonald told anyone."

"I doubt it. Not Larry's style to share. Besides, whatever his reasoning, this was way beyond kosher, even for a chief."

"So what's the plan?"

"The plan? The plan is you dig up what you can on the Dexter Mayweather murder while I try and figure out what Larry Mac was up to with this wire."

"You think they're related, the wire, the Mayweather thing, and the chief's suicide?" she asked.

"If it was suicide."

"Right, if it was suicide," she agreed. "But do you think it's all related?"

"Maybe, maybe not. Depends what Larry was fishing for."

"Huh?"

"Sometimes trawlers catch sharks in their nets. Even if you go to throw the shark back in, it doesn't mean it won't bite you."

HER NAME WAS Nancy Lustig, a forlorn little rich girl whose looks bordered on the ugly side of nondescript. I'd met her in 1978 when I was looking for my *now-you-see-him-now-you-don't* brother-in-law, Patrick. They'd dated long enough for him to knock her up and abandon her after the abortion. I hadn't thought about Nancy Lustig in years, but as I drove home along the Belt Parkway in the suddenly unwelcoming fog, she was on my mind.

I guess maybe there was something in Melendez tonight that brought Nancy to mind. Not her looks, certainly, but there was something in Carmella's eyes, a sadness, a yearning, an old wound that struck the same chord Nancy had struck a dozen years ago.

I don't know, maybe it was my guilt again, screaming at me like the cranky old steps. It wasn't lost on me that in the midst of Melendez's revelations about Larry Mac and her planting the wire, I had kissed a woman in a way married men are not supposed to kiss women who are not their wives. Sure, from the outside it probably didn't look like much of a kiss, but it was on the inside, and on the inside there was fire.

In a way, I think I was grateful for the bomb Carmella had dropped on me about her dealings with Larry Mac. It put the fire on hold, at least for now. There was only so much I could handle all at once, only so many hands to juggle so many balls. Tonight, I'd run out of hands.

CHAPTER TWELVE

FISHBEIN MET ME at a coffee shop in Elmont, just over the Queens border with Nassau County. The D.A. didn't like being summoned. He was careful not to say so, though his expression spoke all too clearly. Fishbein may have been good at keeping his yap shut when the situation called for it, but he wore his heart on his face. It was forever getting him in trouble, especially during his ill-fated run for governor. His media-savvy handlers spotted the problem right away, making certain Fishbein never appeared on camera in his own commercials. His ads were always full of testimonials, newspaper clippings, and still photos.

The bigger problem was that his handlers couldn't control the TV news, and whenever they showed tape of Fishbein making a stump speech, the D.A.'s boredom and condescension showed through. It was especially evident when he'd be in some upstate county speaking to a bunch of dairy farmers. Bad enough that he looked so out of place to begin with—Groucho Marx in a Dickies shirt, stiff Levis, and Wolverine boots—but when he started talking about price supports . . . Jesus, you could just see the man wanted to be any place else.

"So, what can I do for you, Mr. Prager?" Fishbein asked, pulling a face as bitter as the coffee. He put his cup down.

"That's the right question, Mr. D.A., but first I wanna talk about my brother-in-law a little bit. You said—"

"I know what I said, but you might as well not ask. Results. Results. Results. They're the only things that'll get you answers, so I suggest you get to work."

"Can you find out if there was any monkey business going on in the Six-O?"

"Monkey business?"

"Was anyone in the precinct a target of an I.A., local, or federal investigation? Do I really have to spell it out for you?"

"Not really, but can you be a little more specific? Even with good hearing, it helps to know what you're listening for."

Clever man. I knew we'd eventually get to where we now were. I just hadn't counted on it being so soon. I'd spent the better part of my sleepless last night trying to sort through everything I had on my plate, never mind the kiss. *The kiss*. It was all I could do not to let it consume me. But looking across the table at Fishbein's snide expression made the task that much easier. I went with the truth. An edited version of it, at least.

"Chief McDonald had a wire installed in an interview room at the Six-O."

Fishbein's eyes got big and greedy. It was all he could do not to salivate. "A wire, huh? And you know this how?"

"I heard a tape."

"Of what?"

"For now, that's my business and it's beside the point. What I need to know is why."

"You're presupposing this wasn't authorized," said the D.A., taking a second sip of his coffee. He didn't like this one any better than the first.

"I'm not presupposing anything. I'm eliminating possibilities. So, can you find out?"

"I can." Fishbein stood over me. He liked that. Suited his personality much better than speaking to dairy farmers. "I'll be in touch."

I didn't bother shaking his hand, nor did I wish him well. The better I got to know the D.A., the more I hoped he'd get hit by a bus some day. I stayed and finished my coffee. It was bitter, but not so much as Fishbein's. His lips hadn't touched my cup.

LIKE A LOT of towns on Long Island, Massapequa, or Matzohpizza, as the locals jokingly called it, was a popular destination on the white flight express. So many city cops, firemen, and school teachers fled there in the '60s and '70s that people said Massapequa was Algonquin for civil servant. If you screamed "Help, Police!" at midnight, half the porch lights in town went on. One of the those porch lights had once belonged to Larry McDonald—Larry having made the move to the Burger King landscape of the Long Island suburb years ago. Margaret had gotten the house in the divorce settlement.

Long Island gave me the chills to begin with, and the thought of visiting Larry's old house wasn't making me feel any better. I parked in front of the tidy colonial on Harmony Drive in Massapequa Park and took a slow walk to the door. Yeah, even out here the stratification of neighborhoods had taken hold. The collars were bluer in North Massapequa than in plain old Massapequa, and the houses were a little nicer and the lawns a bit more trim in Massapequa Park than in Massapequa proper. But if you had some *gelt*, some *'scarole*, you lived down by the water in Nassau Shores.

The first thing I did was look at the numbers on the front of the house when a squat man of sixty pulled back the door. Who did I expect, Larry McDonald's fucking ghost? It's weird how humans are so good at denying reality. I suppose I thought Margaret would answer. Maybe hoped is the better word.

"Is Margaret home?"

"She's not around. Who are you?" he asked, but without guile.

"Moe Prager. I'm—"

"Sure, sure, Moe. I heard all about you. You were friends with Marge's first husband. Come in. Come in." I stepped inside. The interior of the house was as clean and tidy as the outside. "Frank Spinelli," he said, offering me a thick hand. I took it. Had the grip of a working man, but the skin of a retiree. His accent was Bronx Italian, maybe with a taste of the old country mixed in.

"Pleasure to meet you, Frank."

"Same here. Glad for the company. Gave up the pizzeria a few years back, but I can't get used to this leisure thing. I tried golf a little bit, but I figured if I wanted to suffer so much, I'd just stick pins in my eyes. I'm home so much, sometimes I think I make Marge a little *ubotz*, crazy, you know?"

I liked this guy. "Yeah, I can see that."

"For almost forty years I'm working twelve-hour days, and then this beautiful young woman walks into my shop and she takes my heart. She come in for calzone and winds up with a husband. Life is crazy, no? Hey, I'm being rude. You wanna drink? A little homemade red?"

"Sure, but only with some ice and lemon slices."

That stopped Frank Spinelli in his tracks. "Hey, who taught you how to drink homemade like a guinea?"

Rico Tripoli. "Another ex-cop. A friend of Larry and me."

"Come on in the kitchen."

Frank Spinelli stood at the island with two jam jars filled with ice cubes and lemon wedges. He poured the red wine into the jars from a big jug. He corked the jug and slid a jar my way.

"*Salude!*"

"*Salude!*"

"So, Moe, you know your friend Larry, he really hurt Marge."

"I know, Frank."

"Why did he do that? Marge is a beautiful woman, a good woman."

"The best. But Larry's loss was your gain, right?"

For the first time since I stepped inside the house, Frank stopped smiling.

"Marge, she loves me, but she never loves me like Larry. I knew that when I married her. That is a once in your life thing, the way she loved Larry. Me, I'm a chubby old wop from the Bronx who respects a woman, who knows how to treat her right, but I never fool myself. My poppa," Frank said, crossing himself, "he always said the only real fools were people who tricked themselves. I'm no fool, Moe."

"No, Frank, I don't suppose you are."

"So why you wanna talk to Marge, you don't mind me asking?"

"About Larry. Something was going on there. I knew Larry was an ambitious bastard, and he could do some incredibly cold and calculating things, but suicide . . ."

"Marge, too. She don't understand."

"That's why I wanted to talk to her. Maybe she knows something she isn't aware of. You know, something that happened a long time ago."

"Sure. Sure. Makes sense."

We went out to their back deck and stood in silence, drinking our wine and watching the cardinals and robins darting from branch to branch. Before I left, Frank promised he would have Margaret call me. We shook hands and said our goodbyes, but Frank wasn't quite finished. With the front door nearly closed behind me, I could hear Frank mutter, "Why did he hurt her like that?"

It was a good question. Larry seemed to have left a lot of those behind.

I MADE ONE more stop on my way back to Brooklyn. I pulled off the L.I.E. at Queens Boulevard and drove into Rego Park. Mandrake Towers was a ten-unit apartment building complex. The buildings were red brick boxes that were as homey as an off ramp and as cozy as a prison cell, but I wasn't apartment shopping, thank God!

The security office was in the basement of Building 5. Although the incinerator had been replaced years ago by a garbage compactor, the stink of the fire and ash remained. Didn't matter how many coats of fresh paint were laid over the cinder block walls, it seemed the odor was there to stay. Maybe it was in my head. My friend Israel Roth, forty-five years removed from the nightmare of Auschwitz, says he can still smell burning flesh in pure mountain air. He told me once, "There's no forgetting some things. Some things, Mr. Moe, demand to be remembered."

Who was I to disagree?

The security office was unchanged since the first time I'd seen it in 1983, but the man behind the desk had grown a little grayer, a little thicker around the gut. He no longer wore a trooper's hat and there were now shiny captain's bars on the collar of his khaki shirt.

"Shit!" he said looking up from his book. "Security sure do suck in this place they let broken down old white people like you in here."

"Security's fine, but their leadership's a little shaky."

"Y'all don't want me to come around this desk and kick your scrawny little Jewish ass up and down the block."

"You'd have to catch me first."

"Good point. Come over here and let me give y'all a hug, man."

Preacher Simmons stood up in pieces. When you're six-foot-eight and close to three hundred pounds, you're allowed to unfold yourself one part at a time. In the mid-'60s, Preacher "the Creature" Simmons was an all-city, all-world forward from Boys High in Brooklyn. These days, he would have been drafted directly into the NBA and given a few million dollars to sit on the bench and learn the pro game. But back in '64 he wound up at a basketball factory down South and in the midst of a point shaving scandal. Unlike Connie Hawkins, Preacher didn't have the resources to resurrect his career. He was a power player and lacked the soaring grace of Hawkins. Instead, he fell on hard times and was rescued by a cop named John Heaton. Heaton was the father of the political intern that had gone missing in 1981. It was two years later, when I'd been hired to do a last ditch investigation of Moira Heaton's disappearance, that I met Preacher. We'd been friends since. We even played ball together sometimes in local two-on-two tournaments. We were quite the odd couple: me with one knee and Preacher lumbering in the paint, carrying forty extra pounds around his gut and the occasional defender on his back. But between my outside shot and his power game we made it work. Katy liked to bring Sarah to watch us play. Today, thinking about that stung.

"What brings you down to the bowels of hell today, Moe?"

"You busy tonight?"

"Busy? Nah, man, why?"

"Feel like helping me with something?"

"A case?"

"Yeah."

"Help how?"

"Meet me in front of Nathan's at nine tonight."

"Coney Island Nathan's or Oceanside?"

"Coney Island."

"We investigating hotdogs and beer?"

"Maybe after."

"After what?" he asked.

"After you teach someone a lesson in basketball."

"Y'all talk some shit, Moe. You know that?"

"Can you meet me?"

"See you there."

"I'll explain later," I said, waving my goodbye.

"Why later?"

"Because I hope to figure out what the hell we're supposed to be doing by then."

CHAPTER THIRTEEN

I CAME UP with something, but like the rest of my ideas about being a detective, it was half-baked and spur of the moment. You make do with what you have, I guess. As scheduled, Preacher Simmons met me out in front of Nathan's at nine. I always liked playing ball on an empty stomach. Preacher had different ideas on the subject. He had four hot dogs, two large fries, and two enormous lemonades before I dropped him off at the courts. They didn't call him "the Creature" for nothing.

"I guess sitting on your ass all day in that security office makes for hungry work."

"Man, you know me going on seven years, Moe. For me, breathing makes for hungry work."

Argue that.

When I picked him up at the entrance to the courts about an hour and a half later, Preacher had toweled off and changed into some fresh clothing. Even after a full day's work, the drive in from Queens, and ninety minutes of ball, his eyes were on fire. He'd once told me that the only place he ever felt truly alive was on the court. That was never going to change. He was forty-three now and I wondered where the fire would go when his hips and knees started to breakdown. You can't carry as much weight as he did and pound your legs on concrete and asphalt courts for as long as he had without paying a big price.

There was a burning in me, too, but mine was envy. At least Preacher had a place in the world where he felt alive. All I had now were French Cabernets and California Chardonnays. A stupid piece of carbon paper—did they even have carbon paper anymore?—had taken that place away from me forever. Being a cop, putting on that blue uniform every day, knowing every inch of the pavement I patrolled, that was being alive. The rest of it was sleepwalking.

"So?" I said, trying not to let my envy show.

He thought my scouting report on the Nugget kid was right on. "For such a big head, he don't seem to have nothing in it. You can't tell that boy nothing."

Preacher said he'd caught a lucky break, that another old timer had recognized him from his Boys High years. Reggie Philbis was his name and they'd played against one another back in the day—Reggie for Thomas Jefferson. Currently, Reggie worked as a drug treatment counselor for the city, having come upon his education the hard way. Knowing Reggie paid off in two ways: it helped open up lines of communication with the guys waiting winners, and it got Nugget's grudging attention.

"Anybody have anything to say about Malik?"

"You mean Melvin? Shit, yeah, but none of it kindly. He was like the neighborhood joke, you know what I'm saying?"

"Every neighborhood's got 'em, guy's that fancy themselves something they're never gonna be. Guys that think they're cool, but can't get outta their own way with a tour guide."

"That's the boy."

"But what did they say about him?"

"Strictly small-time, you know, a loser—"

"A loser that could afford half a key of coke."

"You didn't let me finish, Moe. My man Reggie say Melvin not only got a new name, but he got hisself some new friends in recent years."

"New friends?"

"Wiseguy types."

"Wiseguy *types*, not wiseguys?" I asked.

"Well shit, ain't like old Melvin been introducing his new white brothers around, if you know what I'm saying. The boys at the court seem to think they was sorta like Melvin in their own way."

"Wannabes."

"Sounds about right."

"And Nugget?"

"Boy's got some severe offensive game, but on D he moves his feet like a statue."

"Did you talk to him?"

"Some. He ain't ready to hear me."

"He'll learn the hard way."

"Nah, man, some go the hard way, but they don't never learn a thing."

It was getting close to midnight. Preacher wanted to treat for a nightcap, but I took a raincheck and dropped the man back at his car. He asked me what was wrong. I lied and told him nothing. He left it at that. Preacher was good that way, he knew when to push and when not to push.

I HAD IN mind to pay a visit on Malik Jabbar's girlfriend, Kalisha. Given Mable Broadbent's less than glowing commentary on her late son's taste in women, I didn't figure on asking her to make formal introductions. So I just sat in my car across from Rancho Broadbent and waited, hoping Kalisha would appear. I hadn't a clue as to what Kalisha might look like, but somehow I just felt I would know her.

It was getting late and I was beginning to worry that Mable had exaggerated about the hours Kalisha kept. Another few minutes and I'd have to head back home or risk passing out in my car. When I looked up from my watch, a streetlight flickered and I noticed Mable Broadbent's backlit silhouette in the front window of her flat. She, too, was waiting. I wondered if this was how she dealt with her grief, keeping tabs on a woman she despised, a woman who had somehow replaced her in her lost son's life. It's hard getting inside other people's emotions, but grief is, I think, the hardest to slip into. Grief is a dark place, the darkest place.

The stoop light popped on, the front door swinging open. A woman came out onto the concrete landing and closed the door behind her. She hesitated at the top of the short stairs, turning to her left to stare directly at Mable Broadbent. Mable did not move. It was a test of wills. After an endless ten seconds, the woman on the stoop shouted, "Fuck you, bitch." By any standard, Mable had won that round. The woman I took to be Kalisha made a left and moved toward Surf Avenue. I got out of my car. As I did so, I looked to where Mable had sat in her front window. She was gone.

I stood in the shadows across the street from Kalisha. She checked her watch and paced as if she were waiting for someone to pick her up. The smell of the ocean and sewerage was strong in the air. Calling Coney Island the ass end of Brooklyn was both a figurative and literal expression because around the bend of Sea Gate towards Bay Ridge, sewerage was dumped out into the Atlantic. When I was a kid, swimming with my buddies at Coney, Brighton, and Manhattan Beaches, I never gave it much thought. I did now. I walked across the street.

"Kalisha?"

"Whatchu want?" she barked, her pride still hurting from losing her stare down with Mable Broadbent.

She had a svelte, angular body. Up close, she was a pretty woman with almost yellow-brown skin and green eyes, but she exuded a kind of hardness that argued against her looks. She wore an expensive, grassy perfume, and way too much of it, so much that it dominated the scent of the sea and sewerage. Kalisha's clothes cost some bucks, but cheapened her somehow. She stared at me as if I were a lone roach caught out in the light. I realized I had crossed the street fully prepared to dislike her, and nothing about her was changing my mind.

"You want some company, baby, you a long way from Mermaid and Stillwell. Twenty bucks'll get you all the black pussy you can handle down there." My silence made her uncomfortable, and she reached a hand into her bag. "I ain't in that life no more."

I showed her my old badge, bluffing to the max.

"That supposed to get y'all a discount?"

"No, just your attention."

"Now you got it, whatchu want with it?"

"To talk about Malik."

"He dead."

"No shit. That's why I wanna talk."

"Fuck y'all."

"Sorry," I said, "not interested. Now it looks to me like you're waiting on somebody. I bet he won't be thrilled if he has to come collect you over at the 60th Precinct. You think?"

"Whatchu wanna know 'bout Malik?"

"Where'd he get the money for half a key of coke?"

The belligerence in her face was replaced by blankness. The question scared her and she didn't like being scared. She liked showing it even less.

"I don't know whatchu talkin' 'bout. Malik didn't—"

"Bullshit, Kalisha. Malik was a loser, a guy that didn't have two nickels to rub together his whole life. Then he scores a fine looking woman like you and he's dealing weight. Something changed. Maybe he got some new friends, some white boys, maybe. You wanna talk to me about that?"

"Fuck y'all. Ain't met a cop had a dick bigga than my pinky." She demonstrated, waving a ringed little finger my way. It was false

103

bravado. She'd grown shrill and any sense of composure was gone from her voice.

"That may be, but it doesn't answer the question. Listen, Kalisha, you don't talk to me now, okay. But there's gonna be some detectives coming around on a regular basis starting tomorrow. So even if you aren't talking, maybe Malik's buddies will think you are. You know, maybe I should just wait here with you till your ride shows up. Maybe I should chat with him. What do you think?"

"Oh fuck, man! Why you gotta fuck with a girl's life like that?"

"It doesn't have to be this way if you just talk to me."

"Ask your damned questions, man."

"Malik ever talk about a cop named McDonald?"

"E-I-E-I-O. He the guy owns that farm, right?" She smiled, and for just a second, I saw there were still remnants of a little girl inside the hard woman in front of me.

"No, Kalisha, Larry McDonald bought the farm. He didn't own it."

Took her a second to process that. "Oh, he dead too. Well, Malik didn't never talk about no cops, not by name, anyway."

"Okay, how about Dexter Mayweather, Malik ever mention him?"

"You crazy? D Rex been dead almost as long as I been alive. Malik was just a boy when that man was killed. How he gonna know anything about that?"

"I don't know. Maybe one of Malik's new friends mentioned something. Just a question."

Something flashed across her face—unease, maybe. If I had blinked, I would have missed it.

"Whatchu talking 'bout, Malik's new friends? He didn't have no friends but me. And why's all the questions you ask 'bout dead men? Dontchu know nobody but dead men?"

"I know lots of people, Kalisha, but I'm most interested in Malik's friends."

"Look, I told y'all, I don't know nothing 'bout friends."

"Then where'd he get the money for the coke?"

She checked her watch again. "Look, my john— I mean my new man gonna be here any second. Won't look good, me standing here talking with you. Can't we talk another time?"

"Tomorrow."

104

"Not tomorrow."

"When I say tomorrow, it's not a question. I'll meet you at this corner at two."

"Okay, then, just get outta here now."

I did as she asked, retreating into the shadows across the street. I turned to look back at the hard girl. Yet, as hard as she was, Kalisha just seemed a sad, bitter woman from the darkness in which I now stood. She couldn't have been more than twenty-five years old and life had already beaten all the good out of her. I couldn't help but wonder what another twenty-five years would do to her. What small percentage of her soul would remain? I needn't have worried.

I heard the rumble of a loud engine coming down Surf Avenue. Even before its brakes squealed and the car pulled over, I knew something was wrong. But what? I couldn't seem to think fast enough. My head was foggy, my mouth dry, my heart racing. *What's wrong? What's wrong? What's wrong?* It rang in my head like church bells. Kalisha took a step toward the passenger door and stopped. Her face went from falsely happy to blank to genuinely panicked. *The car!* I recognized the car. It was the same Camaro that had tried to make me its new hood ornament.

"Look—"

Before I got the second syllable out of my mouth or taken a full step, the barrel of a shotgun stuck through the open window of the passenger door. There were two flashes and roars. Kalisha's head fairly exploded and her lifeless torso sat down, one rubber leg under her, the other kicked out toward Sea Gate. The Camaro gunned its engine and fishtailed, smoking its back tires as it went.

I was swimming in quicksand as I came back across the street. The acrid cloud of burned rubber swallowed up the twin puffs of gun smoke like finger food, and its stink overwhelmed the cordite, the sea, the stench of human waste. Strangely, I could still smell grace notes of Kalisha's grassy perfume, although the neck and ears on which she'd dabbed it had been chewed to shit by the close range barrage of pellets. I looked down at what was left of her and didn't need to touch her to know it wouldn't take twenty-five more years to find out what she'd become. All she was fifteen seconds ago was all she was ever going to be.

I ran to my car and took off. No lights had come on since the shooting. No new faces had appeared in second floor windows, at least none I could see. They were there all right. When the cops showed, no one would have heard or seen a thing. When I was on the job, I used to think the lack of cooperation was just pure hatred of the cops. Not anymore. Some of it was hatred and resentment, sure, but mostly it was resignation. This is how life worked. This is how it was in the Soul Patch. What was another dead nigger? What was another murdered prostitute to the cops?

As I tore down the street, I once again found myself thinking of Israel Roth and Auschwitz. "You can get used to anything," he'd say. "The very essence of humanity is adaptability. Some people think it's what makes us great. Me, I think it's a curse. There are things we shouldn't be able to live with."

I also thought of Mable Broadbent. What would she do with her grief now that Kalisha was dead?

I found the Camaro down by Coney Island Creek. As I turned the corner it was already in flames. And when I saw the long, wet rag sticking out of where the gas cap should have been, I knew it was only a matter of seconds until the whole thing blew apart. It didn't disappoint. For decades, the city used to have free firework displays along the boardwalk on summer Tuesday evenings. Those displays were fun, but nothing compared to an exploding Chevrolet. I split before New York's Bravest and Finest appeared.

I USED A booth on Mermaid Avenue and got Melendez at home. If I felt weirder making a call in my life, I'd be damned if I could remember it. For fuck's sake, talk about mixed emotions. My guts were twisted in bunches. I had stood there for five minutes with the phone in my hand, rehearsing what to say. But there was no rehearsing a conversation that might cover lust, guilt, murder, and betrayal. When she picked up, I found I could not speak.

"Moe, Moe is that you?"

"Yeah."

"You don't hate me?"

"I feel a lot of things about you, Carmella, but hate isn't one of 'em. I think I wish it was. Things would be easier that way."

"You were all I thought about today."

I ignored that in self-defense. "That's about to change."

"Why?"

"Malik's girl, Kalisha . . ."

"What about her?"

"Someone blew her head off with a shotgun about fifteen minutes ago."

"How'd you find out?"

"I was standing across the street."

"What happened?"

"We talked, Kalisha and me, and we agreed to meet again to talk some more. I walked towards my car and that Camaro that tried to run me down the other day pulled up. She walked over to the passenger door and . . . *Bang! Bang!* She was a mess. I found the Camaro in flames over by the creek."

"Why kill the girlfriend?"

"I've got some ideas about that. You on tomorrow?"

"Uh huh."

"Think you can get away from Murphy for lunch?"

"I'll call you."

"Okay."

"Moe."

"I know," I said. "I know."

I said I did, but I didn't know a goddamned thing anymore.

CHAPTER FOURTEEN

MUNDANE.

Given that in the last few days Larry Mac had either been killed or killed himself, that someone had tried to kill me, that I'd kissed Carmella Melendez, and that I'd witnessed a woman's head being blown off and was reading about it at the breakfast table, you'd think mundane would be the last word to come to mind. But I had a family and a business and a house and taxes to pay. I had pancakes to serve to a little girl and I had to catch the mailman.

"Yo, Joey!"

But when Joey the mailman turned around, he wasn't Joey. Years ago, there was a local New York kids show called *The Merry Mailman.* Well, not only was this guy not Joey, but he was as merry as mortuary.

"Sorry," I said, handing him some letters to be mailed.

"Gee, thanks, just what I need."

I let that go.

"Did your neighbors move?" he asked.

"The Bermans? Yeah, they moved down to Boca about two weeks ago. Why?"

"Look at this crap!" Mr. Mortuary said, shoving a fistful of envelopes at me. "I have to carry all this shit around with me all day because some idiot screwed up their change of address card."

I was seriously considering telling this numbnuts to go fuck himself, but thought better of it. You never want to piss a waiter off before he brings you your meal and you never want to screw with the mailman after you've just handed him the envelope containing your mortgage payment.

"Have a nice day . . ." *Asshole!*

When I got back inside, Sarah was talking to someone on the phone. "Un huh . . . Yeah, I'm in fifth grade . . . Sometimes I help my mom out downstairs with her design work and my daddy takes me to the stores with him . . ."

"Who is it, kiddo?"

"Excuse me a second," she said into the phone. "A lady named Margaret," she said to me.

"Okay, kiddo, I'll take it from here." Sarah handed me the phone.

"Hi, Marge."

"Frank tells me you came by yesterday to talk to me about Larry." Her voice was grave. "What is it? What's wrong?"

"It's not like that, Marge. I just wanted to talk, to try and jar your memory a little about Larry."

"My memories of Larry don't need any jarring, Moe." She began softly sobbing.

Frank Spinelli was no fool. He understood his new wife very well. Margaret's love for Larry was, indeed, a once in her life thing. Although crushed by the divorce, Marge had probably kept the faint hope of some sort of reconciliation alive. She had married Frank Spinelli as revenge. It was foolish, of course. You can't poke someone in the eye when they're not looking at you. My guess was that when Larry had called Margaret a few weeks back to arrange for dinner, she had gone to the Blind Steer fully prepared to do whatever she had to, to recover at least some small part of what she had lost, her own dignity be damned. I can't imagine how much it hurt when Larry failed to show.

"I'm sorry, Marge."

"Don't be. I just . . . I just really miss him."

"I know. He could be a real jerk, but . . ."

"Christ, help me, I know."

"I like Frank a lot," I said, trying to change the subject, but her sobbing only got worse.

"It's so unfair to him, to Frank."

"I don't think he'd see it that way. He loves you and he understands more than you think, Marge."

At that very moment, Katy walked through the basement door, waving her portable office phone at me. Her face was as grave as Margaret's voice had been.

"Excuse me for a second, Marge." I covered the mouthpiece. "What's up, Katy? What's wrong?"

"There's a Detective Melendez on the phone for you."

"Tell her to hold on for one second while I get off this call, okay?" She shook her head yes and walked out of earshot. "Marge, listen, I've gotta go. Can we meet later, maybe someplace you and Larry used to go when you first started seeing each other?"

"Cara Mia," she said, without hesitation and without tears. "Do you know it?"

"In Bay Ridge?"

"That's it."

"Eight okay with you?"

"Eight."

Katy must've heard me hang up, because she reappeared, portable in hand. I mouthed, "Thanks," and took her phone. My day was about to take a sharp turn away from the mundane.

"Yes, Detective Melendez, what can I do for you?"

"They got your tag number," she said.

"Who got my tag number?"

"We did, the cops."

"From last night?"

"That's right. Somebody gave up your plate number."

"Fuck!"

"It gets worse, Moe. Detectives Bento and Klein are coming to talk to you."

"When?"

"Like now, so start thinking of something to say."

"Listen, write this number down." I gave her Preacher Simmons' phone number. "Call it and tell the man at the other end what you just told me. He'll know what to do."

"Give you an alibi, you mean."

"Yeah, something like that."

There was a loud silence on the other end of the phone. I thought she began to say something, but maybe not. I probably imagined it. She was already compromised and she knew it. Calling Preacher for me wasn't going to make it any worse.

When I hung up and turned around, Katy was standing right behind me. Her expression hadn't brightened any. No one, not even the wives of ex-cops, like getting unexpected calls from the police. But there was something else in her eyes beyond concern and curiosity, something I had never seen in her eyes. And before I could ask about it, Katy explained it all with a question.

"How did you know Detective Melendez was a her?"

"I met her before. She's the one who drove me to where they found Larry's body." *She was the beautiful, dark-skinned detective who was hanging around the cemetery. She was the one who pushed me out of the way of an oncoming car. She was the one who I—*

110

I resisted the urge to say more. The guilty talk too much and in the back of my mind I heard the old steps creaking with the weight of my guilt. Katy opened her mouth to say something, when the doorbell rang. Whatever was in her eyes had gone, at least for the moment.

"Those are the cops for me," I said. "I'm going to go with them."

"The cops! What happened?"

"They think I saw something."

"What?"

I ignored that. "Where's Sarah?"

"She went down to my studio," Katy said. "Why?"

"I don't want her to hear us."

"Well, what do they think you saw?"

"This!" I held up the *Daily News* and showed her the story about Kalisha's execution.

"Oh my God! You saw it, didn't you?" There was no fooling Katy. She could see it in my face. That ability of hers gave me pause.

"I'll explain later. I've gotta go."

She didn't argue. The doorbell rang again and this time there was knocking as well. I opened up the door and stepped out, rather than letting the detectives in. Sarah was downstairs, but I didn't want to risk her hearing anything at all. Kids always know more than their parents think they do, but I didn't feel obliged to help the process along.

FOR THE FIRST time in or out of uniform, I was on the wrong side of the desk inside a police interview room. I can't say how exactly, but it seemed fitting that it should happen at my old precinct house. I doubted familiarity was apt to make interrogation a more enjoyable experience. On my way back to the interview rooms, with Klein and Bento behind me, I looked for Carmella, even Murphy. I might just as well have been looking for Judge Crater or proof of Atlantis.

I did stop to stare at the spot on the squad room floor where one misstep and a careless piece of litter had combined to forever alter the course of my life. There was no plaque, no ersatz memorial to the death of my undistinguished police career. Shit, they'd probably redone the floor two or three times since I'd slipped and twisted my knee in a way that neither God nor Darwin had ever intended. But I was lucky, I think, to be able to trace the course of my adult life back to one single thing. When most people look in their rearview mirrors, all they see are faint ghosts; tiny, intermittent steps that don't seem to add up to where they are. How the fuck did I get here? is a question most people take to their graves for consideration. Not me. I'd have secrets to keep me warm through eternal night.

"What the fuck you lookin' at?" Bento wanted to know.

"Can't you see him?" I asked.

"Who?"

"Elvis' ghost."

"Get the fuck in the room, Prager."

They'd spruced up the Six-O's interview rooms since last I stepped inside one over twelve years ago. It's not like they'd painted the walls a snappy orange or added potted plants, but it was brighter somehow.

Wasn't it Pascal who said that if you had to wager on whether or not God existed, the safe bet was existence? Although I don't think he had my situation in mind when he wrote it, I went with Pascal's advice. I didn't know if I was in the interview room in which Carmella Melendez had planted the wire, but I acted as if I were. Even if I were so inclined to trust Klein and Bento with the truth—which I wasn't—I couldn't be sure of who else might be listening. My answers would be as much for those invisible ears as for the two detectives.

Detective Klein was maybe thirty-five, a lean and quiet type with steel-gray hair and eyes to match. He was the kind to hang back and watch. Bento, an impatient, barrel-chested Sicilian, was about my age. He held his hands curled as if holding an invisible salami hero and cold Heineken. He liked his food. I wasn't stupid enough to think one detective more dangerous than the other.

In the car on the way over, Bento had done most of the talking, mostly about the Mets. *They should have won three championships by now. Gooden's a piece-of-shit drug addict. They never should have traded Kevin Mitchell.* It was all crap meant either to make me feel at ease or to disorient me. It did neither. Now inside the box, Bento changed his tune. He was probably a fucking Yankee fan anyway.

"Do you know why we want to speak to you?"

"What happened, you're not interested in talking Mets' baseball anymore?"

"That's not what Detective Bento asked you, Prager," Klein jumped in. "So let me ask it again. Do you know why we want to talk to you?"

"No."

"Lying's no way to begin a friendship," he said.

"I got all the friends I can use, Detective Klein."

"Then why just march into our fucking car when we showed up at your door?" Bento asked, already looking pissed enough to rip my head off.

"Because I used to be a cop and when two detectives from my old precinct show up at my door and ask to speak with me, I go with them."

Klein opened a folder and laid out various photos of Kalisha's body on the table in front of me. Although I had watched the murder take place and had stood closer to her lifeless torso than I was now to either Klein or Bento, the pictures were worse. Recorded after death had fully taken hold, when the blood had settled and the open wounds had begun to attract the local insect population, the photos caught the ugliness and horror of murder in a way the filtered human eye could not: a tangle of blood-soaked hair caught on a wire fence, a piece of skull lying on the sidewalk next to a crushed soda can, a lone fly crawling into a vacant eye socket, a blood-splattered leather jacket.

"You recognize her," Bento stated more than asked.

"It's hard to tell."

"Name's Kalisha Pardee," he said.

I never did know her last name. "Who was she?"

"Come on, Prager. We know you knew her," Klein said.

"Oh, yeah? Maybe you can refresh my memory a little."

"She was a working girl. Used to have a boyfriend, a small-time dealer named Malik Jabbar, a.k.a. Melvin Broadbent. Ring any bells."

"Nope."

"Malik beat his girl into the long hereafter by only a few weeks." Klein made a gun of his forefinger and thumb, pressing the barrel to my temple. "Took a few to the noggin."

"Sorry," I said. "It's not helping."

Bento exploded. "Look asshole, I don't care if you was a cop in this house. I don't care if you built the fuckin' place. I don't care if you was a friend of the chief's. We got a witness places you at the scene."

"Really? Anyone claiming I did this?" I asked, pointing at the crime scene photos.

"You're here to answer questions, not ask 'em."

"Listen, I'm not saying I wasn't in the neighborhood last night. I was, but I had no connection to this poor woman."

The light switched on in Klein's head. "What were you doing there?"

"Basketball."

"Basketball what?"

"I had dinner with my friend at Nathan's and then I dropped him off at the courts over by the projects. I couldn't find a spot by the courts, so I parked on a side street a few blocks away. I walked back to the courts and watched through the fence for awhile. When my friend was done, I drove him back to his car and then I went home."

"This friend of yours got a name?" Klein asked.

"Preacher Simmons."

Bento's eyes got big. "Preacher 'the Creature' Simmons?"

"Yeah, we're friends. We play in two-on-two tournaments sometimes. We were scouting this kid to maybe play with us on a three-man team."

"Kid got a name?"

"Probably, but I don't know it. They call him Nugget."

"Big-headed, dark-skinned nigger, about fifteen, with quick hands and a wicked crossover dribble?" Bento asked, "nigger" rolling off his tongue as easily as "Merry Christmas." "I go down there and watch sometimes. That boy got some game."

"That's him."

Klein looked like he swallowed someone else's throw up. "Before you two start humping each other . . ."

Bento flushed, chastened by his partner.

"Anybody see you at the courts?" Klein continued.

"I don't know. Like I said, I watched from outside the fence. Preacher was the one playing in the games. I didn't make small talk with anyone, if that's what you're asking."

114

"Hey partner," Klein turned to Bento, "you seem to know every fucking thing about these courts. What time they close up shop down there?"

"Officially, like ten, but I seen games go on there till midnight sometimes."

Klein thought about that for a second, opened his note pad and said, "Midnight, huh? Well, the 9-1-1 call came in at twelve fifty-two. Our witness says she saw your car pull out around that time."

"What can I tell you, Detective? Your witness is wrong. Like I said, I was definitely around the neighborhood, but . . ."

"That's your story?" Klein prodded.

"That's it."

"All right. Get outta here. Detective Bento'll give you a ride back to your house."

"That's okay. I'll take the subway. It's only a few stops."

"Have it your way."

I stood to go and made it as far as the door before Klein stopped me.

"You know I don't believe a word of that bullshit story. It's gonna fall apart the minute we start checking into it."

"Look, Detective, I'm an ex-cop, a successful businessman with a family, two cars, and mortgage. Not for nothing, but what the fuck would I want with the hooker-ex-girlfriend of some small-time drug dealer?"

"That's the million dollar question, ain't it?"

CARMELLA MELENDEZ WAS waiting for me in the shadow of the el. I wanted to run in the other direction. Between the longing and guilt, I could barely breathe. And the stress she wore on her face made it worse. It angered me. She hadn't earned the right to be that upset on my behalf. Who was this woman to worry about me? Only Katy had earned that right. We had suffered, laughed, had a life together, made a beautiful child together. Wanting and longing are empty things. They come with no privileges. But in the end, I didn't turn. I didn't run. And by the time I reached her, the anger had washed away.

Melendez said something, but I couldn't hear her for the screeching and squealing of a train above our heads. Sparks rained down into the false darkness that shrouded us. As a kid I was fascinated by the grinding of steel wheels against steel tracks, at how the grinding produced sparks like shooting stars, shooting stars that burned so brightly and so briefly against the shadows beneath the el that ran along Brighton Beach Avenue. Standing close enough to feel her warm breath on my face, I also felt an overwhelming discomfort. It wasn't guilt, not this time. There was something in her eyes, the same things I'd seen the other night, something both frightened and frightening. I was so lost in her eyes that I barely noticed the deafening rumble had faded into a distant, almost pleasant clickety-clack.

"Are you all right?"

"For now," I said. "My story won't hold up for long. You made the call, right?"

"I did. What did you tell them?"

"Basically that I came down to watch some basketball."

"Did they buy it?"

"Would you?"

"No."

"Let's talk, but not here," I said.

"Where? I only have about an hour and I can't be seen with you."

I turned and pointed toward the ocean and began walking away. "Meet me in the aquarium in five minutes."

Wedged between the boardwalk and Surf Avenue, the West Fifth Street handball courts and the Cyclone, the New York Aquarium was no more than a hundred yards away from where Melendez and I had stood beneath the subway station, and not more than two hundred yards from the front door of the 60th Precinct. In spite of the aquarium's proximity to the Six-O, it was highly unlikely we'd run into anyone we knew. The only time I'd ever been there in uniform was back in '74, when Ferguson May and I had to pull some drunk out of the seal enclosure. But as a dad I'd been there many times, taking Sarah at least once or twice a summer.

Strolling around the grounds, just two anonymous adults lost in a sea of school kids and their bored-to-tears teachers, I told Melendez about what Preacher had picked up at the courts and about my meeting with Kalisha Pardee. But as I spoke about what had transpired during the previous evening, I realized there was very little of substance to tell.

That seemed to be par for the course, because when I looked at the big picture, there was no big picture. It was more like a random collection of splotches on an artist's studio floor. People were being murdered, but I'd be damned if I knew why or how the homicides were related.

I stopped at the tank where the rays and small sharks lived out their time, and leaned over the railing to watch them swim. I turned to look back at Melendez, who had stopped several feet short of the tank.

"Sarah, my little girl, she loves to watch them swim," I said. "When she was really little, I used to worry that she'd jump in just to swim with them."

"Don't wony about me, Moe. I ain't jumping in. I hate the water."

"The ocean?"

"Uh huh."

"Pools?"

"Especially pools."

"Really, why?"

"I almost drowned once."

"What happened?"

"I was a little girl and someone saved me, but I don't like talking about it."

"Okay, but look into the tank." Melendez took a few tentative steps forward. I held my arm firmly across her back to anchor her. "Don't worry, I won't let anything happen to you."

"I know you won't, Moe."

"You see how they swim in circles sometimes and just dart straight ahead other times? No matter how I stare at them, I can't figure out why they swim the way they do."

"So?"

"But just because I can't decipher the pattern doesn't mean one doesn't exist, that it's indecipherable."

"This isn't about the fish, is it?" she asked.

"Not really. I'm just frustrated, you know? None of the staff that's going on hangs together. Larry having you plant the wire. A desperate little schmuck like Malik Jabbar getting arrested with half a key of coke in his car and then claiming to know who killed Dexter Mayweather. How the fuck would he know who killed D Rex? He was like eleven years old when Mayweather was murdered. And even if he did know, why would anybody give a shit? But somebody cared enough to kill Malik. Larry cared enough to come to me with the tape, to threaten me, and then he winds up dead too. Somebody cared enough to try and kill me and blow Kalisha Pardee's head off. Why, for chrissakes?"

"Maybe we should find out who Malik's new friends were," Carmella said, quickly stepping away from the tank. Her face was white with fear, beads of sweat on her upper lip and brow. She wasn't kidding about not liking water.

"Yeah, I was thinking that. Who was the A.D.A. who showed up that day you and Murphy arrested Malik?"

"I don't know. Once we went to our C.O., Captain Martello, with Melvin's story about D Rex and wanting to make a deal, he told us to put the little shitbag back in holding and that he'd handle it from there. That was the last time we saw the asshole. Then he turns up dead."

"It was your case, right? Didn't you—"

"— ask Martello what happened? Sure we did, both me and Murphy, but he took the file and told us not to worry about Jabbar anymore."

"Okay," I said. "I think it's time for me to have a chat with your C.O."

"Moe, watch out for Martello. He's a rough bastard. Ice cold, inside and out."

"Don't worry about it. You work on finding out about the company Malik kept and try and get any files you can on Mayweather. I'll handle the rest of it."

"Is that it?" she asked, sharp edges in her voice. "Am I being dismissed?"

"What is it, Carmella?"

She was silent.

"Oh," I said, "the kiss."

"The kiss, yes."

"What do you want me to say?"

"Something."

It's all I can do not to obsess over it. It's difficult to control myself when you're near me. I want to do it again, right here, right now. I . . . I disappointed her with silence of my own, and watched her disappear into the crowd.

CHAPTER FIFTEEN

BAY RIDGE WAS a tale of two restaurants.

Within spitting distance of the Verrazano Bridge, Cara Mia was an old-style Italian joint on Fourth Avenue. It was cheap and charming and perfect for first dates. The waiters had been there so long they bled red sauce and there was more garlic in the air than oxygen. The tablecloths were red and white and frayed with age, and Chianti bottle candlesticks caked thick with wax stood at the center of each table. The neighborhood lore was that they used a chunk of old lasagna as a doorstop.

Across the street from Cara Mia was Villa Conte. Villa Conte was everything Cara Mia was not, and less. Renowned for its Northern Italian cuisine, it was almost as well known for its snooty wait staff and Manhattan prices. The decor featured polished marble, marble, and more marble. And there was enough white linen in the place to supply the Ku Klux Klan for the coming decade. Villa Conte had style, a touch of class, and all the charm of a chest cold. I hated the place, but not for its pretentions.

On February 18th, 1978, at the best table in Villa Conte, Rico Tripoli broke my heart. It's one thing when a woman breaks your heart. You understand that when you take the dive with a woman, heartbreak is always a risk. But there's no expectation of betrayal between best friends, brothers, really. That's why it hurt so much, why it still hurt so much. The story was that Rico had invited me to lunch to celebrate getting his gold shield. Was I jealous? Yeah, a little bit. A lot. In those days, with the city on the verge of bankruptcy, a gold shield was nearly impossible to come by.

I knew my chance had come and gone. Marina Conseco's rescue had been my ticket to make detective, but, for whatever reason, the department had failed to punch my ticket. In February of '78, my head was spinning. I'd met Katy Maloney, found and lost her missing brother, and had already made my pact with the devil himself, my future father-in-law. Aaron and I had yet to find the money for our first store, and my knee still ached so badly that my nirvana was shaped like a pain pill. So yeah, I guess the last thing I wanted to celebrate was my best buddy getting his gold shield. What an ass I was.

At that lunch, Rico confessed that he'd sold something even more valuable than his soul to get his gold shield. He'd sold me out. He had played me, using our friendship to manipulate me, to insinuate me into the tragedy of Patrick's disappearance, to use me as a tool to ruin Francis Maloney's political career. The worst of it was that he thought I would come as cheaply as he had. Rico and his boss offered me the two things I once would have given nearly anything for: my police career and a shield of my own. It was three years before I spoke to Rico again and another eight until I knocked on his door at the Mistral Arms. And fuck me if it didn't still hurt just to look across the street at the entrance to Villa Conte.

"Moe," Margaret whispered, "are you alright? You seemed lost there for a second."

"I'm fine. Just remembering things. That's all."

"I've been doing a lot of that myself lately."

"Come on, let's go in."

We were greeted by Señora. She was a frail woman with white hair, a faded white dress, puckered pale skin, and impish smile. Señora was the matriarch of the family that owned Cara Mia. She had been called by her honorific for so many years, I wondered if even she remembered her given name. She sat us at a quiet two-top in the darkest corner of the restaurant.

Margaret seemed very far away. It was a night to feel far away. A teacher of mine once said that history was everywhere you looked. She was right, but there just some places where you almost didn't have to look. You could smell it, taste it. It came up to you wagging its tail and tugged at your pant leg, demanding your attention. Cara Mia was that kind of place.

"First date?" I asked.

"How'd you know?"

"It's in your face, in your eyes."

And they were startling eyes, blue flecked with gray. She had put a few pounds on her once perfect body and there was some gray mixed in with her satin, blond hair, but it was easy to see why Frank Spinelli considered himself blessed. Twenty years ago, Margaret McDonald was the gold standard for the rest of us on the job. We all measured our girlfriends and wives by her and, until I met Katy, my companions always came up woefully short. The thing about her wasn't her looks. She was calm and understanding. Married to Larry, she would have to be.

"Larry didn't have much money back then, so he took me here. It was perfect. He was a real gentleman, and so nervous."

"Larry, nervous! I'm having trouble picturing that."

"I know, but with me back then . . . That's how I knew we were meant to be. He made me nervous too. Even now . . . Let's order."

"Come on, Marge. No secrets between us, not tonight."

"Thinking about him, I get . . . I can't say it."

"Okay," I said, "I'm sorry."

"Please don't apologize, Moe. Do you know that night when I was waiting for him at the Blind Steer, I was going to throw myself at him? *I* would have begged. I would have given up everything to have him back. Attracting men has never been a problem for me, but no man ever made me feel the way he did."

"But he walked away from you."

"He did. Larry could be a very selfish man."

"You would have taken him back?"

"In a second."

"Why?"

"I can't explain it so that it would make sense to you."

The waiter came by with a basket of semolina bread and two complimentary glasses of Chianti. We ordered and said very little during the meal. Margaret pushed her veal cutlet parm away from her. She hadn't eaten it so much as push it around the plate. I hadn't eaten much of my eggplant.

"That what you ordered on the first date?"

"Yes," she said. "I didn't eat much of it that night either. Larry ordered lasagna and a bottle of Mateus Rose. Christ, remember when we thought that was real wine?"

"Don't remind me. We have a few bottles in each store. Every now and then somebody'll come to the register with one. It's always someone my age and we sort of laugh quietly to each other. We never have to say anything. It's just understood, you know?"

"We didn't know anything back then, did we, Moe?"

"I guess not."

"I really grew to love this place. At least once a week for a year, Larry and me, we'd eat here. You know, he proposed to me right over there." Margaret pointed at an empty table across the room. "He got down on one knee and everything. Señora came over and kissed us both and refused to let Larry pay. I'd give my soul to have those days back." A silent tear rolled down her cheek. I didn't wipe it away.

"You said you came here once a week for a year."

"I did."

"What changed?"

"We stopped coming here and went across the street."

"Villa Conte?"

"The food's great, but it just wasn't the same," she said. "It didn't feel . . . It didn't feel like home."

"Believe me, Marge, I understand better than you think."

"And we'd meet some of Larry's old friends from the neighborhood."

"Old friends?"

"Frankie Motta."

"Frankie 'Sticks and Stones' Motta!"

"No one ever called him that to his face, but yeah, that was him."

Life never failed to bite me in the ass. It was getting so that a few more bites and my pants wouldn't stay up. I'd known Larry McDonald for over twenty years and, though I was never as close to him as I had been to Rico, I thought I'd had Larry covered. Apparently not. I suppose you never do truly know someone else. It was a lesson I kept learning over and over again.

Frankie "Sticks and Stones" Motta earned his nickname on the streets as a kid, because no matter what you hit him with, Frankie kept coming at you. He became a capo in the Anello crime family—the family that ran things in the Sheepshead Bay, Brighton Beach, and Coney Island sections of Brooklyn before the Russians overwhelmed them. Word on the street was that Frankie was a particular favorite of the don, Tio "the Spider" Anello. The old man was long dead and I hadn't heard a word about Frankie "Sticks and Stones" in years.

"How close were they, Larry and Frankie?" I asked, trying to sound casual.

"Why?"

"I'm just wondering. I never knew Larry was friends with Frankie."

She was defensive. "It didn't last. After a few years, we stopped seeing Frankie altogether."

"Did something happen between them?"

"Is it important?" She answered with her own question.

"I don't know, Marge. Probably not."

"It was so long ago."

I was tempted to share a quote that I picked up during the few years I had kicked around the city university system before entering the police academy. Faulkner once said, "The past is never dead. It's not even past." I wanted to shake Margaret and tell her that so long ago is never long enough. Just ask my father-in-law.

"Yeah, Marge, you're right. One more question about this and I'll drop it completely, okay?"

"Sure, Moe, anything."

"Can you remember when you guys stopped hanging around with Frankie?"

She didn't answer right away, but gave it some thought. Although the subject made her terribly uncomfortable, Margaret was a woman of her word.

"I can't remember any particular incident between Larry and Frankie. It was like a few months had passed since we'd seen Frankie and whatever woman he was dating at the time. I tried bringing it up to Larry, but he told me to drop it. That was okay with me, because as pleasant and charming as Frankie could be, he made me uncomfortable. It wasn't a sexual thing, like he was interested in me or anything. He just . . . I don't know."

"Okay, but can you remember the timing?"

"Sure, it was the same year you rescued the little girl from the water tank."

"Marina Conseco."

"It was right around then, a few months after that. Late spring, maybe. Early summer. I think that was the last time we saw Frankie."

There was nothing that struck me about that timing, so, as promised, I dropped it. Maybe Larry's friendship with Frankie Motta was nothing. Hell, I had friends from my old neighborhood who were connected to the Anellos, the Gambinos, and the Lucheses. None of them had achieved the level of success of Frankie Motta, but they were connected just the same. Maybe Larry wised up and understood that his relationship to a known mob figure would hurt his rise up the career ladder. It was definitely Larry's M.O. to shed anyone or anything that might hinder his ambitions.

"Do you want some dessert, Marge?" I asked, moving on.

She shook her head no and took my hand. "Do you think he killed himself, Moe?"

"I don't know. I wanna believe that Larry wasn't the type of man who would run away from things, but he was really worried the last time we spoke. I'd never seen him so shaken. I just don't know enough."

"But I knew him. I slept in his bed. I spent hours with him inside me. It's different for a woman, having someone inside her. A woman can know a man in a way he can never know her. I can't explain it, but I don't think Larry would have killed himself and not left a note. He wouldn't have done that."

"Maybe. Who knows? A person on the verge of suicide maybe isn't thinking clearly about who they're going to hurt."

"I just can't believe Larry would leave that way without explaining why it wasn't his way."

She seemed really haunted by his suicide. I understood haunting.

"C'mon, Moe, let's get out of here. I'm feeling sad and I don't want to feel sad here."

Outside, I hugged Margaret and kissed the top of her head. We didn't really speak. There were looks and shrugs and silent understandings. I had lost a lot with Larry's death, but nothing compared to what she had lost. I watched her pull away from the curb and I followed her taillights until they disappeared near the bridge. In an hour or so, she'd be home with Frank. I wondered if his kindness and understanding made it better or worse for Marge. Then I turned and stared at the entrance to Villa Conte. I wondered if there were any answers behind its doors or just more hurt. It's weird what you think about sometimes.

CHAPTER SIXTEEN

I HAD SPENT the night drifting in and out of sleeps staring at Katy as she slept. I couldn't get Margaret Spinelli's words out of my head. *A woman can know a man in a way he can never know her.* I was torn between disbelief and wanting more than anything for it to be true. Did she feel the unspoken distance between us? Was every day along, boring ride for her as well? Was the problem me? Her? Us? Before I left the house that morning, I pulled Katy aside.

"We need to talk," I said, brushing her cheek with the back of my hand.

"About what?"

"Nebraska."

I expected puzzlement in her eyes, her too-thin lips to turn down in confusion, her brow to furrow, at least a little bit. But she seemed to understand.

"Long, flat, uneventful," is what she said.

"Exactly."

I pulled her close to me and for the first time in what felt like years, my wife pressed herself against me, threaded herself through my arms in that way she had of breaking down the walls between us.

"When I'm done with whatever this is about Larry, we're dropping Sarah at Aaron and Cindy's and we're going to dinner."

"Okay, Moe." She kissed me on the cheek. "Then you better hurry and finish this up."

D.A. Fishbein was happy to get me the name and home address of Captain Raymond Martello, the 60th Precinct's commander. I imagined the D.A.'s mouth watering on the other end of the phone. Uncontained ambition, I thought, must be an incredible burden for a political monster like Fishbein. The better I got to know him, the more I missed Larry. He was so much less obvious about it. When he sucked the blood out of you, you barely noticed. Fishbein would just rip your throat open.

Fishbein also used the opportunity to inform me that he'd come up empty on another front. As far as any of his contacts knew, there was no ongoing or recent investigation into wrong-doings at my old precinct. No one, apparently, not I.A., the city, state, nor federal governments seemed the least bit interested in the 60th Precinct.

That didn't confuse me any more than usual. For me, confusion was a preexisting and chronic condition.

Martello lived in Great River. Unlike Massapequa, Great River was not a frequent stop for folks fleeing New York City. Tucked quietly away in Suffolk County between an arboretum, a wooded state park, a golf course, and the Atlantic, it was insulated from the neon signs and strip malls that dominated so much of the local landscape. It was a lovely old hamlet with clapboard and wood shingle churches and well-appointed houses on healthy-sized plots.

Across the street from Timber Point Golf Course, Martello's house began life as a modest L-shaped ranch. It had since grown a second floor, an attic with shed dormers, an extension, a separate three-car garage, and a fancy brick driveway. Although the work had been quite skillfully done, the original ranch house still shone through.

Ringing the bell and knocking on the door got me nowhere, and I was about to write a note to stick in the mailbox when I heard a lawnmower start up around back. I walked the curvy, bluestone path that led to the rear of the house. I figured the worst that could happen was that I would meet the Martello's landscaper. Before I made it to the back gates the mower crapped out.

Short, broad, fierce, and looking at his riding mower as if it had just disobeyed a direct order, Martello had C.O. written all over him. Before announcing myself, I took a moment to admire the backyard. A two-level, red cedar deck led down to a kidney-shaped swimming pool, a basketball hoop, and a brick barbeque pit. Even with all that stuff, there was half a football field's worth of grass to mow.

"Did you prime it?" I asked by means of introduction.

He stared at me like something shit wipes off the bottom of its shoes. "Who the fuck are you?"

"Moe Prager. I used to be on the job. I was a friend of—"

"—Chief McDonald's. He smiled with the warmth of a hacksaw. "You're the guy that figured out what happened to John Heaton's kid, Moira, right?"

"With Larry's help, yeah." I approached Martello cautiously.

"You know a lot about mowers, Prager?"

"Nah. I still live in Brooklyn. My lawn's the size of a pillow case, but I figured I'd say the only semi-intelligent thing I could think of."

"Well, I primed the fucker, but you're not far off. I think I'm outta gas. So, if the John Deere people didn't send you, I hope you don't mind me asking what you're doing here."

"I don't mind. I wanted to talk to you about Larry Mac."

"What about the chief?"

On the ride over, I'd worked through scenario after scenario. Not in a single one did Martello react well. Cold bastard or not, I couldn't see any precinct command reacting well to the news that a bug had been placed in his precinct house by the department's chief of detectives. And that was just the half of it. I couldn't wait to see Martello's reaction to my questioning him about Malik Jabbar's arrest.

"What about Chief McDonald?" Martello repeated, his jaw tightening.

Reaching into my pocket, I came out with the cassette that Larry had given me a week and a lifetime ago. I made a concerted effort not to wince, steeling myself against the inevitable barrage of questions, denials, and accusations. *What's that? Where'd you get it? A wire? Not in my house! No way! I run a clean house. It's a plant. It's bullshit! Who sent you, I.A.? You're a cocksucking rat, you cheese-eating motherfucker! You're a . . .*

But instead of thunder and lightning, I got quiet resignation and a cold drink.

"I figured the tape would surface sooner or later. C'mon, I guess we better sit on the deck and talk."

Martello offered me something stronger, but I opted for iced tea. He had a beer. I sat and sipped, waiting for him to speak. We both knew the questions. Only he knew the answers.

"My wife and the kids are away upstate, so we're alone here," he said. "How's the tea?"

"Fine."

"You're not gonna make this easy, Prager, huh?"

"That's sorta up to you, no? I don't really know anything except that there's an illegal wire in one of your interview rooms and that you obviously know it's there. That whatever Malik Jabbar said on this tape scared the shit out of Larry, got Malik and his girlfriend murdered, and maybe even Larry too."

"Chief McDonald, no way. That was a textbook suicide, pal."

"Exactly."

"What's that supposed to mean?"

"How well you know Larry Mac, Captain?"

"Well enough. We weren't friends or anything."

"He strike you as the suicidal type?"

"What's the suicidal type? Half the fucking people who commit homicide aren't the murdering type. You push anybody hard enough and they can kill you or themselves. It's just a matter of how much of a push and in what direction. Type is besides the point."

"All right. Let's say Larry killed himself. It doesn't change the rest of it," I said. I was doing an awful lot of talking for someone who intended to listen. "So what about the wire?"

"McDonald came to me and told me he had heard a few things, that stun had filtered back to him about some of my detectives."

"What kinda things?"

"Drug stuff. You know, the same old bullshit about shaking down the local dealers, protecting the bigger ones for a fee, stealing cash and drugs. Blah, blah, blah. Nothing new under the sun, right?"

Just ask Rico Tripoli. "Which detectives?"

"Now you're crossing the line, pal. I'll talk to you about McDonald, but that's where it ends."

"Okay, skip it. So Larry Mac comes to you and he says he's heard some things and . . ."

"And he says he don't want a scandal involving detectives, not on his watch, not while he's their chief."

I laughed with no joy. "He wouldn't. It might hurt his ascendency. I used to joke with Larry that he thought 'Stairway to Heaven' was his theme song."

"You musta known him pretty well, huh?"

"I used to think so. We came up together." I sipped my tea. "So, Captain, he comes to you and says he's heard some things. It's a leap from that to planting a wire in an interview room."

Martello squirmed in his chair so much that it made me uncomfortable watching him. The beer seemed to turn to vinegar in his mouth and he spit it out onto the grass.

"The chief said he wanted to handle things quietly, that if he could get some proof on these detectives that they were using trumped up arrests or threats to shake people down . . . You know, he could pull them aside and warn them to put in their papers before it got ugly for them, their families, and the department. This way the whole thing goes away and nobody gets hurt. It worked for me."

"That's an interesting view of justice," I said.

"Look, Prager, no C.O. wants to get caught in the middle of a corruption scandal. My head would've rolled along with those guilty motherfuckers."

"But even so, what's this got to do with Malik Jabbar and a seventeen-year-old murder case?"

"I don't know. McDonald said I was to call him anytime a drug suspect came in wanting to make a deal. After my detectives—"

"Murphy and Melendez?"

"Yeah. After Murphy and Melendez came to me, I phoned Chief McDonald. He sounded weird."

"Weird how?"

"Just weird. I don't know. Different. Strange. Unnerved, maybe. Anyway, he told me that he'd handle everything. He came down, talked to this Jabbar guy and had me release him. He took that cassette from my office and told me to just keep my mouth shut and that he'd protect me."

"And you believed him?"

"What choice did I have?" Martello asked, crushing his beer can. "I was fucked no matter what I did. I had knowingly let a wire be planted in my house without a court order and by someone who had no authority to do it. I have the fucking receiver in my office, for chrissakes! Even if I could convince somebody it wasn't my idea in the first place, I'd failed to alert anyone about what the chief was doing. And besides, McDonald had juice. Everybody with a brass button owed him favors. If anybody could protect my ass, it was him."

"I guess I see your point. What did you do with the paperwork on Jabbar?"

"C'mon, Prager, you were on the job. Shit gets misplaced all the time. It's a fucking miracle more shit doesn't disappear."

"But with the new computers . . ."

"Never got entered into the system."

"And you didn't called the Brooklyn D.A.?"

"Nope. So . . ." He strummed his fingers on the arm of his deck chair. "What are you gonna do about the tape?"

"This?" I twirled the cassette on the table. "I got no beef with you and I'm not looking to jam anybody up. All I want are some answers about why a small-time shithead like Malik Jabbar scared Larry so much. Nothing really scared Larry. Like you were sayings he had juice and he had balls. What could this Jabbar guy have known that got him and his girl killed?"

"Sorry, Prager, can't help you there."

"Okay, captain, thanks for your time. I won't say anything to anyone about your part in this mess."

"Thanks. One thing I gotta say."

"What's that?"

"I wasn't tight with Chief McDonald, and maybe I'm talking outta my ass, but I think you're being a lot more loyal to him than he woulda been to you."

"You're probably rights but in the end, I don't suppose it's really about who Larry Mac was. It's about who I am."

I stood and offered my hand to Martello. He took it, looking mostly relieved. Mostly.

"About the tape . . ." he said, clearing his throat.

"Keep it. The answers I'm looking for aren't on there."

On the ride back into the city, it occurred to me that I probably should've kept the tape as a bargaining chip for Fishbein, but I wasn't out to hurt people. There was already too much hurt to go around. In the end, I'd find Fishbein some raw meat to chew on. There was bound to be a lot of that around too.

CHAPTER SEVENTEEN

THE FIRST TIME Yancy Whittle Fenn and I met, we had drinks at the Yale Club across the way from Grand Central Station. It didn't start out well for the two of us. I like drinking, but I don't like drunks. An odd position to take, I realize, for a man owns three wine shops, but there it is. Wit had been an especially nasty drunk, because he was a cruel drunk. As a cop, you kind of get used to belligerent drunks, fist-swinging assholes who start throwing punches at the first whiff of alcohol. Sad, stupid, angry, even hateful drunks were one thing, but I could never abide cruelty. Maybe that's why I hated my father-in-law so.

Near seventy, Wit had begun to show his age. He was thinner these days, almost too thin without the Wild Turkey course of each meal. His perpetually tan skin now hung loosely off his jaws and there was a rounding of his shoulders that wasn't there six years ago. But his gray-blue eyes still burned as brightly as ever behind the lenses of his trademark tortoiseshell glasses. And the man could dress. No matter how much my clothing cost, when I stood between Wit and Larry McDonald, I looked like a vagabond.

Wit and I had been back to the Yale Club several times since we'd met, but I don't think I'd ever fully taken the place in. It was of a completely different time. A time when a certain class of white, Christian gentleman ruled the world, and proximity to Grand Central Station mattered in the scheme of things. It was of an era when black waiters wore white gloves and swallowed their anger like table scraps. Katy loved the place. Not me. I would always be more comfortable in steerage with the fish.

"A good day to you and your guest, Mr. Wit," Willie said. He was an overly polite black man equal to Wit in age, if not older, who had waited on us that first time back in '83 and every time since. Willie didn't do white gloves, at least not anymore.

"And to you, Willie," said Wit. "You're getting a little old for waiting tables, aren't you?"

"That well may be, Mr. Wit, but I'm not too old to stop eating, if you catch my meaning, sir." We both caught it, but these two always went on like this. "Would either of you fine gentleman like a beverage this afternoon?"

"Dewar's rocks," I said.

"Club soda with a wedge of lime, please, Willie."

"And for lunch?"

"A Cobb salad."

"The same," said Wit.

"Very good, gentlemen."

Wit took a minute to look me over before saying another word. He did have a way of making me feel like a specimen under a microscope. For most of the rest of the world, he masked his electron beam beneath oodles of charm and tales of the rich and debauched. I guess I should have felt honored that he didn't try to camouflage his inspecting me.

"Are you gonna wait till I squirm before you say something?"

"You've crossed the line, haven't you?"

"You're the second person to accuse me of that today. At least I knew what he was talking about, but what are you referring to?" I asked, already knowing the answer.

"The dark-haired beauty."

"No, Wit. I stepped up to the line, yeah, but I didn't cross it."

"There's only trouble there, Moses."

"So you've said. Right now, that's the least of my worries. What have you found out?"

"Very little, actually. The silence surrounding the late Chief McDonald continues to astound me."

"You said you've learned very little, but very little isn't nothing."

"Our Larry was not beloved," he said.

"Ambitious men usually aren't."

"I suppose not. When people feel they're being reduced to an exploitability quotients I imagine they find it less than endearing. I have hit upon a number of sources willing to tell me this or that about how Chief McDonald screwed them or used them or walked on them. There's no shortage of people griping about how Larry managed to get the bump to deputy chief and then over to chief of detectives, but no one's talking about the suicide."

"No one thinks it's murder?"

"Why would they? There's nothing to indicate it was anything other than suicide."

"He didn't leave a note," I said rather feebly.

"Come, Moe, many, many people have taken the pipe and not left a note. There was a time not long after my grandson's murder that I came very close to doing myself in. I had my neck in the noose and my feet on the stool. I didn't leave a note."

"But people would have known why. They would have understood it was grief over you grandson even without a note. Larry would have wanted people to know why."

Wit opened his mouth to responds but Willie came by with our drinks. He and Wit engaged in a second round of their patented banter before Willie politely excused himself. Wit and I clinked glasses, my host looking rather too hungrily at my Dewar's. Discussing suicide and the murder of his grandson probably weren't the best things for his continuing sobriety. Thankfully, I hadn't ordered bourbon. The time had come for a change of subject.

"So Wit, in all your travels, you ever do a piece on organized crime?"

"I have had the occasion, but not in many years. Why do you ask, other than to change subject?"

Not much escaped Wit.

"Frankie 'Sticks and Stones' Motta."

"Quite a colorful moniker," he said.

"Never heard of him, I guess. How about Tio 'the Spider' Anello?"

"Tio Anello, the man who had his arms in everything? Absolutely! He was the subject of one of my first pieces for *Esquire* back in the early '70s. After Anello's wife died, he started dating this society brat named Ceci Phelps Calvin. It doesn't get any WASP-ier than that. Of couse she was doing it to rub her parents' faces in the shit. One look at her and you knew why he was doing it. Once the story leaked, that was that. Broke his heart. Had a stroke a few months later and nearly died, the poor bastard."

"Sounds like you liked the guy."

"I'm not certain I had any great affection for the man. The Mafia holds no particular romance for me. However, I did respect Anello. He was very old school. And you realize how us Yale men feel about old-school types. He was never once arrested. Never sold anyone out. Avoided publicity like the plague. Moe, as foolish as it was, he really loved this girl, but he put a stop to their relationship before the ink was dry on the first newspaper story about their affair.

"And unlike Carlo Gambino, Anello had a serious no drugs policy in his family. It's the one thing he didn't have a piece of. Gambino gave lip service to it and looked the other way while he shoved the drug money under his mattress. I know for a fact, Anello had people in his own family seen to for selling drugs."

"Seen to?" I teased. "Interesting turn of phrase."

"Must I explain the facts of life to you, Moses?"

"No. But his no drugs policy cost him in the end. Probably why he didn't have the money or the troops to withstand the Russians moving in on him. The Red Mafia doesn't have a no drugs policy."

"That's a shame."

"Stop it, Wit. You sound like the Spider's campaign manager."

"I'll send you a copy of the piece."

"I'd like that."

Willie brought our salads and we were too busy stuffing our mouths with bits of bacon, chicken, and avocado to do much talking. But not a second had elapsed between the time his knife and fork hit Wit's plate and he was back at it.

"You've piqued my curiosity, Moe. Why bring up Anello and this other fellow, Motta?"

"No reason, their names just came up in conversation. Larry's ex and I had dinner the other night. I was hoping she might remember something, but it was sort of a waste."

"Who was this Frankie 'Sticks and Stones' character?"

"Forget it, Wit."

"Satisfy an old man's curiosity, will you? I am paying for lunch, after all."

"Capo in the Anello family. Real tough guy, hence the name. He did a stretch in federal prison and I haven't heard about him in years. Apparently, him and Larry were tight when they were kids, but Larry never mentioned him to me."

Wit rubbed his little, gray beard and stared off into space. "And the dark-haired beauty, what of her?"

"Like I said, the line didn't get crossed. Let's drop it, okay?"

"Very well, my friend."

"Thanks for the help."

"Better to thank me for lunch. I'm afraid I wasn't much help," he said.

"Yes and no. Sometimes it's what you don't find that's revealing. From the way Larry was acting and the things he said, I thought there might have been something going on recently that was the problem. But no, it's definitely about the past."

"What is?"

"Everything."

I NEEDED TO clear my head. The weight of the case, of my lack of sleep, and of my flirtation with Melendez was getting to me. I felt like a fighter pilot pulling too many Gs, losing consciousness, the blood unable to feed my brain.

I started driving over to the Mistral Arms, then turned away. Rico would have no answers and being with him would only add to the weight. Seeing him now, his life in the world of crack whores, cigarette butts, and one-eyed cats, made things worse than when he was completely out of my life. The Rico Tripoli I had known was gone. The harder part to accept, I think, was that the Moe Prager he had known was gone too. You can always rebuild burned bridges, but not the people to cross over them.

I made my way toward Columbus Avenue, to City On The Vine, our first shop. I parked at a meter across the street, but couldn't manage to get out of the car. I stared at the store. I'd had mixed feelings about the wine business way before I got into it. Like I said, the business was Aaron's dream, a dream of redemption for our father's failures, and of security and of a hundred other ingredients that didn't belong to me. As I gazed through the rush of traffic at the store, I realized it wasn't mixed feelings that paralyzed me. It might not have been hate, but it sure felt like it.

Once I made the decision to move on, the paralysis was gone. I drove into Brooklyn across the Brooklyn Bridge, but instead of exiting onto the streets and going to talk with Klaus, I continued on the B.Q.E. to the Cowanus and finally onto the Belt Parkway. Even the thought of hanging with Klaus wasn't enough to get me inside one of our stores, not today. Halfway across the bridge, it began drizzling rain. *Perfect!* But the rain had stopped before I made it to Bay Parkway and I found I was pulling off the Belt at Stillwell Avenue.

Coney Island is a dirty, dark-hearted place, a place that once was and no longer is. Rain washes nothing but the good away in Coney Island. And when the weather drives the visitors back to their cars and subways, they take their happy memories with them. In their wake, only the truth of the place remains: the moldering garbage, the rusted and crumbling rides, empty arcades and sideshow spielers pitching their rigged games to the crush of absent hordes. I looked up and noticed that the top of the parachute jump was lost in the low clouds that covered the beach. I knew just how that felt, to be lost that way.

CHAPTER EIGHTEEN

I COULD SEE the future.

A few weeks from now I'd think about the circumstances surrounding Larry McDonald's suicide or homicide or whatever-icide, and I'd put them away as if I were sliding a few singles change back into my wallet. How many times in my life had I been so completely preoccupied with something or someone that there wasn't enough room in my head to think, in my heart to feel, in my lungs to breathe? Christ, if we could turn our preoccupations into occupations, we'd all be fat and happy.

And then there was Carmella Melendez. Was my obsession with her any different than with Andrea Cotter, my high school crush, or the ten other women whose paths I'd crossed in the course of my life and thought I could never be without? Now, I barely remembered some of their names or faces or why it was they so consumed me. No doubt, there's something magical in obsession, a spark, the ultimate reminder of what it feels like to be alive. Yet, afterthought is the sad fate of all obsession. Some obsessions rush out like the tide; others recede slowly like middle-aged hairlines, but they do recede.

Yes, I could see my future. It included vague, half-remembered questions about Larry's death and wistful smiles about a foolish kiss. Time would bleach out the color and sand off the sharp edges of these things like everything else that seems pressing and urgent at any given moment. Unfortunately, there were people in the world whose vision of the future didn't jibe with mine. Wish I had known that before I got Carmella's call. Guess my powers of prognostication had their limits.

THE LOW, MISTY clouds of the late afternoon had turned darker than the night itself and the romantic pitter-patter of earlier showers was now long forgotten. Rain fell in solid sheets, landing on the roof of my car like swipes from a dull axe. I took it slow over Red Hook's slick and vacant cobblestone streets. Between the blinding rain and the black streams of overflow sewer water, I couldn't be sure of where the street might dip or where the next pothole was looming.

In spite of the awful weather, or maybe because of it, Crispo's was booming. Above the pounding rain, I could hear the buzz of the crowd and the thumping jukebox bass halfway down the block. The noise left me cold. Driving past, I couldn't shake the sense that all the revelry had the vibe of a party at the end of the world. What the fuck? I was a Cold War baby and my mother's son. Either way, I was brought up believing we were always on the verge of extinction. At least, thank God, the Cold War was over. My mom's legacy of pessimism would be considerably harder to outrun.

Although I'd found a spot near the corner, no more than forty paces from Rip's front door, I managed to get soaked to my skin. Inside, the place was even more crowded than I expected, but it didn't take me fifteen seconds to spot Melendez at the corner of the bar, not far from where we'd met the last time. The broad smile that had graced her lovely face that last time was gone. Even after making eye contact, her demeanor remained much the same as it had been the first time I saw her in the vestibule of the 60th Precinct house. She wore her scowling, *Don't-fuck-with-me!* face. I didn't have to look more than five feet to her left to see why. Detective John Murphy, her partner, was there, staring at me like a plate of cold leftovers.

And then, in the tangle of damp bodies to Murphy's right, I caught a glimpse of something else, something familiar. It wasn't so much a face as a part of a profile in silhouette. I couldn't quite make it out, but it registered. For a reason still unknown to me, I found myself looking back—not at Melendez, but at Murphy. He had followed my gaze and the silhouette had registered with him as well. He turned his eyes my way and in them there seemed to be a mix of confusion and worry. *Something was wrong.* I peeked over to Carmella. She had been watching the exchange of glances. Now she, too, seemed worried and took a step toward me.

Murphy's eyes got big with panic and he shouted something at Melendez. His mouth worked in super slow motion, his gaunt face contorted by the movement of his lips, it was impossible to make out his scream above the music. Some wiseass had played *Dominick the Donkey (The Italian Christmas Donkey)* and gotten the bartender to turn it up. The crowd started clapping and singing along with Lou Monte:

> *A pair of shoes for Louie*
> *And a dress for Josephine*

The labels on the inside says
They're made in Brook-a-lyn

With the mention of Brooklyn, everyone cheered. Murphy began pushing his way to his partner.

That's when the shooting started. I caught the first flash out of the corner of my eye, felt the burn on my right cheek, heard the explosion. When the shots come from over your right shoulder, handgun fire is fucking loud. It doesn't sound like firecrackers or a car backfiring in the street. Murphy got hit flush in the neck, spraying blood and panic everywhere as he collapsed. Carmella was going for her piece when the second shot whizzed by me. The frightened girl next to Melendez ran right into the path of the bullet. She fell into the crowd. A third shot. This one hit Melendez, spinning her sideways against the bar, and she crumpled.

I tried to run to her, but the crush of bodies was too great. I reached under my jacket for my .38. As I did so, I saw an automatic, maybe a 9mm, sticking out of the mass of bodies from the spot where the silhouette had been. I didn't wait around for the muzzle flash. I dropped. Now the shots came in a hurry one blast almost catching up to the next catching up to the next, and one body, then another, fell on top of me. The lights went out, glass showering down. I crawled through a moving web of legs to where I thought Carmella would be. I called her name and felt a hand, sticky and wet, grab my forearm.

"Moe, it fucking hurts. Oh, Christ, Moe!"

I felt for her mouth and clamped my hand over it. "Can you crawl?"

Her head shook no against my hand.

"Can you climb on my back?"

This time her head shook yes. I laid flat on my stomach. She rolled on top of me and as I raised up to crawl, only one of her arms curled around me. I headed directly to the kitchen. Almost everyone was running in the other direction, toward the front door. Although there seemed to be a momentary cease fire, the screaming and the chaos went on unabated. I wanted to check Carmella's wound, but I was afraid to stop just yet. I pushed through the kitchen door with my head and shoulder. The galley was deserted, as near as I could tell.

"I'm gonna lay you down and then fireman carry you. It'll hurt like a bastard, but try not to scream, okay?"

"I won't."

"Where are you hit?"

"Right shoulder."

"Okay, here we go. One, two . . ."

I rolled her gently off my back onto the tile floor. Then I gathered her up and placed her over my shoulder. As I placed my hands under her armpits, her body writhed in pain. I'd been shot at but never shot, so I could only guess at her agony.

Shit, just thinking about the sound of my snapping knee ligaments made me nauseous. Making my way through the lightless kitchen, it occurred to me that the .38 had been in my hand this whole time. My knuckles were scraped and raw from crawling and from having been trampled on.

I kicked open the back door and waited. Nothing. I ran down the alleyway. Rip's was close to the corner, so it was a short run back to my car. I laid Carmella on the front seat next to me and pulled away before the cops arrived. This had set-up written all over it and I wasn't in a cop trusting mood at the moment. As I pulled away, I pressed a wad of glove box napkins against her wound to stanch the flow of blood.

"How's Murphy? How's Murphy? How's . . ." she kept repeating, her breathing growing shallower and faster. Her skin was almost colorless and clammy to the touch.

He's fucking dead! "I don't know. I sorta lost sight of him. Just keep quiet and calm."

I pulled over by a public phones removed the soaked napkins, and looked at the wound. It seemed small, but I knew that meant nothing. It's what the bullet does after it enters that matters. I pushed her forward and saw the back of her blouse was also completely covered in blood. Wiping the back of her shoulder, I saw a rip in the fabric. The bullet had passed through, but in the dim light and with all the blood, it was impossible to tell how big the exit wound was. I was afraid to take her to a hospital, and afraid not to.

"Listen, Carmella, do you trust me?"

"I do."

"I'm gonna get you some help, but I can't take you to a hospital."

"I understand." She took rapid little gulps of air.

"Okay, good, I'm gonna make a call and then I'll be right back. I'm not gonna let anything happen to you."

"I know you won't. You always save me."

Good thing she believed it. I sure as hell didn't. For all I knew, I had just condemned her to death.

MY BROTHER-IN-law Ronnie had been a trauma room surgeon at Kings County Hospital before he and my little sister moved to New Mexico a few years back. If there's one thing you learn to deal with at Kings County it's gunshot wounds. These days, he teaches at the university medical school and works at the trauma center. Suddenly I was feeling very grateful Miriam and Ronnie had decided to use the timing of our grand opening party to vacation in the city and show their kids where mommy and daddy had grown up.

"She's sleeping now. The shot was a thru and thru. The wound is pretty clean, but I have no way of knowing exactly how much damage was done. I know it looks like she lost a lot of blood, but the slug didn't hit a major artery. In any case, you should get her to a hospital as soon as you can," Ronnie said, slipping the latex gloves off his hands.

"I don't know how soon that will be."

"Why not?"

"Because the cops will be all over it."

"So . . ."

"Like I told you on the phone, someone killed her partner tonight and tried to kill her, and I can't trust the cops right now."

"But—"

"Look, Ronnie, I have my fucking reasons and I don't have time to explain."

"Well, you can't leave her in the fucking basement of a wine store, Moe!"

"Don't you think I know that? But her life's in danger. What if I bring her to a hospital on Long Island or Westches—"

"Forget it! A blind doctor would spot this as a gunshot wound and it would get reported immediately. At best you'd be buying her a couple of hours. Besides, the long ride in a car could do her more damage."

We stood there in the basement of Bordeaux in Brooklyn, trying not to stare at each other. I couldn't afford to tell him any more than I already had. He was in deep enough and I didn't want to dig him a hole he might never get out of. He was about to do that all by himself.

"You look like shit yourself," he said.

"Thanks, brother-in-law. I love you too."

He slipped on another pair of gloves. "After I clean you up, help me get her into my dad's car."

"Ronnie, you—"

"Shut up, Moe. Just know this. The minute I feel she needs to go to the hospital, I'm going to drop her at Kings County. Deal?"

"You can't bring her back to your parents' house."

"She's my patient now. She's my responsibility. Where I bring her is my business. Do we have a deal?"

"Do I have a choice?"

"Not unless you want her to die."

"Deal."

I'D TAKEN THE deal, and the world, as is its wont, had since moved on. Katy and Sarah were already on their way upstate to stay with my in-laws. It's what they did whenever I managed to fuck up our lives by getting involved in things out of my purview. Katy didn't even bother asking why. The damage had been done. Knowing how and why was beside the point.

I loved that Katy had supported me and got how badly I missed being a cop. She alone knew what it had cost me to twice turn down reinstatement and that gold shield. Years ago, she'd even given me a replica of a NYPD detective's shield. These days it collected dust and lint in my sock drawer with my P.I. license and the remainder of an unfulfilled promise. In spite of it all, I couldn't help but feel she had come around to Aaron's point of view: That my time as a cop had come and gone. That it was time to snap out of it, to grow up and embrace the fact that the wine business was my life now. I'd never much cared for Peter Pan until just recently. Who wants to grow up, really?

Klaus had gone clothes and car shopping for me. The clothes were mine. The car was rented. Klaus, too, had learned not to ask too many questions, especially about the big splotches of blood on my clothes, the bandages on my hands, or the two big plastic bags I'd asked him to drop into another store's dumpster. He'd probably put two and two together by now. Klaus was good at simple math, and the Red Hook Massacre, as it was already being called, was all over the news. Five dead—including a decorated NYPD detective and two underage girls—seven wounded, and a neighborhood in shock was the stuff of tabloid wet dreams.

Luckily, the cops hadn't quite sorted things out as yet. They still didn't know if Murphy was a target or if he had simply gotten caught responding to a gunfight between at least two other shooters. There was no mention of Carmella Melendez on the radio or in the papers. But she wouldn't stay under the radar for very long. The cops would be suspicious by now that she hadn't called in or shown up at the first news of her partner's murder. Maybe they already knew she was missing and or wounded. For most anyone else it would have been impossible to find out just what the cops knew or didn't know, but not for me. No, not me. I had a pipeline into the NYPD and his name was Robert Hiram Fishbein. He got to the phone pretty quick.

"I thought you might be calling, Mr. Prager."

"Why's that?"

"Give me a little credit, will you? Almost everything you've asked me for to this juncture has to do with Coney Island and your old precinct, the one in which you served with the late Chief McDonald. So when I wake up this fine morning and hear a detective—and not just any detective, but one from the Six-O—is gunned down in Red Hook . . . And when I recall that he's the partner of that hot Puerto Rican honey you couldn't keep your eyes off at Fountain Avenue, well, let's just say I did some discreet checking around."

"How much do they know about Red Hook?"

"Are you asking me what they know or what they think?"

"Both."

"They know very little, about as much as they say in the papers. What they think is that maybe Murphy was a target and not collateral damage. They don't know whys but none of the witnesses recall an argument prior to the gunfire breaking out.

"They're also worried about Murphy's partner. She hasn't shown up or checked in and she's not at home. There's also some speculation she might have been at Rip's as well. Some witnesses remember a pretty, black-haired woman getting shot at the end of the bar, but, alas, no body. Curious, huh?"

"Very."

"You wouldn't happen to know anything about that, would you, Prager?"

"I might."

"Care to share?"

"Not yet, Mr. D.A. First, I need to find out everything you can about another detective in the 60th. His name's Bento. Fax the stuff to my Brooklyn store."

"As you wish."

"And Fishbein, in case you're feeling a little impatient and want to cash me in for the short end money, don't do it. I won't be at the store and I'll cut my own balls off before you get a thing out of me. Understand?"

"Understood."

I gave Klaus some instructions about where to forward the faxed documents and what to do with my car.

"Look, there's a lot of blood on the front seat, so throw a blanket over it and park it in the underground garage down the street. Where's the rental?"

"At the meter directly in front of the store."

"I owe you."

"No, boss. You don't owe me a thing. Just promise me you won't get killed. I don't make friends easily."

"I promise."

"Liar. You're just like all straight men."

"I don't know how to take that, Klaus."

"Forget it. Just remember, if you get killed, I'm not coming to the funeral."

"I'll remember."

Looked like I was going back to the land of one-eyed cats and disgraced ex-cops. True, I made friends more easily than Klaus, but at the moment, the ones I had—even the former ones—would have to do.

CHAPTER NINETEEN

I WOULDN'T SAY that Rico Tripoli was thrilled to see me, given the woman from the next room was topless and on her knees in front of him. Marisa was a kid herself, bone skinny, with a plain face and disinterested brown eyes. Given her method of fundraising, that disinterest would serve her well. On the other hand, her addiction to crack would not. It had already begun to erode her body. Whatever humanity she had left wouldn't be far behind. With a few more months of wear and tear on her, she'd be getting five bucks a throw and a lot less picky about her clientele. Two things you never see in this world: baby pigeons and old crack ho's. I wondered if her daughter would ever consider drug abuse as a victimless crime.

I was in no position to judge and no mood to preachy but I was feeling impatient. I waved four twenties at her, putting a basketball-sized dent in her disinterest. She didn't even bother getting up, hobbling over to me on her knees. When she reached out for my zipper I snatched her hand and folded it around the money. Then I lifted her up and told her to go buy her daughter some new clothes and the cat some decent food. I didn't delude myself that she would do anything other than sailor-spend it on crack. She was out of the room before her shirt was buttoned.

Good thing I had too many worries of my own to look for evidence of shame in Rico's eyes. Good, because I wouldn't have found any. He was beyond worrying about redemption, maybe completely beyond redemption itself. The alcohol, drugs, and prison time had beaten all the hope out of him.

"What do you want besides to fuck up my good time?"

"I want your help."

He thought about that for a second. "What's it worth to you?"

I guess I didn't react very well to the question.

"What's the matter, Moe? You just gave that bitch eighty bucks *not* to blow you. What's my help worth? Or maybe you're thinking I owe you something, something like loyalty maybe. I don't owe you shit."

"Okay, Rico, you're right. You don't owe me shit. I heard this speech the last time I was here."

"And you'll hear it again."

"No, I won't," I said, noticing the near empty bottle of no-name scotch next to his bed. "I'm going now. Maybe I'll be back. If I bother coming back, then we'll negotiate the terms of our deal. I'm making a lot of deals these days, old buddy. Don't be stupid and fuck this one up."

YOU HAVE A better chance at winning the lottery than finding a fully functional public phone in that part of Manhattan. If it wasn't the homeless rigging coin slots to trap quarters to be fished out with a crooked piece of wire, it was inept crackheads and a sprinkling of other assorted assholes who ripped apart phones in futile attempts to get at the coin boxes.

Not a month ago, Aaron bought a cellular phone. The man spends his entire life in two places: the Manhattan store and at home. What, he couldn't be without a phone on his car rides to and from work? I mean, who the hell wants to be tethered to a phone twenty-four hours a day? Talk about an invention destined to fail. Then again, the idea of a portable phone seemed pretty appealing to me right at the moment. It was a brief flirtation. I found a working phone three blocks north of the Mistral Arms.

Miriam picked up. "Hello."

"Hey, little sister."

"Don't little sister me! How could you drag us into this, Moses? We're on vacation with our kids. With our kids, for chrissakes!"

"I know. I'm sorry."

"Sorry! You've jeopardized Ronnie's career. I can only imagine what would be going on here if his folks hadn't left for a cruise yesterday."

"If I could've thought of any other way of doing it, I wouldn't have called Ronnie. You know that. But her life was in danger, *is* in danger and—"

"No kidding! You mean people don't get shot for fun?"

"Miriam—"

"Isn't this what they have cops and hospitals for?"

"No, not for situations like this, they don't! Look, I can't unring the bell, but I'll try and do my best to clear this up quick. How is she?"

"Better. Ronnie's got her on some heavy pain medication, so she's in and out of it. But she says she needs to see your that it's very important."

"Okay. I'll be there as soon as I can. You guys need anything?"

"Don't ask questions you don't want answers to, Moses. Didn't you teach me that?"

I took that as a cue to hang up.

DITMAS PARK IS a section of Brooklyn that is of a different time and place. It's a small neighborhood of tree-lined streets, period lampposts, and oversized Victorians on plots of land barely big enough to contain them. Some streets even have grassy center islands. With a little imagination, you could almost see horse drawn carriages rolling along the shady thoroughfares, men tipping their hats to giggling young ladies in floor-hugging cotton dresses who twirled their parasols.

Whereas many of the neighbors had let their houses succumb to the ravages of aluminum siding and stucco, Ronnie's parents had scrupulously maintained the spindle work and clapboards and character of their old manse. But I wasn't there to admire the turrets and wraparound porch, nor was I thrilled at the prospect of squaring off with my sister. I hated when she was right.

Ronnie answered the door. "Come on in. Mir took the kids to the movies, so you don't have to put on your body armor."

"She's right about this, Ron. I shouldn't have gotten you involved in this shit."

"Well, no, but that sort of doesn't matter at this point."

"I guess not, but for what it's worth, I'm sorry. My sister tells me the patient's improved."

"Improved, but not out of the woods. I flushed the wound and repaired what damage I could find. I have her on pain medication and antibiotics to prevent infection, but she still needs to get X-rayed and have a more thorough examination than I can do here."

"I understand."

"You've got one more day, Moe. Then she's going straight to the hospital."

I ignored that. "Where is she?"

"Downstairs in my old room."

"Is she lucid?"

148

"Pretty much."

"Thanks, Ronnie. I'll call you if I need you."

"Moe, take it easy on her, and don't stay too long."

"Got it."

It was so odd seeing Carmella Melendez in what was essentially a high school boy's bedroom. Although she wasn't particularly tall, she seemed too big for the bed. Maybe that's the wrong way to put it. She seemed too grown up for the bed. Her skin was pale, but her breathing was regular and unlabored. Her eyes were shut, so I pulled a chair up and waited.

"Moe," she whispered.

"Hey, nice to have you back." I brushed a strand of hair off her cheek.

"Murphy's dead, isn't he?"

"Yeah."

"And the girl, the one who stepped in front of me?"

"Her too."

Carmella clenched the sheets, tears pouring out of eyes. I let her cry.

"Listen, you've gotta stay calm. Doctor's orders. You can't open up that wound again."

"I'll try."

"My sister said you needed to see me."

"I got a call at home from Murphy yesterdays about an hour after I left work. He said he got tipped off about Chief McDonald. I told him that you needed to hear about it. That's why I called you to come to Rip's."

"What about Larry?"

"The informant said he was dirty."

"Is that so?"

"You don't seem so surprised, Moe."

"I think I've assumed that Larry was dirty all along. I mean, something had to be going on here to push Larry over the edge or get him killed. Did the informant say *how* the chief was dirty?"

"If he did, Murphy didn't tell me."

"Did Murphy tell you who tipped him off?"

"Just that it was another cop."

"We were set up."

"I already figured that out for myself. I am a detective, you know." She tried smiling, but it didn't work.

"Okay. So you have no idea who the cop was that tipped Murphy off, huh?"

"No."

"I do. Detective Bento was also in Rip's last night. He was standing in a crowd about twenty feet to your right. I didn't recognize him at first, but Murphy did and that's when he realized we'd all been set up. When Murphy tried to warn you, all hell broke loose."

"Bento? But I didn't get hit in my side. I got shot from—"

"—the front. I know. The first shooter, the one that clipped Murphy and hit you, was standing over my right shoulder. His piece was so close that my ears are still ringing. Then Bento started firing at me."

"That's weird," she said. "If the guy who shot me was that close to you, why didn't he just—"

"—shoot me in the back and then go after you and Murphy? Good question. I guess I've had my head stuck so far up my ass since last night I hadn't thought about it. Maybe he didn't recognize me from the back. Did you get a look at who shot you?"

"Not really. You know how dark Rip's is. I saw his outline, mostly, his hair. He was a big man, big shoulders, taller than you. Older too. I couldn't pick him out of a lineup."

"It's a start."

"Moe, there's something else."

"What?"

There was a light knock on the door and Ronnie stuck his head in. "Only another minute or two, Moe. She's got to rest."

"Okay, Ron. I promise. And bring some stuff down for her pain." He shut the door.

"Your family's been great to me. Your sister is so pretty."

"Someone had to get the looks in the family."

"There are plenty of looks to go around with the Pragers."

"So what's this other thing?"

"I have a snitch, Vinny Cee, a real lowlife cokehead. He does some dealing to support his habit. He says he's got something for me on Malik Jabbar."

"Like what?"

"I don't know. I—" She began coughing. "I was planning on seeing him with you today, but I—" The coughing was getting worse. "I guess someone had other plans."

"Take it easy."

Beads of sweat poured down her forehead. "No. Listen. He works off the Cropsey Avenue Bridge or sometimes in the parking lot of the Nebraska Diner. Show him some money and use my name."

"Okay, okay, relax."

She was starting to gulp for air like she had the night before and I could see blood seeping through her dressing.

"Ronnie! Ronnie, get down here!" I screamed.

"One more thing," she said, "somebody's got to go check on my grandma. She doesn't speak much English and she gets frightened when she's alone for a long time. Please go check—"

"Ronnie! Get the fuck down here!"

The door burst open. "Shit! I told you not to push her. That's it. She's going to the hospital."

"I'll take her," I said.

"No, you won't. I know the people at Kings County. Just give me a few minutes to stabilize her. Go on, get out of here."

"Wait, call this guy," I scribbled Fishbein's number on the back of my card. "He'll help you out."

"Who is it, some mob guy?"

"You know, Ronnie, Aaron and me didn't use to think you had a sense of humor."

"What's that supposed mean?"

"Forget it. Just make sure she gets to the hospital and call that number."

Being in over my head was par for the course, but this wasn't just about me anymore. Looking back, I'm not sure it ever was. Unfortunately, things had gotten to the point where I could no longer ditch the case. Now I had to wait until it ditched me.

Standing on the Coney Island side of the Cropsey Avenue Bridge, Vinny Cee was about as hard to spot as a cotton ball on a sea of black velvet. He was pale, skeletal, fidgety, and squeezed his too prominent beak between his fingers every few seconds. Christ, if this guy didn't have LOSER tattooed across his ass, he should have. It was easy to see why he made good snitch material. He probably didn't deal

151

enough to hurt anyone but himself, so the cops could leave him on the street. And depending upon his level of desperation, he'd probably sell out anyone, from his birth mother to the Holy Ghost.

I folded too much money up in my palm. Money was the second best way I knew to cut through bullshit. Fear was best, but I'd hold that in reserve. As I approached him, Vinny Cee got even more twitchy, his eyelids beating like hummingbird wings. I guess I still had the cop vibe about me. I liked that, I guess. I slapped the folded bills into his hungry hand. He took a peek. That got his attention.

"Only half grams, buddy. I can't—"

"This isn't about coke and I ain't your buddy."

"Hey man, no reason to be that way." I thought he might burst into tears.

"We have a mutual acquaintance. Detective Melendez sent me your way."

Vinny Cee smiled at that. "She's fine. You a cop? See, I fuckin' knew it. I was jus' thinkin' to myself, dis guy's a cop."

"I'm not a cop anymore, Vinny, and you talk too much."

I'd hurt his feelings again. "No need to be that way. Whadaya you want?"

"Malik Jabbar."

"Whadabout him?"

"You tell me."

"Maybe I don't feel like talkin' no more. Maybe I—"

"Vinny, don't try and shake me down for more than what's already in your palm. 'Cause, you see, I'll throw your skinny fucking ass off this lame excuse for a bridge if you don't just answer me."

He flinched. "Okay, okay, man. Easy, easy."

"We're good. Now tell me what you had for Melendez."

"I been copping from Malik since his name was Melvin and I know the pretty lady was askin' around about Malik's new friends. Am I right?"

"You're the new fucking Kreskin."

"Who?"

"Forget it."

"Whatever. Well one day, a few months back, I went around to Malik's and I seen him with dis guy I went to Xaverian with and they was doin' some business, if you know what I mean."

"This guy have a name?"

"Frankie Motta."

I twisted my hands around Vinny Cee's collar and lifted him over by the railing.

"Listen to me you lying piece of shit. Frankie Motta has to be fifty-five, sixty fucking years old. I don't like having my time and money wasted."

Vinny Cee flailed his arms and kicked his legs frantically as he tried choking out some words. I relaxed my grip enough to let his lies flow a little more easily.

"Frankie Junior."

"Frankie Junior what?"

"His son. I went to school with Frankie Motta's son."

I let him down, but not free. "How many years ago was that?"

"We got out in '76, I think."

"Were you tight, you and Frankie Junior?"

"Nah, Frankie was always braggin' about how tough his old man was. He thought he was tough too, but he was a punk. Nobody would touch him because a his dad's rep."

"I can see that. Second generation's always got it too easy."

"Huh?"

"Never mind, Vinny," I said, smoothing out his rumpled clothing. "Nothing you've got to worry about."

"I understand stuff." Oy, there were those hurt feelings again. "I ain't stupid, ya know."

Who was I to argue? Maybe he hadn't looked in a mirror just recently. Or maybe he had, and all he saw were thin white lines and razor blades.

WHEN I FIRST met Wit, he literally lived out of a suitcase. It's not like the guy went from one Motel 6 to another. From the Pierre to the Plaza to the Waldorf was more likely. Sometimes I think his rootlessness was a hedge against the grief over his grandson's murder. It was as if he hoped having no permanent address would make it harder for the grief to find him. Worked about as well as his drinking.

These days he lived in a tidy, three-bedroom apartment on Fifth Avenue in the Village. For Wit, this was blue collar stuff. Of course, it was really about as blue collar as a private jet. But given the polo pony world out of which he'd fallen, it was a start. The package of documents that Fishbein had faxed to Klaus, and Klaus to Wit, was waiting for me in the lobby. There was also a copy of the *Esquire* piece Wit had done on Tio Anello.

I was going to leave it at that, but then I remembered about Carmella's grandmother and the promise I'd made. Earlier, I had intended to ask Ronnie to ask Miriam to do it. But under the circumstances, I figured I'd asked quite enough of them, too much. Wit, on the other hand, always liked to be asked favors. Made him feel needed.

"Wit," I said when I got upstairs, "how's your Spanish?"

RICO WAS A lot more receptive to my presence when I showed back up at his place. It was late. He was less drunk and, as he was quick to mention, Marisa had thrown him a freebee because of my financial largesse.

"A fuckin' freebee! Man, I almost felt like a cop again," he cooed.

I felt sick.

That summed up the difference between us. He had seen his being a cop as a means to an end, something to use for his own good. Naïvely, I suppose, I'd come to see it as a way to do some good. Strange, I had almost laughed at Carmella Melendez for voicing that same sentiment to me. What's that they say, you criticize in other people what you despise about yourself? I'd outlived my naïveté. I hoped Melendez would as well. I suspect that hole in her shoulder would go a long way to that end.

"What's that?" he asked, pointing at the envelope in my hand.

"The personnel file of a detective who I think tried to kill me."

"This have anything to do with what happened in Red Hook last night?"

"You know about that?"

"Name me five people in New York that don't."

"I get your point. And yeah, it's got everything to do with Red Hook."

"You must be getting close."

"Not that I'm sure exactly what it is I'm close to. All I know is that Larry must've been mixed up with the Anello Family."

"The Anellos. Get the fuck outta here!" Rico was skeptical. "They ain't even an active family anymore, not since the Russians swallowed up their territory."

"You kept up on things when you were—"

"—away. Yeah, they have papers and TV in prison. When you do your bid in isolation, you got all the time in the world to keep up and think."

"Sorry."

"You and me, we're way past sorry, Moe."

"Way past."

"So . . ."

"So I think the Anello Family is trying to make a comeback. At least with the drug trade."

"Drugs? That don't sound like Larry. Not his style, especially him knowing what happened to me."

"I know, but Marge told me he grew up with Frankie Motta."

"So what? We all grew up with connected guys. That don't mean shit."

"They were close there for awhile when Larry first got on the job. Then Marge said they had a falling out, but Larry wouldn't talk about it."

"Maybe Larry owed him."

"We're talking a long time to owe somebody," I said.

"You owe somebody, you owe somebody. Owing these guys a favor don't come with a time limit. Believe me, I know."

"Larry never owed anybody anything. It was everybody that owed Larry. It was his strategy, the way he built the rungs on his ladder."

"Not for nothing, Moe, we didn't know Larry Mac before we all served together. Could've been an old debt."

"But it's Motta's kid fronting the drug move, not his old man."

"Don't mean the old man ain't behind it, even if the kid's leading the charge."

"I guess not. Look, Rico, I'm beat. I'm gonna crash out on your floor, okay?"

"You don't mind the roaches, they won't mind you."

"That's comforting."

"Hey, toss me that file. I don't sleep so good sometimes."

"Here." I handed it to him after removing the *Esquire*. He wasn't the only one who had trouble sleeping.

Although a lot of what Rico said made sense, there was definitely something else at play. There was more here than an old debt and new drugs, there had to be. No one kills cops without a good reason, especially not the mob. Bad for business, killing cops. And what about Malik Jabbar, Kalisha Pardee, and Larry Mac? I was missing something.

I know the world is a messy place and that to expect things to snap together like Legos is crazy, but I couldn't escape the feeling that they should. Einstein spent the last decades of his life looking for a unifying theory, one thing that tied all the forces of the universe together. He failed. Thinking about it that way, my task was considerably less daunting. Trouble was, I didn't have decades to putz around, and failure didn't seem like a viable option.

CHAPTER TWENTY

IT CAME TO me in my sleep. Who knows, maybe a roach whispered it in my ear. More than likely it was Wit's article. What can I say, the man's my good luck charm. Six years ago, it was his exposé on the career of a New York politician that was the key to my discovering Moira Heaton's true fate. But this time it wasn't so much one detail or a particular sentence that made it come together for me. I had simply drifted off reading Wit's piece, "Said the Spider to the WASP," and when I woke I up, I knew it all revolved around '72.

Although there were guesses I was making to help things fit snugly into place, I felt pretty confident. I also felt like an idiot for not seeing what was in front of my face from the day of the grand opening party. Larry had been trying to give himself away, not only at the party but that last time we spoke on the boardwalk. I just hadn't been listening carefully enough.

"Rico." I jostled him, Bento's file spread over him like a paper quilt. He stank of cigarettes and sour scotch.

"What?"

"I'm heading out."

"Whatever."

I left most of the money in my wallet on the shelf in the bathroom. When I closed Rico's door behind me, there were the usual ambient odors of urine and crack smoke in the air. Mostly there was a weary silence, emptiness. Even one-eyed cats have to sleep sometimes.

IT WAS EARLY yet, so I rode back into Brooklyn, back to my house. I showered and made some calls. Waited for some answers. My house felt even emptier than the Mistral Arms and nearly as desperate. I was reminded of what my life was like before Katy before Sarah. That's why I was so distraught when I was injured and kicked to the curb by the NYPD. That's why I was so eager to jump onto Aaron's dream and ride. I felt empty and alone and untethered. Before Katy, all beds were too big. My apartment, too. There didn't feel like there was enough of me to fill up even the small spaces. Katy made me fit into the world.

At a little after ten, I headed out the door and bumped into our regular mailman, Joey.

"Hey, Mr. P."

"Joey, no more vacations for you, man. That guy who replaced you was—"

"—a dick. Yeah, I know."

"There are guys on death row with a happier outlook on life than him."

"Not only is he a miserable fuck, but he's an incompetent one too. Here, Mr. P." Joey handed me a neat stack of banded letters.

"What's this?"

"That shithead delivered some of your mail to the Bermans even though he knew they moved."

"Thanks for looking out for us, Joey."

"No sweat, Mr. P."

I tossed the banded pile of mail on the front seat and drove to Mill Basin.

Mill Basin is sort of Brooklyn's anti-Ditmas Park. The area's unifying theme seemed to be bad taste. Surrounded by water on three sides, it's the kind of place where people who make a little bit of money turn perfectly lovely houses into things that would make Salvador Dali scratch his head. *Yeah, it may be ugly, but it's big and it's mine!* Just lately it had become quite popular with the Russians, who had recently began to wander beyond the confines of Brighton Beach. I took perverse pleasure in the fact that most of Frankie 'Sticks and Stones' Motta's neighbors were people he probably despised.

I came fully prepared to do battle, my .38 in its usual spot and my replica shield in my back pocket. I might as well have come with a cap gun and cowboy hat. The big, but tasteful brick house on National was, as near as I could tell, unguarded. There were no obvious security cameras, no *Beware of Dog* signs, no nothing. The toughest thing I had to cope with was avoiding a medical supply truck backing out of the driveway, its bomb-like metal tanks clinking against one another as it rolled past me down the street.

I parked at the curb, strolled up to the front door, and pressed the bell. It didn't play the theme from *The Godfather*, but did the usual *bong—bong—bong—bong.* The way I figured it was that Motta was the shooter in Rip's that night, that his kid had gotten in way over his head, and Dad was trying to fix the damage. When the door pulled back, I got the sense that maybe I needed to reassess the situation.

A petite Filipino woman in a white nurse's outfit smiled up at me. "Can I help you?"

"I'm here to see Fran—Mr. Motta." I was reaching around to my back pocket, ready to produce my fake shield. I needn't have bothered.

"Oh good," she said. "Visitors really perk up Mr. Frankie's days. Come with me."

I followed her through the house, barely noticing the décor or layout of the place.

Just outside a door, near what I assumed was the back of the house, she stopped and whispered.

"He's having a good day, but don't let it fool you. He becomes tired very quickly. My name is Anita. If you need me, just call out. There's a monitor in the room so I can hear if he should fall or have trouble breathing. Okay?"

"Thank you, Anita."

"I'll be just down the hall." She pushed open the door.

It was a spacious room, probably once a den, with high, angled ceilings. Long-necked fans hung from exposed beams, their lazy, spinning blades creating a gentle breeze. Large rectangular skylights let in the sun and the smell of salt air. There was a large stone fireplace surrounded on either side by a black granite ledge. The mantle was black granite as well, but that's as far as the "den-ness" of the room went. Now a hospital bed sat where a leather sofa or loveseat might once have faced the big French doors that looked out onto the back deck and canal behind the house. Next to the bed was all manner of medical equipment and two large oxygen tanks.

In spite of the sun and salt air and fans, the nose stinging medicinal tang and the stink of decay were heavy in the air. Frankie Motta was sitting in a wheel chair, staring through the glass of the doors that stretched from one end of the room to the other. A forty-foot boat crawled along the basin behind the house, slowly working its way toward Jamaica Bay and the Atlantic beyond. It was hard to tell if he even noticed my presence. Maybe he had or maybe he just didn't give a shit. His nickname might have been "Sticks and Stones," but

"Sticks and Bones" was now far more appropriate. There couldn't have been more than a hundred and thirty pounds of gray flesh hanging on his big, bent frame.

"Used to have one a them myself. Big motherfuckin' boat. Didn't do shit with it except let it impress my friends. Sat at the marina a few blocks from here. What a waste a fuckin' time and money, boats. But now I like watchin' 'em, you know?"

I didn't say a word.

He turned the electric wheelchair at an angle away from the French doors and toward me. "I know you?"

"I'm an old friend of Larry McDonald's."

If I laid a glove on him, he didn't show it. He rolled the chair closer to me and gave me a squint. "I seen you before. You was on the TV a few years back. Solved that girl's murder, the cop's kid."

"Moira Heaton."

"Yeah, her. I watched the press conference. Larry Mac got the big bump after that case."

"You got a good memory there, Mr. Motta."

"I got lung cancer, idiot, not Alzheimer's."

"Sorry."

"Makes at least two of us. You got me at a disadvantage. You know my name, but I only know your puss."

"Moe Prager."

"Oh yeah, the Jew. Larry used to talk about you sometimes."

"That's funny, because Larry never once talked about you, Mr. Motta."

"Frank." It wasn't a suggestion. "He wouldn't, now would he?"

"I guess not, Frank."

That pleased him, me calling him Frank. "Larry was always the smartest guy in the neighborhood when we was kids. He picked things up right away." Motta snapped his fingers weakly. "Took stuff in like a sponge, you know? He always understood shit without being taught it."

"Sounds like Larry," I agreed. "Always knew how to get what he wanted without asking."

Motta laughed at that, but the laugh transformed itself into a coughing fit. I grabbed a white towel and handed it to him. He sounded like he was hacking up what was left of his lungs. When the coughing subsided, he put the towel down and slipped a green plastic oxygen mask over his nose and mouth. He took shallow breaths. Shallow was probably the only option left to him. Finally, some color came back into his face, and the panic in his eyes, which he hadn't bothered hiding, subsided.

He removed the mask. "You ain't from Meals on Wheels and you ain't a respiratory therapist, so what you doin' here, Prager? Not that I don't enjoy the company."

"Wanted to talk about Larry with you, talk some old times."

"Old times is all I got. No time to make new memories."

"Does it scare you, dying I mean?"

"I used to be scared of it, but when you die this way, in little pieces . . . Hey, when it comes, it comes. This!" he said, making a sweeping gesture, "This ain't really living and it ain't really dying, pal. It's waitin'. I always hated waitin'."

"I hate waiting too. Bad news is better than no news."

"Exactly. I jus' hope the lungs crap out on me before the shit spreads into my brain. I can see why you and Larry Mac got along. You think like he thought."

Finally, an opening. "Not really. I wasn't an ambitious cocksucker."

If I thought that was going to make an impression on Frankie Motta, I guess I was going to be disappointed. Coughing out his lungs might have concerned him, but he was still a tough motherfucker.

"Come over by the doors a second," he said, the electric motor whirring as his chair moved ahead of me. "How long you figure it's been since that boat passed? Thirty seconds? A minute?"

"Something like that."

"You see the water? Even though the boat's gone, the water's still telling you it was there. I hear there are some weird little seafaring cultures in Asia where they can read the ripples in the water like the Indians here can read tracks."

"And this relates to Larry how?"

For the first time since I stepped into the room, the real Frankie Motta reared his head.

"Shut your mouth and pay some attention, then you won't have to ask no stupid questions."

"Your house, your rules," I said.

He liked that too. Maybe he'd give me a gold star on my Delaney card for being such an apt pupil.

"See," he continued, "Larry didn't understand that stuff like about the boat. It was a big blind spot for him. He thought you could sometimes float a boat by without leaving a wake. Maybe I thought the same thing there for awhile, but I learned. There was this time once when I had a boss, a foolish old man who had some silly ideas of honor."

"A guy like Tio Anello, for example."

"Yeah, hypothetically speakin', a guy jus' like him." Motta smiled at me. He had a smile not too dissimilar from my father-in-law's, as warm and welcoming as a lobster claw. "Well, old men, they lose focus sometimes and look backwards instead of the way ahead. They forget what's important and what's not. They think because a thing used to work one way for a long time, it should always work that way. You catchin' this, Prager?"

"You mean like this old man maybe having rules against getting involved with the drug trade? Like that?"

He showed me the lobster claw again. "You're pretty fuckin' sharp."

"Sometimes."

"What does a guy like me do with an old man who taught him everything about the world, about survivin', about all the important things? What does a man like me do when he can see the future in a way the old man he works for can't?"

"Depends on what he thinks is more important, the future or the past."

"From where I'm sitting today, it's the past. But that's only because I got no future, so that don't count. Back in them days, I thought the future was important. I thought survivin' was everything."

"And anyone who thinks the future is important has to plan for it."

"So I planned, but I tried to do it without hurtin' the old man. I hid it from him, because if he found out about it—"

"You'd have to survive and that would mean clipping him . . . hypothetically speaking, of course. And he meant too much to you for that."

162

"There was that, but even if he had a sudden change of heart and decided drugs was the best thing since cheese fries at Roll-n-Roaster, he'd a had to . . . you know . . . make an example of me for challengin' his authority."

As Motta spoke, things about the past were falling surely into place like tumblers on an old combination lock.

"Dexter Mayweather! You bankrolled D Rex." I could feel my mouth turn up into a self-satisfied smile.

Frankie Motta bowed his head in respect. "That's good!"

"This way Anello couldn't connect you to the drugs, but you could salt away the profits and a have a network in place for when the old man died."

"Hey, that Dexter, he was one sharp fuckin' nigger, let me tell ya. A little too sharp for his own good, maybe. We coulda been the fuckin' kings of Brooklyn, the two of us," he was screaming. "We coulda run this town and them cocksuckin' Russian scumbags woulda had to come beggin' to us for a piece a the pie. But—" Motta was gasping for air again, his chest racking violently.

"Anita!" I shouted and slid the green mask over Frankie's face.

Motta flailed his left arm at the little table next to the bed. He made a C out of his right forefinger and thumb and squeezed the tips together. "Inhaler! Inhaler!" he gasped.

I found a mustard yellow inhaler on the bedside table and curled his fingers around it, then removed his mask. He took two blasts from the little plastic device and his breathing eased almost instantaneously. Anita bolted through the door, took a glance at the inhaler, and eyed me in that same disapprovingly way Ronnie had. I was beginning to feel like Typhoid Mary's intern.

"Mr. Frankie cannot get excited. It puts too much strain on his lungs."

"I'm sorry."

"You'll have to go now."

"No!" Frankie rasped. "He's stayin'. I'll keep calm, Nita."

"Mr. Frankie, this is not good for you to get excited."

"I promise. Cross my heart and hope to die."

"You are not dying yet!" Anita chided as if she had a vote in the matter. She turned and wagged her little index finger at me. "Don't make me have to come back in here. I come back and you are out, no matter what Mr. Frankie says. Understand?"

"Perfectly."

"Okay." She eyed me skeptically as she closed the door behind her.

"She's a tough cookie, that one," Motta said. "Woman cares more about me than my ex-wife did."

"She gets paid to care."

"So did my ex-wife. We pay 'em all, one way or another."

Argue that.

"Before, you said something about D Rex being too smart for his own good."

"Everybody's a team player up to a point. Dexter thought he saw an opening and he went for it."

"Got him killed, huh?"

He rolled the chair over to me and began patting me down before I could answer. His movements were practiced, familiar, but his touch was weak. "You wearin' a wire?"

A wire! Talk about coming full circle. Then again, it wasn't the wire Larry had planted that started this mess. The wire and Malik Jabbar's taped interrogation simply marked the end of the intermission, an intermission to a drama whose opening act was played out nearly two decades ago.

"You're clean."

"Would it have mattered if I was wearing a wire?"

"I guess not."

"Then why don't you just tell me what happened, Frank?"

He thought on that. "Sure. Why the hell not?"

"I'm listening."

"We had the distribution network in place. We had a ton a cash to expand as soon as Tio died. We were gonna be patient with him, wait him out. He was a man of respect and if we whacked him it woulda caused trouble with the other families. Then he did us a favor and he had that fuckin' stroke."

Another tumbler fell. "You jumped the gun. You thought Anello was gonna die when he had that stroke."

164

"The fuckin' doctor said he was a dead man. That it was a twenty to one shot that he'd ever regain consciousness, never mind anything else."

"But he did."

"Like three weeks later, the stubborn old fuck. Sometimes I wish that society bitch had just fucked him to death. He was months in therapy. Even so, he talked like he had rocks in his mouth and walked like a fuckin' gimp. But he still knew what was what. He heard things. Those was dangerous days to be me."

"I bet. D Rex saw his opening."

"He knew I was in a bad place and he tried to renegotiate percentages."

"Pissed you off, huh?"

"Nah, like I said, he was a sharp nigger. He was only doin' what I woulda done in his shoes. Problem was, once the old man recovered, it wasn't about percentages no more. It was about survival, *my* survival, my crew's survival."

"D Rex had to go."

"I had no choice. I hated doin' it. I kinda liked him and he had a real head for business. With the money we woulda generated, we coulda turned the Anellos into a powerful family, not a fuckin' afterthought. But Dexter was the only link to me. He's the only person I ever dealt with directly. With him dead, Tio coulda heard all the rumors in the world and it wouldn't a mattered."

"But you didn't kill him," I said. "You *had* him killed."

"If word ever got out inside the family that I clipped Dexter Mayweather, people would start to wonder why. I couldn't risk that. Had to keep my distance, you know?"

"So you couldn't use anybody from your crew or even bring in a guy from another family. You had to use outside help, people who were insulated from the family and maybe even from the law. And it had to be done messy, nothing that could look like a pro hit. Something that would seem to be the work of one of D Rex's rivals or an ambitious one of his own looking to move up the quick way."

"You musta been a helluva detective, Prager."

I let that go. "It's easier to see things looking down when you're standing on seventeen years of history I guess the guys working the case back then thought exactly what you wanted them to think. It's

165

what everybody would think. And who would really give a shit about some black drug dealer?"

"Good question. Why do *you* give a shit?"

"I don't give a rat's ass about the vic. I'm interested in his killers."

"Why?"

"Because one of them was a cop and a friend of mine, someone I thought I understood."

"Oh, I get it. This ain't about him. It's about you, huh?"

I thought about that. So far I'd barely touched Frankie Motta, but he'd gotten a few hard, straight rights in through my gloves.

"Yeah, Frank, I guess maybe it is about me. Larry must've owed you something big to do this for you."

He started laughing again; laughter even blacker than his lungs.

"Larry didn't owe me shit. Wasn't you payin' no attention before when I was talkin' about not leavin' a wake?"

"I thought I was."

"Larry McDonald was a friend a mine too, you know? We went back a long fuckin' ways, him and me. He was just as hungry for stuff when we was kids as he was the day he took the pipe."

"Fuck!"

"That's right, Prager. Larry Mac come to me with the idea, not the other ways around. He was smart and, like Dexter, maybe too smart."

"But you said no one else knew about you and Mayweather."

"He didn't exactly know, but this is Larry we're talkin' about here. He was on my pad to keep an eye on Mayweather and he was on Mayweather's pad too, to keep an eye on the cops. How long you think it took Larry to figure out what was really going down?"

"Probably not too long, knowing Larry."

"When Tio come outta the coma, Larry Mac came knockin'."

"And you answered the door and let him in."

"You bet your fuckin' ass I did. Listen, it was like havin' my prayers answered. I could trust Larry and with him being on Mayweather's payroll, he could get in close to Dexter. He wasn't connected to me business-wise, not so's anybody knew about it, and, like you said, he was insulated from the law."

"Perfect."

"Almost."

"Something's perfect or it isn't," I said. "The difference between almost perfect and perfect is like one and infinity."

"Huh?"

"Never mind. So what went wrong?"

He smirked. "The ripples in the water."

"We're back to that again."

"We never left. See, Larry found out that muderin' somebody leaves ripples in the water that don't never go away. He had trouble living with that."

"You're telling me he had a conscience."

"Nah . . . Well, maybe a little one, but that wasn't the thing of it."

"Then what *was* the thing of it, Frank? You don't mind me asking?"

"Dexter was a big boy, wide and country strong."

"I remember."

"Took more than just Larry to do what needed doin'. Yeah, they fucked up poor old Dexter pretty good; broke his fingers, smashed up his knees, beat him bad."

"I heard, but what's . . ." Then it dawned on me. "The guys who helped him. The ripples in the water."

"Pat yourself on the back there, Prager. You got long arms."

"So who helped him?"

Motta stared at me in a way that could've frosted glass. "I ain't never ratted nobody out in my life. I coulda saved myself a ten year stretch in prison, I opened my mouth. What makes you think I'm gonna talk now? And to you?"

"You talked about Larry."

"Larry's dead, God rest his soul." Frankie crossed himself. "Nothin' can hurt him now. Not even sticks and stones can break his bones no more."

"That's almost funny. Well," I said, "at least I know the guys who helped Larry out are still alive, otherwise you'd talk about 'em."

"Maybe, maybe not."

I didn't pursue it further. He wasn't going to discuss it. And though I would have been happy to waste every second of time he had left on earth, I wasn't inclined to waste mine.

"Marge tells me you and Larry had a falling out."

"She still hot, Marge? Man, Larry had some good taste; always the finest threads and finest pussy."

I ignored that. "So what happened?"

"Guess Larry didn't like having his balls in someone else's hands."

"What's that supposed to mean?"

"It means that if he killed for me once, maybe he'd have to do it again."

"Did he?"

"Let's just say Larry didn't have much of a heart for me after . . ." He didn't bother finishing his sentence.

Frankie Motta was spent. The frosty looks and lobster smiles were all gone now. Only strain showed on the scarecrow. He was exhausted, but couldn't quite bring himself to admit it. Not only had my presence been a distraction, it had breathed a few minutes of life back into him. He remembered what it felt like to be powerful, to make decisions about other people's deaths instead of watching boat wakes and waiting for his own.

"So, you happy now?" he asked. "You gonna sleep better tonight? A dead fuckin' nigger and a dirty cop . . . I mean, who really gives a shit besides you?" Motta spun the chair about and wheeled back over by the French doors. "It's been nice talkin' to you, Prager, but you're startin' to gimme *agita*."

He was right. No one gave a shit. If that was as far as it went, I might actually have been inclined to let go and toss it into the water with the rest of the world's sins. But this wasn't just about Larry. There was too much blood and too many bodies to ignore and simply move on.

"You still here?" he asked.

"We're not done."

"I disagree. Now get the fuck out."

"Can't do it. You'll miss the part about your son."

Motta flinched. It was barely perceptible and he kept his eyes on the water the whole time, but I hadn't imagined it. "What about him?"

"You should be proud of him. He's following in your footsteps."

"Stop talkin' outta your ass, Prager. My kid ain't like me." But this wasn't a proud father jumping to his son's defense. If I could have pricked holes in Motta's words, his disdain would have drowned the both of us. "Junior couldn't wipe his ass without an instruction manual."

"Nice."

"Nice got nothin' to do with it."

"I guess not."

I opened my mouth to say something else, but I can't recall what.

"Quiet!" Motta whispered, rolling his chair up next to me.

There was a conversation out in the hallway between Anita and a man. I couldn't make out their words. I thought I recognized the man's voice and though Motta didn't quite tilt his head like a curious dog, it seemed to me that he recognized it too. I didn't like that. *Why would Frankie Motta know Captain Martello's voice?* What I heard next, I liked even less. Something thumped hard against the wall— *Anita?*—and the conversation came to an abrupt halt.

Motta started panting again and there was real fear in his eyes. It was hard to tell whether Frank's concern was for himself or his nurse. I reached around for my piece, but when I brought it forward my hand slammed against the wheelchair and the pistol fell a few feet behind Motta's back. Never mind retrieving it, I didn't even have time to bend my knees before Martello strolled fully into the room. He was pointing a cocked .38 of his own vaguely in my direction.

"Ripples in the water," Motta whispered to me.

"Shut up, Frankie! And don't look so disappointed."

"Whadya do to Anita, you cocksucker?" Motta asked, trying to slow his breathing and failing.

"I put her to sleep for a little while. I wouldn't worry about it, she won't feel a thing. And that asshole kid of yours, you don't have to worry about him either. What an idiot, Frankie. You sure he was yours?"

Frankie Motta clamped his hands on the arms of the wheelchair, trying to raise himself up, but it was no good. He fell back, defeated, his coughing worse.

"That's right, Frankie, sit the fuck back down. All this violence, because your kid had to walk in your footsteps. He had to bring up the past. Now I gotta put an end to it."

"*You* helped kill Mayweather!" I said to Martello.

169

"Prager, you shmuck! Too bad you figured that out seventeen years and two minutes too late. Kenny, get in here!" Martello barked, tilting his head back slightly over his shoulder.

Caveman Kenny Burton walked into the room, a black 9mm dangling in his hand. If I had any lingering questions about who had helped Larry Mac murder Dexter Mayweather, Burton's appearance answered them. No doubt Kenny had enjoyed breaking D Rex's bones.

"Hey Moe, I ever tell you you were a cunt?"

"At every opportunity."

The corners of his lips turned up.

"Stop fucking around!" Ever the commanding officer, Martello shouted some more orders, then turned his attention back to me. "That was some fancy gun handling I saw when I came in, Prager. Pick it up."

If I had any balls, I would have told him to go fuck himself. What I did instead was pick up the gun.

"You told me it was a bad day for you when D Rex was killed," I said to Burton as I knelt to retrieve my gun.

"I guess I lied. Go figure."

"Yeah, go figure."

Violence put Kenny in talkative mood. "Good thing for me your pal Rico got cold feet that night or I woulda missed out on a big payday. You may be a cunt, but he's a real fucking coward. I'm gonna enjoy killing him."

"Not if I get to him first."

"I like my chances better," he said, making some guttural noises that passed for laughter.

"Shut the fuck up, the both of you," Martello groused. "Prager, go stand over by the fireplace."

I did.

"Shoot Frankie!"

At first I didn't think I'd heard Martello right. Several scenarios ran through my head, none of them any good. I might be able to get one shot off at either Martello or Kenny, but not both, and I'd be dead before I found out if I'd hit the target. Didn't seem like a good option, not yet, anyway. Besides, Motta was spasming and coughing up wads of blood-laced phlegm. He was twitching so much I wasn't sure I would've been able to hit him even if I were inclined to shoot. Maybe I could stall for time.

Martello had other ideas. "Then shoot at the fucking floor, but shoot."

"Fuck you!" I thought I heard myself say.

A moment of clarity. He wanted me to be found with gunpowder residue on my skin and sleeve. Considering the volume of raw violence over the last few weeks, I thought this all very silly and elaborate. Homicide according to *Robert's Rules of Order*. Apparently, the Caveman agreed with me.

"This is bullshit!" Kenny whined, raising up his nine mil. "I shoulda just killed you first at Rip's the other night." He saw the stunned look on my face. "That's right, Moe, I was standing so close behind you I coulda licked the wax outta your fucking ear. You're a lucky bastard, you know that? If that asshole Bento wasn't there, you'd be——"

"Shut up, Burton, and let's finish this up."

"Fuck you, Martello." Kenny had chaffed at authority when we were on the job together. He didn't seem to tolerate it any better now.

For the second time in as many minutes, I opened my mouth to say something but was interrupted, this time by gunfire.

Bang!

I looked down at my gun hand to make sure I hadn't pulled the trigger. When I looked back up, Kenny Burton—legless as a drunken teenager, his expression asking, "Hey, what the fuck?"—was doing a London Bridge. He fell down, all right, his head smacking the hardwood floor with a nauseating, hollow thud. I felt it more than Kenny did. He was beyond feeling. Then again, he had always seemed to be beyond feeling.

"Don't worry about him," Martello said to me, "he was gonna die anyway. Now shoot the fucking gun, Prager. If you can't tell, I'm not in the mood for any more bullshit."

My gun hand felt completely detached from my arm. It took all my strength and focus just to raise it up and pull back the hammer. I pointed it away from Frankie, who was now desperately groping for his inhaler. For the heck of it, I peeked at Martello, but he wasn't stupid. He had assumed the proper shooting position, his Police Special pointed right at my belly. Given that he'd hit Burton flush in the heart with a single shot from his hip, I didn't like my chances.

I closed my eyes and squeezed the trigger, but there were two bangs, then a third. When I opened my eyes, Frank Motta was crumpled in a heap in front of his wheelchair, a chunk of his neck torn out, the blood barely pumping. Apparently that wasn't his inhaler he had been groping for. If it had been, he wouldn't be needing it now. Martello was down too, but alive, rolling around on the floor in agony, the right side of his abdomen soaked with blood. He was too busy screaming, "Fuck! Fuck! Fuck!" to worry about me or his lawn or to contemplate his future.

I ran over to him, kicked his gun out of the way, and pressed my foot down hard on his shoulder. That got his attention. With Martello flat on his back, I reached down and stuck the short barrel of my .38 into his mouth. I made sure he saw the gun was cocked.

"Now, you won't have to *tell* me to shoot. Understand?" He did.

I had to hurry as I wasn't sure how long he'd stay conscious and I could hear sirens in the distance.

"I want answers—short, quick answers," I said. "If I believe them, I won't kill you. It's that simple. Ready?"

He was.

"You, Larry, and Kenny killed Dexter Mayweather."

He nodded yes.

"Was Burton telling the truth about Rico?"

He nodded again.

"Where did you fit in?" I yanked the .38 just far enough out of his mouth so that I could I understand his answer.

"I was Frank's man inside the Six-O. He made Larry take me along for insurance. Now get me a fucking doctor, for chrissakes! I'm bleeding to death here."

"Not yet," I said. "Is Bento dead?"

"Yeah."

"Where's the body?"

"Coney Island Creek." He put a clammy hand on my forearm. I shook it off.

"And Motta's kid?"

"The Gowanus Canal."

"How were you and the kid involved?"

He didn't answer. The sirens were close now. Martello's eyelids were fluttering and he'd begun to shiver.

"Okay, listen to me," I said, slapping his face to get his attention. "You tell the cops anything you want about what went on today. You put bullets in two men, so I wouldn't stretch the truth too far. Otherwise, I don't care what kind of bullshit story you come up with to explain what happened here between you and Kenny and Motta. But you mention word one about what happened back in '72 or about Larry, and I'll fucking kill you. That's a promise."

His eyes shut, maybe for the last time. Maybe not. The cops were at the front door. I holstered my gun, stood up, and walked quickly over by the French doors. I slid one open and tossed something into the water behind the house. I did it knowing Katy would understand.

All dreams have a shelf life. The expiration date on my dream of pitching for the Mets or playing point guard for the Knicks had long since passed. And now, finally, I had acknowledged that my dream of getting my career back, of carrying that gold and blue enamel shield, had gone the way of the Mets and Knicks. I took out my silvery old badge, the only one I had earned the right to call my own, and waited for the cops to sort things out.

CHAPTER TWENTY-ONE

AFTER TELLING THE same bullshit story over and over again to detective after detective, my mind pretty well went numb. I said I had come to talk to Frankie Motta on behalf of Pulitzer Prize-winning author Yancy Whittle Fenn. Wit, I told them, was researching a project on the fall of the old organized crime families and I sometimes helped him do his early background work. The last part was true enough. I did sometimes help Wit with his research. Of course, the rest of it was utter crap.

As to the shootings, I feigned ignorance. There seemed to be, I said, some sort of dispute between the three men that had something to do with the Red Hook Massacre and Frankie Motta's son dealing coke. Sure, I knew Kenny Burton a little bit from when I was first on the job, but I was shocked to see him walk through the door with Martello. I guess if they looked hard enough, the cops would find someone who had seen the Caveman and me at O'Hearn's in the city or with me and Rico at Larry's burial. And as no one had seen me at Captain Martello's house out in Great River, I swore that I'd never met the man. Whether anything I said would jibe with what Martello would tell them was something I'd worry about tomorrow. Besides, when they rolled Martello out to the ambulance, he wasn't looking very spritely.

The cops didn't believe five words of what I said. I could see it in their eyes, hear it in their voices. Shit, I wouldn't have bought it either, but they had run out of questions to ask and ways to ask them. And when I got a chance to use the phone, I called Queens D.A. Fishbein. After I gave him a bit of a preview of what I'd learned—specifically that Burton was responsible for the murder of at least two NYPD detectives—he sounded quite pleased for himself and with me. He assured me he'd put in a call to his Brooklyn counterpart on my behalf and that this would all be cleared up soon enough. I had to hand it to Fishbein, he was good to his word. Within fifteen minutes, the Brooklyn D.A. was on the phone to the lead detective.

Whether it was the detective's choice or a fit of pique by the Brooklyn D.A. at being trumped by Fishbein, I am still unsure, but for whatever reason, I was not allowed to go home. The best they were willing to do for me was to let me wait out in my car. There, alone in the front seat, I don't suppose I ever felt so alone. It was difficult to say by whom I felt more betrayed, Larry McDonald or Rico Tripoli. I think Larry Mac—even more calculating and cutthroat than I'd imagined—had tried to warn me in his own way, but Rico had basically let me stroll into my own execution. I couldn't get past the gnawing feeling that he had put in a call to Martello.

I think I was exhausted beyond sleep. After about an hour alternating between forcing my eyes shut and watching aircraft lights glide over the Atlantic, I stretched my legs a bit. As I walked between all the official cars and stared at the curious faces who stared even harder back at me, I realized there were things about the case I would never know. Unless Martello survived, found God, and spilled the parts of his guts that weren't all over Motta's floor or removed in surgery, I would be at a loss. In some ways, not knowing would be the worst part of it for me. I dreaded not knowing.

I asked once again if I could leave or use the phone. The polite version of what I was told was to get the fuck back into my car and wait. I began sorting through the pile of mail Joey the postman had handed me just as I'd left my house to come talk to Motta. Finding three credit card bills ain't exactly like finding a forgotten twenty in the pocket of your blazer. But there amongst the bills and expired coupons, last week's edition of the neighborhood paper, and a letter from the PTA, was something I couldn't quite get myself to believe.

In my hand was an envelope. The return address printed in the upper left hand corner was: New York City Police Department, One Police Plaza, New York, N.Y. 10038.

My address was written by hand in blue ink. Larry Mac's handwriting was as neat and distinctive as the man himself. I noticed my hands were shaking and that my heart was pumping so much blood so quickly I was lightheaded.

There was a sharp rap on the glass. I turned and looked up into the face of some detective or other and watched his lips moving. He rapped the window again and motioned for me to roll it down.

"All right, Prager," he said. "You can go."

I think he said some other stuff about keeping myself available, but I can't really say.

EPILOGUE
1972 Redux

AS IT HAPPENS, my recounting of the events at Motta's house that day is the only thing the cops have ever had to work with. Martello made it through the night and beyond . . . sort of. He went into cardiac arrest on the operating table. The OR personnel managed to revive him, but not before the lack of oxygen had resulted in a near total loss of brain function. These days what's left of him lays in some long-term care facility upstate. If you think there's some kind of justice in that, you'd be wrong. But I won't argue the point. You'll have to excuse me because nothing about this whole thing feels like justice to me.

The cops, as directed by Fishbein, found Bento and Junior Motta's bodies where Martello had told me they were. The bullets they pulled out of both dead men matched Kenny Burton's 9mm. Someone with half a brain might've thought to use a different piece to murder people, but Caveman was never the smartest guy on the planet. Besides, when you've gotten away with so much for so long, you start to think you'll never get caught. He was right, I guess, in his own way.

Detective Klein, Bento's partner, was about as happy to see me as a CAT scan of a brain tumor. As far as he was concerned, I was no different than Burton, worse maybe. If I had been more up front with Bento and him about the events surrounding Kalisha Pardee's death, he said, his partner wouldn't have been curious enough to tail me and he'd be alive today.

"He saved my life, you know," I told Klein. "Apparently, Kenny Burton was standing right behind me and your partner fired over my head to give me cover."

"His mistake," Klein said. "Now get the fuck away from me before I kill you myself."

I did as he asked.

Sorry is so often a meaningless word, but there are times when it's more meaningless than others. This was one of those times.

Fishbein and Kings County D.A. Starr held a press conference about a week after the shit hit the fan. I had told Fishbein the whole truth, as far as I knew it, on the condition that he never reveal Larry McDonald's part in any of it. Maybe I was foolish to trust him given the depth of his ambition, especially in the light of what Larry Mac turned out to be. But Fishbein had always been good to his word and I didn't want to give him any excuse not to hold up his end of the bargain. If he could tell me where my brother-in-law Patrick had gotten to, I needed to know.

The two D.A.s spun an interesting tale of murder, deceit, corruption, and betrayal, including the solution to the seventeen-year-old execution-style murder of one Dexter "D Rex" Mayweather. In their telling, it was Frank Motta himself along with then Patrolman Martello of the 61st Precinct, and Patrolman Kenneth Burton of the 60th Precinct who had tortured and murdered Mayweather. They claimed to have solved the Red Hook Massacre and the execution murders of Malik Jabbar, a.k.a. Melvin Broadbent, and Kalisha Pardee. They went on to say they had broken up a major new drug ring headed by Frank Motta, Jr. This last part was a huge exaggeration, but since all the players were dead or as good as dead, no one was around to dispute their claims.

Fishbein was most happy with the turn of events and had begun interviewing aids to help run his campaign for state attorney general. Maybe he had finally learned a little modesty and realized that he wasn't gubernatorial material quite yet. I didn't think this case was enough to propel him back onto the state political scene, but that wasn't my concern. Busy as he was, I gave him a few weeks before asking him to keep his end of the bargain. When I did ask, he was more than happy to make an appointment to meet me and discuss Patrick's long ago disappearance. On the phone the day we talked, he even asked me if I would consider working as the chief investigator for his campaign.

Are you outta your fucking mind? "Thanks for the offer, Mr. D.A. Let me think about it. I'll give you my answer when we get together."

"One thing, Prager, before you hang up," he said. "Not that I minded keeping Chief McDonald's name out of it, but why bother? This man was a cold-blooded killer, he lied to you for almost twenty years, and he almost got you killed."

It was a good question, one I had asked myself a thousand times in the last few weeks. *Why did I care?* It would be easy to say I was trying to spare Margaret more pain and embarrassment, which I was.

Or maybe it was my reflexive loyalty. Maybe it was a sense of nostalgia for a time when I believed in the love of my friends. But Frankie Motta's words still rang in my head, "Oh, I get it. This ain't about him. It's about you." In the end, I suppose it was. What I told Fishbein was that I owed it to the memory of an old friend no matter what he really was. It sounded good, even if it wasn't the truth.

We were going to meet for lunch at the Pastrami Palace on Queens Boulevard in Forest Hills. Although I had neglected to tell Fishbein, I'd taken the liberty of inviting the devil along for lunch. I may have hated my father-in-law, but Katy's dad had just as much right to know what had become of his son as I did. Besides, I wanted him there so I could see the look on his face when I told him I wasn't going to play the game anymore, that I was done with secrets, that no matter the consequences I was going to confess my sins to his daughter once I found out what had become of Patrick.

It was a little after twelve-thirty p.m. and Fishbein was more than fifteen minutes late. I didn't like it. Robert Hiram Fishbein was a lot of things, but he had never failed to keep his word. I liked it even less because I had to sit there with Francis Maloney staring at me across the table. Though I have to confess it was almost worth it to see my father-in-law so unnerved. It was a sight one seldom got to see.

I'm not certain even now which happened first, whether I heard the sirens or felt the cold chill. Does it matter? All I know is that an old lady came through the doors, tears streaming down her face.

"What's the matter, Sonya, for goodness sakes?" the counterman asked.

"He's dead."

"Who's dead."

"The man, *oy gevalt!* He was crossing the boulevard near Austin Street and he was . . . The bus, he didn't see the bus."

I didn't quite run out the door. Well, maybe I did. All I know is that by the time Francis Maloney caught up to me, I was already laughing.

"What's so funny?" he wanted to know.

"It's Fishbein. He's dead."

My father-in-law seemed to exhale for the first time all day. Our secrets were safe.

As we walked back toward the restaurant, he asked me again about why I was laughing.

"You know what Oscar Wilde once said?"

Francis smirked. "No, wiseass, enlighten me."

"He said that when the gods want to punish us, they give us what we pray for."

"And that means what?"

"Forget it," I said. "If it was true, you'd've been dead a long time ago."

Now *he* was laughing, that familiar all-knowing look on his face. Order had been restored to the universe.

WHEN I GOT home that night from Motta's, I still hadn't opened the letter from Larry Mac. I just didn't have it in me for any more revelations. I was all used up. The light on my phone machine was flashing madly. I ignored it. There were calls I should have made, needed to make. I didn't. I showered and shaved and slept. *Shaved?* Yeah, I know. I'm not sure why I shaved. I guess I wanted to clean as much of me off as possible.

In the morning, I listened to the messages. They were from Katy and Sarah and Wit and Miriam and Wit and Wit and Wit and . . .

I called Katy first and told her to bring Sarah home. It was time, I said, to have that talk about Nebraska. Sarah was really happy to hear my voice, but not nearly as happy as I was to hear hers. Nothing like being a few seconds away from getting shot to death to make you appreciate what you have.

Miriam had heard the news about the shootout in Mill Basin and was relieved to hear I was alive. Wisely, I asked after the kids and Ronnie before checking on what had happened to Carmella.

"She's doing fine," Miriam said. "There was a bullet fragment Ronnie couldn't see or feel that they dealt with as soon as he got her to the hospital. Ronnie called in some favors at Kings County and they kept her presence quiet. It's not like they don't get a ton of gunshot wounds there all the time. The cops had no trouble believing they were just too busy to report her wound immediately. There was no need to call that friend of yours."

"Can I see her?"

"Sure, but there are a lot of cops around. Maybe you should wait a few days."

"Thanks, Mir. Tell Ronnie I owe him one."

"You owe him a lot more than one."

"I knew you were going to say that."

WIT, TOO, HAD heard about the goings on in Mill Basin, but he seemed a lot less interested in my well being than Miriam, and considerably more distracted.

"Did you go see Carmella's grandmother?"

"I did," he said.

"She's okay, right?"

"Fine. She's a lovely old gal. I'm going back to see her later today. You should accompany me."

"Wit, I—"

"It wasn't really a suggestion, Moe. There's something you need to see for yourself."

"Okay. I'll pick you up in front of your building in two hours."

He hung up before I could change my mind or ask more questions.

Once, years before, when we were first getting acquainted, Wit and I had taken a ride out to Long Island. It had been a quiet and uncomfortable trip because we were headed to Lake Ronkonkoma to see if the remains of a young woman were those of Moira Heaton. Our trip into Brooklyn from Wit's place was similarly uncomfortable, but for less obvious reasons. Wit resisted all my attempts to engage him on the subject. I couldn't imagine what was eating him. By the time I turned off Flatbush and onto Atlantic Avenue, I had grown weary of the subject and just wanted to get the visit over with.

The house on Ashford Street looked different in the daylight; older and a little frayed around the edges, but with plenty of character. As we stood at the front door waiting for Carmella's grandmother, Wit said, "Take a close look at the photos in the living room."

After Wit did the introductions, he took Carmella's grandmother into the kitchen to make some espresso for us all. I hung back and did as Wit had instructed, I studied the photos in the living room. One thing was for sure, the woman did not lack for grandkids. She had pictures of them all at all different ages and stages covering almost every inch of available wall space. But it was obvious that Carmella was her favorite. There were so many pictures of Carmella, you could follow her backwards in time, from her receiving her shield to her graduating from the academy to her high school graduation to . . .

Suddenly, I got the strangest feeling. I can't quite describe it. I realized I was no longer staring at Carmella Melendez's face, but rather at the people gathered around her at her high school graduation. There was something disturbingly familiar about these folks, especially about the mart and woman standing to either side of her. I knew these people from somewhere, but where? The man, who I assumed was Carmella's father, was particularly familiar. I gave up, figuring I was still too exhausted to do even simple math.

Then, out of the corner of my eye, I spotted another picture. This one featured a pretty little girl, maybe five or six years old, in the arms of her father. Her father was dressed in his New York City Fire Department blues. When it clicked, I might just as well have been hit with a bat. I knew these people, all right. I had once saved that little girl from the bottom of a water tank.

THE COPS HAD closed off the block of the Mistral Arms, so I parked illegally and walked back to the building. There were two blue and whites, two unmarked cars, a crime scene unit, and the M.E.'s meat wagon parked out front. Pretty fucking convenient, I thought, to have everyone on hand for when I pressed my gun to Rico's liver and pulled the trigger. Or maybe someone had saved me the bother and had already killed the lying prick.

No such luck. Rico Tripoli's wretched little room was empty. He was gone with the wind, or maybe he'd crawled back under the molding with the rest of the roaches. I'm not sure where people like Rico go to disappear. I was beyond worrying about it, because in the pit of my belly I just knew Rico would fall back into my life again someday. He'd be even more desperate and lost, and my anger would have gone by then.

Marisa had been freed from all earthly worries. Apparently, one of her customers was displeased with the indifference in her eyes or her technique or needed money more than she did. Whatever the reason, she'd been beaten to death for it.

A detective stopped me on my way back downstairs and asked me what I was doing there. I showed him my old badge and explained about Rico. I wondered if he was a suspect.

"Nah," he said, "it was the deceased's ex. The kid saw him do it."

As I left, I noticed Marisa's daughter, the chubby girl, sitting in the same wobbly chair in which she sat that first time. The one-eyed cat was in her lap eating meat out of a can held in the girl's hand. The cat had on a fancy rhinestone collar with a bell and a name tag, but the chubby girl was still dressed in the same ill-fitting and dirty clothes she had worn the day we passed in the hall. Not all little girls get rescued.

IT WAS FOUR days before I went to see her at Kings County. By then, it was determined that she was no longer in danger and the guards outside her door had been reassigned. I didn't have to say the words. She saw it in my eyes.

"You know, don't you?"

"I do, Marina."

Just mentioning that name seemed to transform her back into the girl I had found at the bottom of the water tank in 1972. Wit had explained that her grandmother had let Marina's name slip a few times that first night he went to see her. It hadn't taken Wit very long to piece the whole story together.

"My parents, especially my mother, were old fashioned," Marina said. "They were ashamed for me and for themselves. So they changed my name and moved me to Puerto Rico and hoped by never speaking about it that I would somehow forget. There is no forgetting what was done to me, Moe."

"I know."

"But some of the remembering was good. I always remembered about the man who found me. My father told me about you—not your name, but about you. That man who held me in his arms and told me everything was going to be okay was why I always wanted to be a police officer. I wanted to be someone's hero someday."

"When did you know it was me?"

"Not when we met at the precinct."

"When you accused me of stalking you?"

182

She ignored that. "That day, when we drove you to Fountain Avenue, I knew. You mentioned saving the little girl. At first, it almost didn't register. Then it hit me. That night I called my dad. He's retired down in Florida. He told me your name."

I had come prepared with a speech about the kiss, but somehow I just couldn't say any of the words. I think she had prepared a speech as well. Our red faces seemed to say all that needed to be said.

After a few more minutes of uncomfortable silence, I stood to go.

"The doctors think it's a million dollar wound," she said. "I'll need more surgery. I don't know what I'll do if I can't be a detective."

"You'll learn how to swim, Marina. I did."

I'm not sure she understood. I'm not sure I did, but it felt like the right thing to say.

"Thank you, Moe . . . for saving me."

I walked over to her and held her chin in my hand. "Everything is going to be okay. I promise."

LARRY'S SUICIDE CONFESSIONAL had found its way to me. Had it been delivered on time, there's a chance Kalisha Pardee, Detective Bento, Frankie Motta, his son, and Ken Burton might still be alive. Martello, too, if, like me, you don't consider a persistent vegetative state living. But I don't know. Maybe I would have been slow to act or I would have gone to the wrong people. What I can say is that Malik Jabbar would have been just as dead no matter who delivered my mail, because it was Larry McDonald who killed him. I read enough of Larry's letter to know that much.

I read enough of it to know that Frank Motta, Jr. had somehow found out about the circumstances surrounding Dexter Mayweather's execution and that he was using that knowledge to blackmail Captain Martello into protecting him and Malik from the cops. How Junior found out about D Rex, the letter didn't say. Probably because Larry didn't know. But Martello understood that Frankie's kid and his partner were incompetent fools who would eventually self-destruct and bring him down in the process. That's why he had Larry plant the wire. If Martello was going to get into bed with these clowns, he would need to be aware of any trouble before it tainted him. He figured he could do damage control if he had enough advanced warning. And if Larry hadn't killed himself, Martello would have been right.

Once Jabbar got arrested and yapped about Mayweather, as he must have been instructed to do by Junior Motta, Martello decided he wasn't going down and he wasn't going to do the dirty work himself. So he enlisted the help of his fellow executioners, Larry McDonald and Ken Burton. It wasn't the first time either Martello or Burton had blackmailed Larry into aiding their causes. Martello's making captain and Caveman Kenny Burton's remarkable career survival were no longer mysteries. Larry had called in a lot of markers over the years on their behalf. After all, what choice did he have.

Like I said, I didn't get through the whole letter. When he got to the part about how I knew him, *really* knew him, better than anyone and how I had always understood him, I stopped reading. Even in death he was trying to work an angle, to manipulate me, to gain the upper hand. He was right, of course. I did understand him. He hadn't taken his own life out of guilt or some sense of justice. Larry Mac could live with the murders without losing a second's sleep. What he couldn't live with was the loss of control, because no matter how high he climbed he would never be able to climb past blackmail. The closer he got to being king, the better pawn he'd be.

ON A SATURDAY night, about a month after the shootout at Martello's, we dropped Sarah off at my brother's house and I took Katy to dinner. Things had gotten better for us, but we never did have that talk about Nebraska. I guess my brushes with death and infidelity had woken me up to what I had. Sometimes, though, I still wonder about what would have happened if Fishbein hadn't died under the wheels of that bus. Would I really have had the courage to confess my sins of omission and complicity to Katy? I guess I'll never know.

"Where are we going?" she asked.

"It's a secret. Don't worry, I think you'll like it."

After I parked the car, I reached in the back for the brown paper bag I'd brought home from work that day, and tucked it in the crook of my arm like a baby.

"What's that?"

"It's a surprise," I said. "I think you'll like it."

184

When we strolled up to Cara Mia, Señora greeted us at the door.

"Table for two," I said. I pointed to an empty two-top in a dark corner. "Can we sit over there?"

Señora smiled approvingly and showed us to the table.

"What's this all about?" Katy asked.

I didn't answer and asked the waiter for two empty wine glasses and a corkscrew. When he brought them, I pulled the bottle out of the brown paper bag.

"Mateus Rose! Moses Prager, I haven't had Mateus Rose since—"

"Do you remember the first time I kissed you?"

"On the corner of Second Avenue and East Ninth Street in the Village. You called me a *vance*. You said it was Yiddish for a wiseass woman who wants to be kissed."

"That's right."

"Moe, come on, what's this about?" she asked again.

"It's about the past, and about leaving it behind."

AUTHOR'S NOTE

I grew up very close to Coney Island; in the shadow of Coney Island Hospital, actually, on Ocean Parkway, which was sort of the borderline between Sheepshead Bay and Brighton Beach, not Coney Island. Then again, Coney Island isn't an island, but a peninsula. Go figure! So given the fictionalized nature of the world in which I grew up, I felt it only proper to invent a part of Coney Island called the Soul Patch. Don't bother doing Google searches, because, as far as I know, the only two places in which the Soul Patch exists are in my head and on the pages of this novel. I suppose my hope is that it will now reside in a third place.

Afterword
by Reed Farrel Coleman

NOTHING IN WRITING, maybe nothing in most professions, is so hard as following up success. Therefore *Soul Patch,* coming, as it did, on the heels of my most popular novel, *The James Deans*—a book nominated for the Edgar, Shamus, Barry, Anthony, Macavity, and Gumshoe Awards—was quite a difficult task. I had been faced with a similar situation after the first book in the Prager series, *Walking The Perfect Square,* had received unanimous critical acclaim. It was on the strength of that acclaim that Penguin (Viking/Plume) bought the rights to *Walking...* and the next two Moe books. Unfortunately, given my experiences with the follow up to *Walking...,* *Redemption Street,* I was less than optimistic about the book that would be *Soul Patch.* As I've often joked—half-joked, really—*Redem-ption Street* was the first book to ever go directly from the printer to the remainder bin. Why, I wondered, would things be any different this time around?

But things *were* different this time; they were worse. Because, in spite of the fact that *The James Deans* went to a second printing and of all the nominations and the book winning the Shamus, Barry, and Anthony Awards, Penguin was considering dropping me. To their credit, they made no secret of it. So here I was riding high on my most successful book, but unable to fully enjoy it as the axe was always visible out of the corner of my eye. Normally, I would have begun writing the next book in the series three weeks after finishing *The James Deans* and would have had it finished within six months. However, because of my predicament, I didn't write the next book in the series. I had been advised that it was nearly impossible for a series like mine—much acclaim, but middling commercial success—to move from one house to another. Writers write, that's what we do. So instead of sitting on my hands and waiting to hear from Penguin or writing another Moe book that might never see the light of day, I wrote a novel called *Hose Monkey.*

Enter Bleak House Books. Bleak House was an independent publisher from Madison, Wisconsin, with a taste for edgy fiction. Jon Jordan, a friend and publisher of *Crimespree Magazine,* had mentioned them to me and I mentioned them to my then agent. One look at the manuscript of *Hose Monkey* and Ben Leroy of Bleak House bought it and its sequel. Trouble was, I still didn't have Penguin's decision and couldn't risk publishing under my own name with a different house if Penguin did decide to re-up me. "Tony Spinosa"—my pen name—was born. In the intervening months, Tony Spinosa began the sequel to *Hose Monkey*, Bleak House Books was bought by a larger independent publisher, and Penguin dropped the axe on me. I still remember the day I got the letter from Penguin informing me that I could purchase my books at a discounted rate before they sold them off to someone else. That was a very very dark day in my life and, for the next few weeks, it was difficult for me to think of myself as anything else but an abject failure. My bank doesn't accept critical acclaim for mortgage payments nor do they see awards as collateral.

Normally, I would shy away from giving you all these business related details, but you need to understand where I was financially and emotionally if you're going to understand where *Soul Patch* came from. Bleak House had indicated that they would be interested in discussing doing more Moe Prager books if Penguin dropped me. They were good to their word, bought two new Moe books, and gave me a fairly generous advance for a small publisher. Generous, yes, but nothing like the money I'd gotten from Penguin. Still, the cloud of failure hung over my head and I was in a pretty dark place. All you need do is look at the cover of the original edition of *Soul Patch*—featuring a photo I chose—to see where I was at.

Although other books of mine are grittier, bloodier, more violent—*Hose Monkey, Empty Ever After, Tower, The Fourth Victim*—none is emotionally darker or more claustrophobic or more desolate. *Soul Patch* is a book of betrayal because in it, Moe discovers that the men with whom he served in the 60th precinct, the men whom he has loved and mythologized, the men he trusted to have his back, had, in fact, stabbed him in the back. Nothing can hurt Moe more because his time as a cop is something he treasures beyond all rationality. For Moe, it is like finding out that the solid steel base on which you've built your life is actually made out of beach sand and can be destroyed by a few drops of rain or by the truth being exposed to the sun. Even Moe's beloved Coney Island is shown to be much less than the romantic vision to which he stubbornly clings. The Coney

Island in *Soul Patch* is a place of unfulfilled promises and lies. It is a rotting hulk, an empty place where the excitement, the rides, the shrieks of laughter, the scents of French fires and hotdogs are artifice, used to cover an underlying violence. Even Coney Island, a tiny peninsula at the tip of Brooklyn, is racially divided.

In *Soul Patch* the reader can see the first hairline fractures in Moe's marriage. And, perhaps more painfully, Moe sees them too.

> "We had hit the inevitable impasse, that stage in marriage when each day is like a long drive through Nebraska. In the absence of passion, I wondered, what distinguished love from habit?"

Later in the book, Moe crosses a line which, when I first conceived the series, I could never imagine Moe crossing. He kisses another woman. So, not only is Moe betrayed, he betrays, if only somewhat innocently. Of course, that other woman is the reincarnation of or, more accurately, the self-reinvented version of someone who predated Katy in Moe's life by five years. Carmella Melendez is yet another human piece of Moe's past, his Coney Island cop past, who isn't what she seems. At every turn, Moe is reminded that he cannot trust anyone, not even himself. He, too, is corrupted. Corruption, particularly political and police corruption, is always a major element in the Moe books, but in *Soul Patch* corruption is pervasive. It's far more than an element. It's what the book is about.

Coney Island, too, is always featured in the books, but in *Soul Patch* it is its own character. And nowhere else in the series is it as allegorical. The first line of the prologue states:

"Nothing is so sad as an empty amusement park. And no amusement park is so sad as Coney Island."

By the end of the book, Moe is as empty and as sad as Coney Island. He has shed all his old friends, his old beliefs, and begun the long painful descent into the dissolution of his family. As Donald Maass writes in his *The Fire in Fiction*:

> "It [Coney Island] has been featured in countless movies, songs, and novels, but one of my favorites is in a recent novel in Reed Farrel Coleman's gritty series of New

York mystery novels featuring ex-cop turned P.I. Moe Prager .
. . The novel begins with a meditative prologue that slowly
zooms in, cinema style, on the boardwalk a number of years
before the action of the story . . .

"What is it that gives the boardwalk at Coney Island
its mythic significance in this passage . . . It is rather that
something violent—and symbolic—happens there. Without
that, the boardwalk is just a place to get a decent hot dog. To
make a place iconic, make something big happen there.
Something bigger than cotton candy."

In the end, *Soul Patch* garnered three award nominations
including a 2008 Edgar Award nomination for Best Novel. I was
incredibly honored to have been placed in the company of nominees
like Pulitzer Prize-winner Michael Chabon, Benjamin Black, John
Hart, and my friend and co-author of *Tower*, Ken Bruen. People
often ask me how much of Moe is autobiographical. It's an impossible
question to answer accurately. But what I can say is that emotionally,
Moe and I have never been closer than when I was writing *Soul Patch*.
The sting of getting dropped by my publisher has faded, but the joy
derived from having written it continues.

Reed Farrel Coleman
January 2010

Recently called "a hard-boiled poet" by NPR's Maureen Corrigan, Reed Farrel Coleman has published twelve novels, including two under his pen name Tony Spinosa, and *Tower*, co-authored with Ken Bruen. He has been twice nominated for the Edgar Award and is a three-time winner of the Shamus Award. Reed is the former executive vice president of Mystery Writers of America and was the editor of the anthology *Hard Boiled Brooklyn*. His poems, short stories, and essays have appeared in *Indian Country Noir, Damn Near Dead, Wall Street Noir, The Lineup, Crimespree Magazine* and several other publications. Reed is an adjunct professor in creative writing at Hofstra University and he lives with his family on New York's Long Island.

CPSIA information can be obtained at www.ICGtesting.com
Printed in the USA
LVOW04s0958301114

416264LV00019B/842/P